THE HAUNTING
OF MODESTO
O'BRIEN

Cover Design and Illustration: Gareth Lind, Lind Design, modifying the following source images:

Denis Pesterev/Shutterstock.com
Cattallina/Shutterstock.com
VasjaKoman/iStock.com

Library and Archives Canada Cataloguing in Publication
Title: The haunting of Modesto O'Brien : a novel / by Brit Griffin.

Names: Griffin, Brit, 1959- author.
Identifiers: Canadiana (print) 20250235552 | Canadiana (ebook) 20250238128 | ISBN 9781997529002 (softcover) | ISBN 9781997529019 (EPUB)
Subjects: LCGFT: Gothic fiction. | LCGFT: Novels.
Classification: LCC PS8613.R535 H38 2025 | DDC C813/.6—dc23
Printed and bound in Canada on 100% recycled paper.
Cover Artwork: Gareth Lind
Author Photo: Lola
Published by:
Latitude 46 Publishing
info@latitude46publishing.com
Latitude46publishing.com

We would like to acknowledge funding support from the Ontario Arts Council and the Government of Canada through the Canada Book Fund for their support.

THE HAUNTING OF MODESTO O'BRIEN

A NOVEL

BY BRIT GRIFFIN

A NOTE FROM THE AUTHOR

This is not an historical novel. It is, however, a story inspired by real-life events. One of these occurred in a small town in Alberta, Canada in 1967, another in the boreal forest of northern Ontario, Canada between 1903 - 1909, on the traditional territory of Timiskaming First Nation. There is a section at the end of the book that identifies other historical events that are referenced in the book. But the rest is speculation, conjuring, and some serious wishful thinking.

This story is for Fox

"… the dark, the speckled easterly wind
Both black and purple."

— *Creation of the winds with their colours from Saltair na Rann*. From Hull, E. (Ed.). (1913). *The Poem-book of the Gael: Translations from Irish Gaelic Poetry Into English Prose and Verse*.

PROLOGUE

"Are you not the depraved son of a bitch that took my sister?" The man squinted up at her—her with a shotgun pointing right at him, her suddenly just appearing, standing a few feet back from the top of the trench. Him at the bottom of it, shovel still in hand.

The trench was about ten feet wide and four feet deep. It ran parallel to the shore of the lake, part of the network of trenches that had been gouged out of the rock by sweat and shovel and dynamite. He felt the sun in his eyes. It was warm now, but he knew the chill would return in the evening. The ice was starting to melt on the lake, leaving patches of open water, but it was still crusted thick along the edges.

Beyond the lake was a forest that had been hacked and dynamited, reduced to stumps, their tops sheared off irregularly. Some of the stumps and forest debris were charred, his partner Moberly telling him that burning was sometimes the best way to clear off the tree cover, to get down to the soil, then the rock. After that it was slow going. It was hard work, chipping away at the rock, but it was going to pay off, he knew it. Wasn't that huge slab of silver found not too far away? The vein itself running over a foot wide, a few hundred feet long.

He'd been hanging around in town when the news about the spectacular find had come in, and he'd joined the steady parade of men, women, and children heading out to see it. As they stood around gawping, some Algonquin fella in the crowd said, "That there silver, it was found right next to my place. Where I am, it's lucky, the silver giving itself, lying right on top of the ground in some places! Secrets, shown just to me! Not like this, taking this silver is going to stir up trouble, bother the lake," and a few fellas had laughed, dismissing him, but then he'd said, "You'll see, that thick serpent of silver is going to uncoil itself right across that claim line, it's going to come to me, I know it."

But the man at the bottom of the trench feeling the sun hot on his forehead knew that the snake was going to be his, and no one was going to get in his way. Not that Algonquin anyways, not anymore. And not anyone else either.

"I asked you a question."

He looked past her, wondering if anyone was close enough that he could call to, but the forest behind her was still, not even any birdsong. Just as well, the situation he was in would take some explaining, and he wasn't too interested in doing that. He'd been working out here on his own—and for good reason. If one area was going to prove out, it was right here. And he sure as hell wasn't sharing any of it with the likes of his deadbeat partner. If only he'd brought Bill with him today, or even Shitty Mitty. But he couldn't trust them to keep their mouths shut, and he hadn't wanted them to know where he was working, or to notice him coming or going. Well, guess she'd noticed.

He said, "I don't have your sister."

"Never said you had her, I said you took her."

"Did no such thing and you got no right to accuse me."

"I saw you."

"Did not."

"Did. Saw her in a wagon with you."

Was it possible this one had been in town then? Down there to meet the train? He asked, "Where? Where did you see this?"

"In my mind. Saw it clear as anything."

The man laughed then, relieved, but she said, "You know I can see things."

"You must have been mixed up, I haven't seen your sister," then thinking he should try changing tactics, flatter her, he said, "You look like her."

"No, I don't."

"Well, seems to me you would if you got yourself one of them nice dresses 'stead of them old trousers and coat you favour. I could take you back to town, get you fixed up. Think you'd look right pretty."

"Not interested in what you think, mister. I want you to tell me where my sister is."

He spat, watching the foam hit the iron-stained rock at his feet. She was right. Didn't look at all like her sister. Lily Nail was a fistful of trouble, that was for damn sure, but she sure was fine looking. Almost worth the trouble. This one was different.

He said, "Oh, the last time I saw Lily Nail was down in Butte, running around with some dark-haired fella. That was some time ago."

"You know that's a straight up lie, mister. I bet you came in on that train from Montreal."

"Not me, been out here working this claim as soon as it got warm enough."

"You keep lying I'm going to shoot you."

He was lying, but she had no way of knowing that for sure. Her gun dropped a bit, the man figuring if he wasn't careful, she might just take off the top of his skull without even meaning to.

He said, then trying the truth, "Honest to god, I don't know where she is right now. But I could help you find her."

"Don't need no help besides you telling me where she is."

"What's your name again?"

"Lucy. But you might already know that."

"No, I didn't. That's a pretty name."

"Is it?"

"Why sure it is, and you're a pretty little thing yourself."

"Folks say that about my sister, but not about me."

He tried, "Maybe they don't see you the way I do."

He thought he saw the beginning of a smile. Maybe he could persuade her to drop the gun, flattery and women after all, 'specially one as plain as her, but then she said, "Mister, you're just a lowdown liar through and through. And by all accounts, you're just plain wasting my time. I don't appreciate that. So, what you're going to do right now is put down your shovel, climb on up out of that trench, and then get your hands up over your head."

He dropped the shovel, thinking she'd want him on her side of the trench, her now stepping back a few feet to make room, so he turned, scrambled awkwardly up over the lip on the opposite side, just as she was telling him not to. He'd be better off keeping the trench between them. What was she going to do about it anyways?

When he stood, glad to be eye to eye with her, she said, "You still ain't far enough away from me if I want to shoot you."

"Why don't you just put that gun down. Don't want to hurt anyone now do you?"

"I believe I might have an appetite for exactly that. Now get those hands of yours up where I can see 'em."

"I swear to you, I don't know anything about your sister."

"Best be quitting that lying, or else a lot of folks around here are going to know what a liar and cheat you really are."

"What does that mean?"

"I've been watching you, seen what you've been getting up to out here. You're a dirty dealer, that's for sure. Didn't get this scrap of land fair and square. You're not supposed to be here, you and that Moberly. Folks don't think much of claim jumpers, they're right down there with horse thieves and rustlers."

Jesus Christ. "Course this is our claim."

"No, it ain't."

"Sure thing, even got our cabin just beyond them trees there."

"I seen your cabin, some run down shack a few claims over where you started out, looks more like a trash heap if you're asking me. This one you're in now is some other man's cabin, a man who was building it to last. You don't got no right to be here, working his ground."

"Not sure you know how this works, but I staked this claim. If a man's got a claim, blazed it and followed the rules, then a man has a right to be here."

"Tell that to the fella that's lying rotting in one of those trenches out behind your trash heap. You out and out murdered him so you could steal his claim. You just figured no one would care 'cause he was one of them Algonquins from across the big lake."

The man laughed. "You best stick to womanly things."

"That right?"

He hesitated answering, eyeing the shotgun, looking her over too, her hat pushed back on her head, old jacket and baggy trousers, hair of no particular colour pulled back, her sharp nose, eyes like iron, and crooked too. He tried a smile, said, "This ain't going to get us anywhere."

"Can you swim?"

"No, not really," he answered, picturing now the lake at his back, the thin coating of ice. The water would be damned cold. That's why there weren't too many fellas out working in the bush yet. Ice too thin to be hauling out sleighs of ore, but not warm enough to fire up the hydraulic pumps. At least those were the excuses he was hearing. After itching to get back out after the long winter, lots of the fellas were suddenly dragging their feet, spooked by the strange goings on around the lake, screams and cries from the bush, then a day ago a fella just up and disappeared. Some said it was just wolves, hungry now after the winter, but wolves leave some trace of a man, don't they?

"If you don't tell me right now where Lily is, I'm sending you out there. Into the water."

He could feel the sweat sticking his shirt, to the skin along his spine. "I'm not going in there. Not there."

"Heard a man drowned out there, but I doubt the water's deep enough. Why don't you go find out."

"I'm not going out there, you know what folks say about that lake."

"That there's a monster living out here?" She was smirking now, eyebrows raised, said, "I wouldn't mind seeing a monster. Nice day for it."

The man felt both ashamed and scared. Felt himself colouring. But he wasn't going to go in there. No matter what. He shook his head, said, "Let's talk this thing through. I'm pretty sure I can talk to a few fellas, find out something as to the whereabouts of that sister of yours."

"Mister, you start walking into that lake. Or I can shoot you right here and now. I'm giving you a choice."

"I ain't going."

She looked past him to the lake, the ice showing the grey-brown water below. "Ice by the shore is thick enough to hold a man. Be entertaining enough to see when exactly it finally gives way under your weight."

"What's the damn point in making me go out there?" He was flustered, hot now in the sun but imagining the cold waters.

"Give you time to make your peace, for what came before, and what you done now."

"What are you talking about?"

"You know what you did."

She was gnawing on her lip a bit. He thought maybe she was getting nervous, thought too of just turning his back on her, walking away. She wasn't going to shoot him. Maybe didn't even know how. That's right, she didn't know what she was doing, woman was crazy. He could probably just jump right over that trench, take the gun away, give her a good beating right there on the rocks. Eyeing the distance between them, gauging it, he readied himself, said, "You stupid bitch."

She shot him, the bullet hitting him in the chest. Second one went through his neck.

The crack of the gunshots scattered the group of ravens along the edge of the lake. A few of them taking flight but then circling back. She went over to the man's body. His eyes open, him staring upwards.

Weren't worth burying, she thought, grabbing hold of his feet, starting to drag him towards the water. He was heavy. She glanced up at the gathering clouds. Rain, maybe even snow. The breeze was picking up too. Soon, everything and anything would be smelling him.

As she got closer to the water, the ravens started raising a ruckus, a few landing close by, big birds, black heads dodging back and forth, keeping an eye on the prize. Black beaks at the ready, and then they started to call, their *kwark, kwark* sounding old and hollow, calling in their kin to share the feast. Lucy dropped the man's legs. They hit the muck with a heavy plop.

The ravens were now closer to a dozen. One landed on the man's shoulder and Lucy stepped back. "Sure, have at him," she said. "Before the coyotes come. Or that monster."

CHAPTER ONE

Several men watched as the sign was hung up outside the store-front. The storefront itself was narrow, squeezed between a tall rambling two storey building and another building that was either being built or being torn down. Hard to tell, things just happened too fast in this town. As for the sign, it read: Modesto O'Brien - Gunman & Detective.

The men had congregated outside the grocery store that was four doors down. Two of the men were sitting on a bench, two more had been carrying out supplies but had stopped to watch the sign go up, curious. They were talking amongst themselves, just shooting the shit, wondering about this new fella with the green frock coat, making some jokes about it. Another man, tall with narrow sloping shoulders, hands in pockets, was using the toe of his boot to dig at the dirt caught between the wooden slats of the sidewalk. Something to do, restless.

Modesto wasn't paying attention to the men, though; he was listening to the buzzing of the flies rising up from the mud. Why were they so loud with their buzz-buzzing, with their fussing? What were they saying?

He looked around, and then saw what had them riled up, a team of horses struggling up the road, the wagon veering close to the sidewalk, the gutter thick with manure and garbage. The horses were pulling a towering load of lumber, a dark bay on the far side, next to it a dapple grey. The horses were moving slowly up the street towards Modesto, hooves caked in mud, flies clustering along their legs and up along the harnesses too.

One of the men on the bench yelled to the driver, "That load ain't making it past this corner." The teamster wasn't listening though, bringing his whip down against the flank of the bay, shouting at it to get a move on.

The horses were straining, leaning into the harness that now dug into their shoulders. One of the bay's knees buckled, the horse staggering, but the harness held him. Modesto could see the thick muscle moving under the grey's shoulder. Ears back, head down, the mare was pulling for the both of them. Modesto took a step down from the sidewalk and stopped to watch, eyes drawn to the lean bay and her labour, to the story whose ending was already being told in the bustling and humming of the fat blue-black flies.

The men outside the grocery store were watching the wagon too, not noticing as Modesto stepped back and carefully removed his green coat and laid it over the railing, then rolled up the sleeves of his crisp white shirt. Felt the chill in the air, smoothed down his burgundy vest just as the wheels on the far side of the wagon hit one of the deep ruts that ran like a scar up the mud road. The wagon dipped, teetered, and then the load started to slide, the teamster yelling, "Get moving!" as if the motion of the horses pulling forward could somehow stop gravity, him looking surprised as the lumber shifted behind him and started to tumble. The whole load, wood and driver, sliding off the wagon as the man on the bench yelled, "Told ya so," and a couple of the other men laughed.

As the load tipped over and spilt out across the street, the horses were jerked sideways, the grey struggling to keep her footing but the bay horse sort of crumpling up and going down. The driver was up fast, cussing, kicking at some lumber that was in his way, yelling at the horses, the grey swaying with the strain, the thick leather harness stretched taut between her and the bay that now lay tangled up in the straps and chains, its head flat against the ground. Modesto saw the horse give up, right before his eyes, it was so unutterably sad, the great head resting now in the mud, a slight twitch of an ear, the horse, defeated, hearing too the loud buzzing of the flies calling her name.

The man kicked at the bay's hind leg, shouted at it, "Get up, goddammit," but the horse wasn't moving, its sides rising and falling slowly, ribs showing. The man who'd been pushing around the dirt with his foot shouted to the teamster, "That horse ain't ever getting up. Best call Shitty Mitty," then added, "Going to cost you though, to have it hauled away."

The driver was angry, kicking at the bay again and yelling, "You fucking lazy..." but then noticed Modesto, crouching down beside the horse's head, big knife out and sawing through the leather. "The fuck you doing, mister?"

A few of the men moved down to get a better view, thinking there might be trouble, interested now. Modesto just kept working, said to the teamster, "As you can see from this angle, the harness is pulling the other horse down. I'm just going to help you a bit with that."

The teamster didn't say anything, what was there to say, the man had just stated a simple truth. But then he saw Modesto's gun, the teamster eyeing the pearl-handled colt, said, "Whoa up there, mister."

It was as if Modesto couldn't hear him, too focused on the horse, stroking now the velvet of its muzzle, the horse taking hot, short breaths.

The teamster said, "I'm talking to you, mister. What are you on about there? Get away from my horse."

Modesto said, "Please, quiet for a moment, I can barely hear her," tilting his head towards the horse, listening, not seeing the man's uncomprehending expression. Modesto took a deep breath, settled his gun on a spot centred above the horse's dull eyes, steadying her with his hand on her muzzle, then pulling back several inches, a slight tip of the gun, and then firing. Behind him the grey mare skittered sidewise as much as the harness allowed, but the bay barely twitched—a small jerk of the back leg, and the teamster came out of his stupor, said, "You shot my horse."

Now standing, Modesto began to unhitch the dapple grey, its head down, tired too, raw sores the size of a man's fist where the harness had rubbed. Again, the teamster said, "Mister, you shot my horse."

Not looking at the teamster, Modesto said, "Yes, very sad isn't it, the loss of a beautiful creature like this, you will miss her," saying it in a tone as if the man agreed with him, had somehow consented to the killing, and was now sharing Modesto's grief.

"You can't just shoot another man's horse."

"You must see there was no other way."

"You're going to pay for this."

A man up on the sidewalk said, "Careful now, he's a gunman," saying it to make the others laugh but they didn't, weren't sure if this new fella in town might be good with a gun. How were they to know? Didn't look the part though, elegant shirt and vest, his face gaunt and pale. And the hair, too long, and a dark auburn. Now that was something different.

"Hey, mister!" the teamster said, "I'm talking to you."

Modesto, now slipping the last of the harness off the grey, said, "I can hear you, sir," but was now looking at the blood splatters on the sleeve of his shirt, the pop of red against the white, thinking then that as the blood dried it would only look like mud, just more mud. This town was nothing but mud. He'd been here only a week or so and it had already been too long.

The teamster glanced down quickly at the tangle of chain and leather between him and Modesto. He could feel the eyes of the men along the sidewalk watching him.

"May I make a suggestion?" Modesto asked, now moving towards the head of the dapple grey.

The teamster hesitated, said, "Get away from my horse. I'm taking her and then I'm going to be back with the Constable."

"Of course, that is one option. But I suggest an alternative. I'll pay you for your team. Fair price."

"Dead horse ain't worth nothing."

"A more than full and fair price for both horses, plus for the damage to the harness."

"Fair price?"

"Dead or alive, yes."

CHAPTER TWO

A man called through the door, "O'Brien? There a Mis-ter O'Brien here?"

Modesto was relieved by the distraction, bored with un-packing the few crates he'd brought with him. Books and papers stacked in messy piles, a few already falling back to the floor. "Yes. Do come in."

There was a delay, as if the man on the other side of the door was reluctant to enter. Then the door handle creaked and a man came through the door saying, "They told me I'd find you here, had the only green door on the street. Maybe even in this here entire town of Cobalt. Guess they weren't lying."

"Apparently not," Modesto said, smiling politely. The man was tall enough but scrawny, bit of a slouch to him and scruffy looking, the armpits of his blue shirt already soaked in sweat even though it was still early in the day.

The man was looking back at the door. "Get the paint in town here?"

"Yes, the place up the street. Are you in the market for some paint?"

"Me? No. Didn't even know there was paint to be had in town, never thought about it I guess. Most folks don't bother painting much of anything round here, 'specially not their doors."

"And why is that?"

"Not sure," the man said, moving a few steps into the room, eyes darting around, nervous but eager, "guess they don't think they'll be here long enough for the paint to dry," snorting at his own cleverness.

"Well, who knows how long I'll be here," Modesto said, changing his mind about the interruption, now wanting the man gone, finding his presence too much, standing planted near the door, blocking the exit, gobbling up the room with his jittery eyes, "but I'm here now. Modesto O'Brien at your service, how may I be of help?"

"Modesto? What kind of name is that?

"Yes, I believe it is an Italian name. Biddy, my Gran, took a fancy to it, think she saw it on a gravestone in Butte, Montana."

"I ain't heard that name before, and let me tell you, I heard all kinds of names around here. Fellas from all over the world here, Germany, Finland, and Americans too, lots of 'em from Montana, but haven't heard that name."

"Well," Modesto said, "now you have. And what is it I can do for you?"

But the man was not to be moved along in the conversation. "You one of them mining O'Briens?"

"No, I don't believe so."

"Must be," he said, but then added, "or maybe a hockey O'Brien. You own one of them there hockey teams?"

"No, I know nothing of hockey. Or mining for that matter."

"This here town's all about mining. All the O'Brien people in this camp are about mining or hockey. You sure?"

"I'm afraid so, but O'Brien it is a well-known Irish name, after Brian Boru, a king of noble house of Munster, eventually became King of all of Ireland. But that's going back a while."

"So just some other O'Brien then?"

Modesto smiled, extending his hand towards the man hoping the gesture might dislodge him from his persistent questioning, said, "Yes, just some other O'Brien. And you are?"

The man reached out his own hand awkwardly, Modesto almost recoiling from the dampness of it.

The man said, "Name's Milton Steam. Some fellas just call me Shitty."

"Ah yes, then you've come about the horse."

Shitty scowled a bit, said, "Alright then, we can get down to it. Now Werner said you'd paid him yesterday what you owed him for up and shooting his horse right out of the blue, and stealing the other one away, so that's the one thing. But now you gotta pay me for hauling the dead one away, pay me fair and square, now if there's a problem…"

"Of course not, there's no problem at all," Modesto said, moving behind the desk, sliding a wooden box out from the top drawer, "I have it ready."

"You bought that other horse? The grey?"

"I did, so in fact it was hardly stealing. I paid Mr. Werner in full."

"You a teamster? That thing won't be able to pull anything for you, ain't nuthin' but skin and bone."

"We're all skin and bone, the horse, myself. You."

"I suppose you're right about that, but it's a funny way of thinking about things," Shitty said, then asking, "What you done with the horse? Didn't see it out front."

"I have her stabled down at Carr's livery for now. She's a lovely creature, just needs some rest, she'll be fit as a fiddle. I'll find somewhere with nice pasture for her."

"Sure won't be around this town, no sir. There's not a single scrap of land left. They say this town's worth a hundred dollars a square inch! 'Cause of the silver, you see."

Yes, Modesto had seen what the silver had done, both to the men who chased it and the land that held it. Gnawed a town out of the forest, scraped bare the rock. He'd only been there a week or so and had seen families emerging from the hovels they'd built out of discarded crates, seen too those same hovels torn down from around those very families—nothing but 'squatters' the mining men had said. And how the family had howled, clinging to the ground, green with sludge and thick with garbage, but they were dragged nonetheless. That dragging, that breaking of homes and families, Biddy had told him all about that.

"It's a hard place," Modesto said.

"Well, maybe for some fellas, but others fella get downright rich. You know that silver vein they just found, well it was almost two feet wide, ran for over three hundred feet. Imagine that! No wonder those fellas are fighting over it. There ain't no place like Cobalt."

"You're correct about that, the noise, the smell. It's unbelievable."

"Well, it sure can get ripe, that's a fact. Just wait till summer. Now mind, I've done some hauling of that old honey wagon, loading 'er up with all those buckets of shit. Do it long enough, you do get used to the smell, just natural I guess. Folks complained about me, but I say that those folks don't mind relieving themselves all over town but sure don't like thinking about it afterwards."

Modesto sighed, tiring of this man's cataloguing of grime and disaster, tired too of the town's chaos, the mining companies tearing up the main street with their trenches, and once the gouging for silver was done, moving on, tearing up more, the trenches filling in with garbage and waste behind them. No room for a dump, no time for clean water.

"A shabby excuse for a town, this Cobalt of yours," Modesto said, "Ten cents for a gallon of water. How do families afford that, for cooking, cleaning? And the stench, all around their homes, how do they endure it?"

Shitty Mitty didn't answer, took his time looking around the office, said, "Probably noticed that there's some horses just get left where they fall, some of 'em dead, some almost dead. Now that ain't so bad in winter, but come spring, whoowee, they get to smelling. You would not believe it. And they bloat up something fierce, then I got to puncture them just to get them into chains so's I can drag them out of town. But you got to take them away," Shitty Mitty concluded, "just 'cause of the smell, and then the pests that come into town on account of the rotting meat."

"Yes, of course, I understand. I should be getting back to my work here, so if we could settle your bill..."

"And Mr. Blackwell down at the livery at the other end of town, he got fined by that Health Inspector fella that come up here from the city. Well, he was hopping mad about that, but he had to pay in the end for not hauling his horses away. Then after the Inspector left, he went right back to leaving them where they dropped."

"Is it a common occurrence that Mr. Blackwell's horses die?"

Shitty Mitty exhaled loudly, "Well, you try hauling through that mud all day."

True enough, Modesto had seen it in the eyes of the bay horse, the hauling day and night, people, timber, metal. And the short rests, cramped stalls, musty hay, the feel of the whip. It was surprising any of the horses lasted more than a couple of years.

"Yes I suppose you're right. Rather unfortunate waste of horses though wouldn't you say?"

"I've heard about fellas like you, always crying for the poor animals. Don't see too much of that around here, no time for it!"

Too busy, yes, busy toiling, moiling, scrounging for wealth. Biddy had said Montana was dark and wild once, the skies thick with birds, then the men standing and shooting as the bodies and feathers and fear piled up around their ankles, Biddy pointing to the ladies' hats as they went to market, would say, see that there, they're wearing the death of the birds on their heads, then getting mad, would say that Montana was nothing more than a boneyard. A stinking boneyard. No buffalo. No coyotes. Grizzlies, wolves, birds, all gone, all bone.

Modesto said, "Montana didn't have time for it either."

"Why, now that you mention it, there's a fella here working as a dynamite man, from your part of the country. Said he learned about dynamiting from blasting wolf dens, said it was the best way to get them wolves out, said a fella could get a bounty of five dollars off each of the pups. That ain't bad money, no siree!"

Shitty Mitty was looking at Modesto, waiting for his reaction, but Modesto found he couldn't speak, found it unbearably hot in the room. The impulse to take Shitty by the back of his neck and pound his face into the desk was almost unbearable. Irresistible. Modesto knew, though, that he had to be patient, not attract any attention, then he could finish what he came for, finally be done with it. Then he could leave, take the grey horse and leave.

Shitty got impatient waiting for a response, chuckled as he said, "From the way you look right now I'm thinking you might take pity on those wolves too, but they ain't like your pet dog, no siree, tear you apart as soon as look at ya. And those horses, a vicious streak can take hold of them too. Why just the other day, one of the horses over at the Hudson Bay mine got itself scared during a storm, the teamster was just unhitching it, taking his time like he does every day, experienced and all, but that horse just up and kicked him in the gut. Tore his intestine right through and through. Died the next day, he did. So, you cry all you want."

Modesto managed, "Yes well, that is unfortunate as well. Perhaps the mines' use of both men and horses is needlessly violent."

"Well, you sure got yourself a heap of ideas and opinions don't you, Mr. O'Brien? Yes sir, you do," said Shitty Mitty, then distracted by one of books stacked on Modesto's desk, picking it up. "Who's this?" he asked, reading the name slowly, "this Captain James Freney? You an army man?"

"No, not at all, Freney," Modesto said, reaching over and removing the small green book from Shitty Mitty's hand, "was a famous Irish outlaw. This was my Gran's favourite book, from her school days I think."

"What kind of an outlaw?"

"Like a Robin Hood, I suppose. He'd had his land stolen by the English. Decided robbing the rich was a fair response."

"What happened to him, he still around?"

"Freney? No, no, this was well over a hundred years ago. I think he managed to find some sort of clemency, but I believe the other men in his gang were hung."

"Well, that doesn't seem right. For one fellow to get off."

"I think the wrong in this case lies in the stealing of the land in the first place."

But Shitty Mitty wasn't paying attention to what Modesto was saying, asked, "You got yourself a heap of books. You read all of them?"

"I try. And yourself, Milton, are you a reader?"

Shitty Mitty's eyes narrowed, searching for the meanness, the trick in it. "What do you mean?"

"I mean do you like to read a good book every now and again?"

"No."

"Each man is different I suppose. For myself I find there is comfort to be found in a good book."

Shitty Mitty was suddenly snarly, said, "I'm not looking for any comfort."

"Oh, that's unusual. So, what are you looking for?"

Silence. Then Shitty Mitty said, "My money. Fair and square, for hauling that fucking nag outta the street."

Modesto nodded and smiled, passed him the money. Thought to himself, that Shitty Mitty, he was one to watch.

CHAPTER THREE

"I'm entitled to my hates, aren't I, Mr. O'Brien?"

"Of course, as are we all."

Mauve sleeves making a faint rustling sound as she leaned forward and placed her pale hands on the desk. Modesto thinking that the veins on her hand were the same colour as her dress. It was lovely but worn, had white buttons. Her hands too showed signs of wear, the knuckles chapped, fingers scratched. That was odd.

"Then you will take the job, find him and kill him." A statement, but she made it seem like a question.

"It has just been my experience that killing a man is not all that easy. Nor often warranted."

"But I have already explained all of that to you."

And she had. He had arrived back at his office from lunch to find her standing outside his door, back to him, staring off down the street that was full of noise and men and horses, wagons loaded and being unloaded, deals being made and broken.

She hadn't turned around as he approached to unlock his office door, just asked, "Are you open for business, Mr. O'Brien?" but before he could answer, she added, "It is a rather urgent matter."

And so she had preceded him in, said nothing as she waited for Modesto to remove a crate from a chair so she could seat herself. Then, not waiting either for introductions or pleasantries, she explained her urgency: the missing sister, and the man who took her. The man she wanted him to find and kill.

"And you are certain he took your sister?"

"He took her. Or one of his associates."

"Well, if that is the case, and you are certain of it, why haven't you gone to the authorities? I do believe there is some sort of sheriff or constable or some such thing in this town."

"The Police Constable won't do anything. He's fit for separating a few bad sorts from their bottles, nothing more. My sister is in danger, I can feel it. I need to find her."

"I see," he paused, glancing at her hands as they rested on his desktop. A deep scratch on the back of her hand, then something emerging along the edges of his mind, running like a thin thread, the violet of her veins, the silver veins of the ground, what a strange coincidence, and she said, "Mr. O'Brien?"

"Yes, sorry, I was just thinking. And perhaps also wondering, why hire me to kill the man rather than find the sister?"

"In my mind they are the same task."

"Perhaps, but for my peace of mind, could we separate the two?"

"That is impossible for me to imagine. He won't give her up."

"As you wish, but perhaps so that I might understand this situation better, could you explain why he has taken your sister?"

The woman hesitated, said, "I'm not altogether certain ..."

"Venture a guess then. You're clearly familiar with the man."

"As bait. He took her as bait."

"Bait?"

"He knows I will come for her."

"Is this man your husband?"

"No! This man is a brute."

"They could be one and the same."

"He is not my husband. He is not my lover. I have barely exchanged a few dozen words with the man."

"I see. This is a perplexing case, engaging me to kill a man you hardly know."

"You're experienced in the business of killing men, why make a fuss about this one?"

"The killing of a man, even when justified, is still a sordid and private business. It is not to be undertaken lightly."

The woman reached into her small handbag, tiny purple flowers beaded onto it, withdrew a lace hankie. Dabbed at her eyes. Modesto kept watching her hands, it was better than taking in her face, not the tears, those did not trouble him, but the hollow of the cheek, the fair skin and dark hair tucked behind her ear. And the eyes. That was too much.

He said, "If I may be blunt, do you have reason to believe that perhaps, well ..."

"That she is already dead?"

Modesto nodded. Waited. Taking the silence to look at her more closely. She must be in her early twenties, younger than him by maybe ten years or so. More scratches there in the curve of her neck. Not an animal's, no, he didn't think so. Maybe tree branches?

She dropped her head slightly, dark blue eyes downcast. The drama was excellent. He could not help but admire that. She then slowly brought her head up to meet his gaze, said, "If she isn't dead by now, she is likely wishing she was."

Modesto was silent, distracted by that—he found that the desire to live was so thick in the veins and muscle that it was hard to imagine wishing oneself dead. But it happened. He knew that better than most. Was everyone capable of feeling that though, did the hare wish itself dead when it felt the tooth of the wolf?

"Mr. O'Brien, are you paying attention?"

"Yes, of course, sorry, to business then. I would like you to start at the beginning. Tell me when and how, as far as you are aware, your sister came to be missing."

Modesto took a minute to rearrange the objects on his desk, pulling out a writing pad. She said nothing, just watched. He said, "You seem to have caught a few small bits of tree in your hair …"

She patted the side of her head. It was swept up and held by pins. She found the twigs, carefully pulled them from her hair, said, "Yes, you're quite right."

"Perhaps we could start with your name, and where I can reach you. Are you are staying in Cobalt?"

"I am clearly here, aren't I? Mr. O'Brien, really, could we please discuss your plan …"

"Yes, you are here, but many visitors stay up the road in Haileybury, a little less, shall we say, rough and tumble. Are you here on your own?"

Her impatience was almost a physical force, like another body was in the room pushing on him, ready to take him by the shoulders, shake him and drag him away from his desk and obsessions, but he took a deep breath, grasped his pencil more firmly as if to ground himself, and said, "I really need some information from you if I am to consider your case."

"Yes, I am here alone. And I'm currently staying at the Cobalt Hotel, near the train station."

"And your name?"

"Theodora Bow."

"Theodora Bow?" he raised his eyebrows.

"What now, Mr. O'Brien?"

"I beg your pardon, Miss Bow, of course you are certainly entitled to call yourself whatever you please, that is entirely your prerogative. But if you want my professional opinion, I would try a less showy name, perhaps it might draw less attention to yourself. Your chosen name has a bit of the vaudeville about it."

"That would have been best discussed with my mother I suppose, god rest her soul."

"No doubt a saint herself as well."

"There is no call to be sharp with me, Mr. O'Brien," she said, "If you are doubting my honesty, I can take my business elsewhere."

"There are not very many merchants in this town for business such as yours, Miss Bow. You are asking murder of me."

"Yes."

"And who is this man? His name?"

She shook her head. "You don't need to know his name."

"How can I possibly take the case of tracking down a man whose identity remains a mystery? I need you to be more forthcoming if I am to find your sister."

She nodded slowly, stood, but left the tips of her fingers resting on the table, said, "That is fine then, consider this matter no longer your concern."

Those hands, slender nails, almost as pale as the skin itself, not letting go, not yet, so he asked, "Am I to assume then that I am fired? Before I was even hired?"

"I would prefer to engage your services," she offered, softening her tone, "you are not wrong when you say there are not many men suited to the job at hand."

"And I am?"

"Your sign outside advertises yourself as a gunman and detective. I think that makes you more than suitable."

"I am quite certain that my sign says no such thing, Miss Bow."

"Mr. O'Brien, I have no idea why you must engage in this ridiculous banter, either you want my business, and my money, or you do not."

Modesto saw colour in her cheeks, she was getting angry now, he supposed he couldn't blame her. And he could certainly use her money, having turned the last of his over to Shitty Mitty for the horse.

He said, "My sign very clearly states that my area of expertise is as a fortune teller and detective. Now of course I am interested in the proposition you have on offer, but I do want to be clear as to where my talents lie, that is all. So that we understand each other."

"I don't really care what you call yourself as long as you think you can help. This is an urgent matter, and I cannot justify wasting time chit-chatting with you while my sister is in danger."

He could leave it, either refuse her business or play along with the charade, but there was that pull at the edges, something just out of sight in his mind, both tantalizing and unnerving. And he was curious too.

"Which is why I would prefer to clear up the matter of your identity now, so as detective and client we know exactly where we stand with one another. A preferable state of affairs, I find, for matters such as a desired murder, wouldn't you say?"

"Why on earth do you insist on this foolishness," she said, her frustration and perhaps now worry showing, "I am quite certain I can locate another detective, there are no doubt some Pinkerton types hanging about in this squalid town. I am sorry to have wasted your time, Mr. O'Brien, and even sorrier you have wasted mine."

"I do believe you are more likely to find a man from the Thiel Agency than a Pinkerton. Try the Colonial Hotel up on Argentite, they tend to congregate there. My advice would be to arrive earlier in the day to avoid excessive drunkenness. But if I were you, I would think twice about rustling up the likes of one of those men, Miss Bow."

"I am sure they are somewhat more motivated than you are to make a decent dollar."

"True enough, Miss Bow, and they may indeed be highly motivated to assist you in locating your sister, after all, there is a handsome reward for the Nail sisters. Even a drunken Thiel man would know that. And I am sure they understand basic arithmetic. Fifty dollars for one of you, but for the both of you? A hundred dollars is a tidy sum of money."

CHAPTER
FOUR

Modesto came around the desk, saying, "Miss Bow, please do have a seat, you're looking pale."

She sat down slowly, said nothing.

"You're alarming me, please, do take a few slow breaths and try and recover yourself."

He went back around his desk, taking a bottle of whiskey from the lower drawer, noticed there were at best two meagre shots left in it, how could that be? He poured her a glass and slid it towards her, poured one for himself too, waiting as the last two drops fell, amber and slow. The bottle now empty.

She drank and then set the small glass down on the desk, looked to Modesto, but he could only shrug. She said, "What a sad state of affairs, Mr. O'Brien."

"The empty bottle or the peril facing your sister?"

"Both."

"Indeed. Not much to be done about the empty bottle but I do believe I can help you and your sister."

"The reward for us could fill more than a few of these bottles. I have to wonder why you would be willing to forgo the reward to aid the notorious Nail sisters?"

"You have made quite an impression on me," he said, "so let's just say it is a gesture of professional courtesy. Or maybe bad judgement. Does it matter?"

She seemed to consider this, then said, "Yes it does matter. It is, as you said yourself, important that we know exactly where we stand with each other."

"Yes, fair enough."

"So? Why then?"

"I am not quite sure myself."

"Cannot resist a damsel in distress?"

"Lily Nail is hardly to be described as a damsel in distress."

She smiled. "I certainly cannot pay you as much as what is offered as the reward."

"Money I could certainly use, if for nothing else but to replenish my store of whiskey. I do find that on certain evenings it is a much needed salve for my soul. But you may pay me what you can."

"I'm not sure I should place my faith in a man whose soul is in such a state as to be revived by bad whiskey, but I find myself with little other choice. I cannot locate her on my own, I have already tried every path or possibility open to me. And as you can understand, I must be discrete. It is a troubling position to be in, but here we are."

"Yes, here we are indeed. I can assure you that I have no interest in turning you or your sister over to the authorities. I am in Cobalt for my own reasons which are of the utmost importance to me. As long as assisting you in finding your sister does not interfere with my purpose here, and as long as you can provide enough funds to replenish this bottle of whiskey, then I think I can be of service to you."

She sighed, and the silence settled in. She was still waiting, he thought, to come up with some other way that things could unfold, but there they both were, stuck on either side of the large wooden desk with the burn marks on its top and the empty bottle between them. He felt that she was drawn to him, as he was to her. The nature of that attraction, if that was even the word for it, was confused and confusing, unfamiliar. And if he had been taught anything by Biddy growing up, it was to keep an eye out for slippages in the familiar.

Finally, she asked, "So how did you know?"

Modesto slid open the drawer of his desk, rustled around, then withdrew a folded newspaper, "The ever-illuminating Butte Miner. Montana's finest tabloid."

He smoothed out the creased page and turned it so she could read the large headline under the artist's sketch of two women: *Notorious twosome in Daring heist, Miners rolled for Grubstake, Nail sisters use their Feminine Wiles.*

Her eyes shifted from the newspaper to his face, said, "Of course, yes, Butte. We never should have gone back there, but it had been a few years since we'd left, we thought it might be safe. But we were recognized right away, had little time to get funds together to move on."

"I wondered why you'd returned. So many rumours about the two of you, about your exploits elsewhere. I followed the stories, of course, your robberies always had a certain elegance to them."

"Were you living in Butte then?"

"Born and bred in the Dublin Gulch."

"Ah, of course. Strange, we could have been neighbours. Do you miss it?"

"I must confess I prefer not to even think about Butte. I have fond memories, but they exist in spite of that dreary place."

"I share your sentiments, Mr. O'Brien," she said, then added, "I often asked myself, how was I, possessed as I am of such charm and rare genius, stuck in that uncouth Montanan town?"

She was smiling as she said it, half joking perhaps, but oh goodness, how dazzling was her smile, and he said, "I remember one day I'd come home from school, said I didn't want to go back, the school, the entire town, so full of bullies and ugliness. Biddy, my Gran, told me we could make things better, that we were going to go out and put a spell on the town, to set things right. We walked to the four corners of the Gulch, and at each corner she took a few grains of dirt from her pocket and dropped it on the road, let the wind carry it. I asked her what she was doing, and she said it was soil from her home in Ireland, a little place called Ardroe in Kerry. She assured me that this bit of her home would protect me. When I asked her how, when Butte was so big and there was so little of her dirt, she said not to worry, that the east winds would take it where it needed to go. I got the sight that day I think."

"The sight? You have second sight?"

"A version of it. You have an interest?"

"My sister, Lucy, she has it. Hers' is very powerful."

Modesto smiled, said, "Mine is unpredictable, unsettling, and usually not very helpful."

"I think that might be the nature of it. Lucy can't control hers either. Sometimes it completely takes her over. And yes, it is often more troublesome than helpful. But we earned a decent living from it for a while, doing readings, mostly with cards. But trouble always seemed to find us."

"As dire as your circumstances are currently, I must say it is a pleasure to finally meet you, I've admired you and your sister for a while now."

"A peculiar attitude for a lawman."

"But I'm not a lawman, I'm a detective."

"Still, you risk running afoul of the local police by assisting us."

"That doesn't worry me. Biddy always said that there was a fine line between lawful and unlawful."

"Your Grandmother held some unorthodox views."

"I suppose she did. Biddy Savage was an independent thinker, and a fine storyteller."

"Such a woman's talents would be wasted in Butte."

"Yes, it was difficult for her in America, but she had to leave Ireland, the famine of course, but she said she still had one foot in Kerry, even though she was on the other side of the ocean. She often told me about her walk to the ship, crying, heartbroken and pregnant, barely any belongings, most sold off to buy passage. She said her only comfort living in Butte were the scraps of her stories, her jumble of memories. She'd tell me all her stories of magic hills, talking animals, fairies, sad tales of sickness and starvation. Just fragments from her childhood and homeland that didn't quite make sense any longer, couldn't quite fit together in the same way. She'd always says they were unmoored without the land that gave rise to them."

"What people salvage and what they leave behind says a lot about their character, good or otherwise."

"I suppose it does."

"Could you explain, then, why you held onto that newspaper, bringing it all the way here with you?"

That was a good question, why indeed? He hadn't really considered it before now, why, of all the things to collect, save, pack and then unpack, why this creased and worn page from a tabloid? Biddy'd say it's not just the slippages in the day in and day out, but the criss-crosses too, watch for those, the ones in the corners and up the walls …

She persisted, "You must have a reason."

"Yes, there is always a reason. I suppose there is a glamour about you and your sister, and growing up I was instilled with a deep fascination of the outlaw. I think I found the existence of the Nail sisters comforting."

"Is this your grandmother's influence again?"

"She did have a soft spot for a decent highwayman. The first books she read to me, and then I read on my own, were about outlaws. So how could I resist when encountering Lily and Lucy Nail?"

he asked, turning the paper towards himself to read aloud: '*The Nail sisters have a special talent for relieving kind-hearted citizens of their money. I have no doubt that they are facing a life of hardship and crime unless they learn their lessons now*'. The Sheriff must have been quite irate to offer such a substantial reward for your capture."

"I must wonder if you're not a bounty hunter of some sort," she asked, now frowning. "Have you been following us for the money? It would be naive to not consider this a possibility."

"Of course, but I can assure you that I find such work distasteful. But it is a reward that would tempt a Thiel man. Not the calibre of reward one would get for the likes of a Billy the Kid, but still, a hundred dollars is a hundred dollars."

She smiled slightly but looked tired now, the stiffness in her shoulders gone. "Am I to trust you then?"

"I think I have made myself clear."

"Alright then. I suppose you have a client. And your newspaper clipping will hopefully make things easier for you."

"And why's that?"

"You now know what Lucy looks like. I have no photograph of her."

Modesto studied the two faces looking up at him from the newspaper's illustration. Not much of a resemblance between the sisters. Lily, large eyes, dark hair piled on her head. The other woman seemed smaller somehow, diminished. Her hair was short, eyes small and staring, set too close together, the artist making her appear almost cross-eyed. Something compelling about the directness though. A defiance. Perhaps the artist's fancy.

"Tell me about Lucy. Is she as bold as she appears?"

"Please, Mr. O'Brien, if you could put aside your fascination with outlaws and focus on the peril my sister is currently in. We need to find her quickly. If we are not already too late."

For a brief moment, Modesto was drawn to the sound of that word, 'we'. Since the death of his family, there was no more *we* for him. To be part of something when he was always so alone, it was tempting, but then no, he had to focus, finish what he started. Otherwise, what use was his search for these past few years? He too, then, would be unfinished, bits of him strewn, and then stranded, across a landscape that was not his own. But still, those strange, crooked eyes. And this woman with her scent of flowers.

"Indulge me, Miss Nail. So that I can understand your sister. It is far easier for me to find someone if I have a real sense of who I'm looking for."

"Alright, Mr. O'Brien, if you insist, but there isn't much to tell. Lucy finds trouble. She always has. Speaks her mind. Makes most people uncomfortable."

"Because she is a blunt speaker?"

"I'm not sure. Could be many things. Her impulsiveness. Boldness. Lack of tact. Her strange eyes. I could go on."

"Was she always like this?"

"Yes, of course. Lucys are born, not made."

"But your upbringing perhaps? The newspaper implied it was colourful?"

"Colourful? Yes, I suppose. My mother was an actress, my father a drunk. After my mother died, he was out drinking most nights. Finally managed to get himself stabbed in an alleyway owing to an overdue debt, backed the wrong horse in a race. After that, Lucy and I raised ourselves. I did my best as the oldest, but Lucy has always been a little feral."

"Did you grow up in Butte?"

"All over. San Francisco, Chicago, a few small, desolate towns in Arizona. We were in Cripple Creek when my mother died, Butte when my father did the same. Lucy and I thought of heading to New York after that, but I guess Butte has a hold on people, so we ended up back there."

"Now you find yourself in Cobalt?"

Lily sighed. "It is a very long story, Mr. O'Brien. But yes, we were to meet here. We thought it could be a place to hide, to start over. Get lost in the crowds. Why does anyone come to a place like Cobalt? Why did you?"

"My motives have nothing to do with the matter at hand. Yours might."

She persisted. "Not seeking your fortune? A second chance perhaps?"

"I don't really believe in second chances. Most of us don't deserve them."

"Running from a dark past are you?"

Dark? No, the past had been bright, all colours of Biddy and his home and tea with his mum. Until it wasn't. Modesto asked, "The trouble your sister might be in, could it be related to her second sight?"

"I love my sister dearly, but she doesn't need the second sight to elicit strong reactions. If she gets herself in trouble, it is impossible for her to not make it worse. She unnerves people. Says strange things. She *is* a strange thing. Men hate her, women find her repulsive."

O'Brien leaned back in his chair, smiled, said, "She sounds delightful. Now tell me, did you and your sister leave Butte together?"

Yes, they had. As Lily explained, they divided up for safety, Lucy to New York, Lily to Montreal. It seems they did things right, heading to the big cities, losing themselves in the crowds. And of course heading to Cobalt, everyone was making their way north to the silver city, nothing to rouse suspicion there. Of course, New York was a rough city, it was possible Lucy came to harm there, but Lily said no, Lucy could handle herself. And she had a strong feeling her sister was here, in Cobalt, even though she'd asked around at the hotels and boarding houses, checked for a telegram and nothing.

"And the date you arrived?"

Lily hesitated. O'Brien knew in that hesitation was the makings of a lie. Lily said, "I was late."

"By how long?"

"A number of days."

"May I ask what the cause of your delay was?"

"Travel arrangements fell through. These things happen."

"Were you delayed in Montreal?"

"In Montreal? No. Yes. Oh, really, is this badgering necessary?"

"I'm just curious, given that you were later than you hoped, could Lucy have gone looking for you in Montreal?"

"We agreed to wait here for the other."

"Does Lucy always do as she is supposed to?"

Lily sighed, "No. I suppose it is possible. But I feel she is here."

Modesto nodded, "I would imagine you would know, so we will start here, though I may make some discreet inquiries down at the train station, just to be sure. And the gentleman in question, the one you believe took your sister, what of him?"

"Gentleman? He's no gentleman, he's a devil."

A devil. Not a demon. That hierarchy of dark, it was wise to pay attention to that. And hadn't he just heard talk of a demon, some presence that had the prospectors on edge, the thing whispered about, was that a demon? A demon that stopped the men possessed by silver fever from going into the woods after dusk. Was the silver fever a demon all of its own? Driving these men to claw and clamber over one another just to scrape a few dollars from the earth. Weren't they all just dragging their own demons along behind them by their skins, the greed and the demon inseparable, bound together by their matted hides?

"Mr. O'Brien? Did you hear me?"

"Yes, my apologies, I was just thinking. And I believe you should come back this evening, let me read your fortune. And in the meantime, during the day, please keep to your room."

The scent of violets as she rose.

"What a lovely scent, Miss Nail, reminds me of home."

"And where do you think of as home? Surely not Butte!"

"Home is in my mind, Miss Nail, in my mind."

"I see," she said, and then asked, "so you aren't serious about reading my tea leaves, or cards, or whatever it is you are proposing? I would prefer to spend the time preparing for our search."

"I find it hard to separate the fortune-telling from the detective work. It is my profession after all."

"Your sign promises otherwise," she said moving towards the door and shaking her head, smiling though, stepping through and pointing up, then looking, reading *Modesto O'Brien: Fortune Teller & Detective.*

She stared for several seconds, as if by staring she could change it back to what she had seen before. Her eyes then returned to Modesto, him watching expectantly, smiling pleasantly, and she said, "Well, I'm not sure," now a bit flustered, glanced back at the sign, said, "I did think it strange in a town known for its law-abiding citizens...." Her voice trailed off, then she said, "I really don't know what has come over me today."

O'Brien slipped the newspaper back into the drawer, joined her in the doorway.

"Do not believe all of that law-abiding boastfulness, there is plenty of six-gun bravado to be found here. Now let me lock up here and escort you back to your hotel."

She murmured her consent, waited as he locked the door. "It is truly a dreadful place," Modesto said, taking her by the arm, moving her down the uneven wooden slats of the sidewalk, the sun harsh and too bright, "much too easy to be jostled by these crowds, so please do be careful."

She said nothing, and Modesto left her alone with her thoughts until they reached the hotel, men hanging over the second story balcony watching the hustle of the street below, the hotel festooned with shabby bunting.

"Remember, Mr. O'Brien, this man we are looking for, he is not to be trifled with."

"Of course, Miss Bow, I take these matters very seriously. When we are finished tonight, I am going to move you to safer living arrangements. Inform the hotel you will be checking out. That you are headed down south on the train."

"Yes, alright."

"Oh, and when you come by this evening, perhaps just after you take your supper, please feel free to bring a nice bottle of whiskey with you. You can send the boy at the hotel to fetch it to your room."

"Does that help with the fortune telling?"

"It certainly does not impede it," he said.

CHAPTER
FIVE

DRIFTWOOD CITY, UP ALONG THE BLACK RIVER, TIMISKAMING

Giving a hard shove to anyone stepping out of the line or dragging their feet, the man walked along the line of workers yelling, "Keep up! Shut your mouths and keep moving!"

Lucy got a shove to her back, sent her stumbling forward, but she kept her footing and the man sounded disgusted when he said, "You ain't going to last a day on the crew. Fucking foreigners, nothing but skin and bone."

"Bone. Bone." Lucy muttering, then gazing upwards said, "Look there, those trees, they look like human bones, those trees there. Bones everywhere. All around us."

No one was listening to her. Not the other workers, not the men in charge. There were four men acting as guards, two of them were squat men who didn't have much to say and kept to themselves. The other two had been at the train station in Montreal and had stayed with the group throughout the trip north. They were mean, one sporting a big beard that stayed littered with bits of his food, and the other had a thick moustache, eyes just slits. The men spent their time walking up and down the line of workers, making sure no one tried to slip away or slow things down too much. Lucy was midway up the line, struggling to carry the big pack and keep up to the rest.

"Are none of youse listening to me?" she shouted. "Look all around us, everything's dead, cut down, we need to be careful out here. All these bones. What if our bones end up here too? Left lying here, alone, no one knowing, not kin or no one. Can no one hear me?"

If they could, no one was showing it, all the workers just kept trudging along, minding their own business. The trail they were on was fairly wide, had been hacked out of the bush by a crew cutting the right of way for the coming train tracks. The ground was uneven, torn up. The edges of the trail were crowded with felled aspen trees, the branches pale with black markings, some thick, thigh-sized limbs, others wraith-like thin, or crooked like elbows, all piled up on top of each other. Victims of dynamite, a tangle of stumps and severed branches. The jagged ends on the blasted trees were left sticking out of the ground. They were sharp and sturdy.

The slit-eyed man came up alongside Lucy, barked, "Shut up, keep moving." He didn't bother to even look at her, just kept moving up the line, but she saw him, saw him there with his drooping moustache, broad forehead and thin chin. She tried to form a picture in her mind: her turning around to face the man, looking into those slits, taking hold of him and raising him up and then slamming him down on top of one of the jagged tree stumps, puncturing him through and through. If only she were a good foot taller and had another hundred pounds on her. She would do it.

"Something bad is going to happen," she said loudly, wondering what it might be. She could feel it all around her, thinking now maybe she was just feeling what had already happened, that it was still hanging in the air like a lament, like when the singing ends but everyone is still listening, still making space for the sadness.

"Not to me boy, not to me," said the slit-eyed man, "but something bad will surely happen to you if you don't shut your fucking mouth." He turned to one of the squat men who was cradling a rifle in his arms, barked, "Hold that thing properly! Do you even know how to use it?"

The man fumbled with it a bit before he got it righted, said, "Sorry JoeBo, just don't think these lazy sonsofbitches going 'cause much trouble."

"Don't give a damn what you think, do your job!"

This man named JoeBo was always mad, threatening or pushing one worker or another, even when they were just minding their own business and doing what they were told. Bullying his own men too, Lucy figuring he was the boss of one of the railway crews. She didn't know too much about railroading, but it looked like another bunch had already been through and blasted the living daylights out of the forest to cut the right of way. There'd been lots of talk in all the newspapers of the railway pushing northward, opening up the country. Opening. Opening up, the words sticking to her as she thought about it. Like wounds opening up? Sutures tested and strained. The railway like the sutures, thinking it could hold things together. Look at the ruptures all around, what could put all of this back together again?

Behind the piles of severed limbs and tangle of branches, the once green leaves of the tree crowns lay decapitated and orphaned, tossed high on top of one another. It was hard to just pass by. Not to feel the pull of their sorrow. Their reproach. Lucy stopped, kneeling to touch the smooth bark of the branches, seeing then the black marks looking like eyes, she felt their hold, mesmerizing, looking up to where the tree tops had once fluttered, whispering to one another and playing in the sunlight, she said, "It wasn't me." Saying it first quiet like but then yelling, "Wasn't me, wasn't me!" and when there was no answer that she could hear, she yelled, "It was them!" pointing to JoeBo and yelling even louder, "It was him."

Between the slapping of bugs, and his own yelling, he didn't hear her at first. He was distracted, turning his meanness on a thick set man who had stopped along the trail just up ahead, the worker winded, bent over and breathing hard. Lucy wondered if her volume was wrong, if she wasn't hearing what everyone else was hearing. Was no sound coming from her when she yelled again, "*It was him!*" pointing towards where the JoeBo man was now putting his foot into the back of the thick-set man's knees, sending the man crumpling down, sending up splatters of grey muck?

"Going to leave you here in the mud," JoeBo raged, puffing from the exertion, "you worthless son of a bitch," and then looking up towards the front of the line he shouted, "Hey, you, up at the front, slow down," now moving up along the line of trudging workers.

The worker at the front was slight, almost as slight as Lucy, and was a good twenty yards ahead of the rest, Lucy thinking maybe he was trying to make a break for it. He kept walking fast, maybe even starting to go faster as JoeBo shouted at him to stop. Maybe he didn't understand, Lucy not sure where these men were from, but she thought maybe they were Hungarian or something, only one or two seeming to speak any English.

Lucy tugged down her hat. The bugs were savage, swarming up from the marshy water with each step that the man in front of her took, getting in her eyes, buzzing loud in her ears. Couldn't think. Could barely walk straight. Not that she knew what direction they were headed. Or even where they were.

The day before, as they had been pushed out of the train car, she asked the man beside her where they were. He pointed to the station sign: Englehart.

"Where's that?" she'd asked, but he just shrugged. Then a group of people on the platform, four, maybe five, men, had approached JoeBo, talking with thick accents and him trying to play the tough guy, then patting his hip, letting them know he had a gun. She already knew he had a gun because she'd seen him jam it into the mouth of one of the workers in the railway car when he protested being pushed around and insulted. It was hard to protest when you had a gun in your mouth.

But then two other men had come up along the railway platform carrying rifles, and Lucy thought maybe this was some sort of showdown and then there were some shots fired, men ducking and running and firing, and her and all the workers got pushed back into the train car where they crouched, almost on top of each other, listening to the shooting and yelling.

When the door slid open in the early morning, all of them hoping to see anyone but that man with the drooping moustache, there he was, outlined by the blood red sky behind him, saying, "Get the fuck out and get moving, we have time to make up. You can eat later."

That had been two days ago. They'd been pushed into another boxcar, hauled a ways over rough terrain, the caboose bumping along and twice slipping off the tracks and all of them getting off and having to right the thing before they could get moving again. When they got to the end of the line for the train, they started walking, some of the men excited after a few miles to see some shanties up ahead, but they were told to keep moving, to quit dragging their feet and get on the scow that was waiting.

The scow was loaded with stacks of hay and oats and camp supplies, the vessel sinking into the water under their weight. They went in two groups, the first one having to wait on the shore for the other to get there. And they'd been walking ever since, half the time in some mixture of mud and water that was up over their ankles, loaded down with sacks of grain or packs or bedrolls or bundles of tools. They were half-dead on their feet.

Lucy, too, felt half-dead, but now JoeBo was on the young kid up at the front, the kid now trying to hide himself in the crowd, probably trying to avoid attention but somehow doing the opposite.

"You lazy ass bastard, think I ain't going to notice when you drop out of sight. I see fucking everything," and with that he took hold of the boy, kicking his legs out from underneath him, and the man starting to drag him, the kid getting all wet, begging to be let go.

"First he's walking too fast, then he's not walking fast enough, just leave him be," Lucy moving up towards JoeBo and shouting even as she knew she shouldn't. JoeBo dropped the kid, the plopping sound of the body hitting the thick tangle of reeds and water, and turned his attention to her, in no rush to come to dole out the punishment, maybe even enjoying dragging it out. Displaying his power in the middle of this stinky swamp.

He barked at a few of the workers to tie the boy up, they were going to drag him the rest of the way like a sack of meat, teach them all a lesson. Then he bunched up his fists, pumped up on his own anger, and headed for Lucy, ready to go. He towered over her. "Fucking little troublemaker!"

Lucy conjured an image in her mind, him swinging, the blow landing, seeing too, as she loosened her body, her skeleton, the frame of it, softening her bones to jelly, and then his fist really did come, but by then she felt her body was weightless, giving way like water under a boot. She went down with a splash, her head going under, the metal of her blood mixing with the brown marsh waters in her mouth. His boot was there then, sending a hard kick to her ribs, her scrabbling up onto her hands and knees, sputtering, but him kicking her again and her thinking thank Christ he was standing in water up to his ankles, his kicks less ferocious than he wanted. She spat out the blood and swamp, tried to clear the mud from her face as he was walking away, satisfied, barking at the others nearby to quit gawking and get a move on.

She felt the reluctant efforts of the men pulling her up, one muttering in a language she didn't understand, getting her on her feet but then leaving her on her own. She didn't expect these men to come to her aid, why should they, she knew none of them. But through bad judgement and bad timing, she was now sharing their fate. Wait till she told Lily what had happened. Lily'd be some pissed. Both at Lucy and the men who brought her here. God help 'em if Lily got a hold of them. And Lucy was hoping against hope that Lily would, she wasn't sure how much longer she could take this.

Lucy used her sleeve to clear the mud from the side of her face, then joined the end of the line of workers, sloshing past the wasps buzzing and bouncing along the cattails.

CHAPTER SIX

He pushed his weight into Shitty Mitty's back, shoving up against him, back-to-back like, then bellowed to the dozen or so men scattered along the bar at the Bucket of Blood Saloon, "Drinks on Mitt the Shit, I'll be damned if he hasn't just been paid."

Shitty Mitty was wedged up against the bar, the rough edge of the wood pressing into his belly. "Hey, Bill, get off of me."

"Bill Beau-dine," Bodine said, drawing out his own last name, "wants a whiskey, make it a bottle."

"Count me in," a man called from the far end of the bar, picking up his glass and moving up, most of the men now gravitating towards Bodine. He was like that. When he spoke, men wanted to be near him, hear what he had to say, whether about mining, women or cards. Didn't seem to matter if half of it was bullshit, because Bodine was just the kind of man most other fellas wanted to meet in a mining camp like Cobalt.

He was big enough, well over six foot and broad shouldered, fair haired and squared jaw. Bodine once told his friend Butch that what he possessed, and Butch lacked, was animal magnetism, but Butch hadn't known what that meant, so Bill had explained it was when folks couldn't stay away from you. 'Like you're a magnet. Folks, 'specially women, are drawn to you," he'd said, and Butch had asked, "Well, what's that got to do with an animal?" and Bill had said, "It means it's in my nature Butch, it's my instinct to be attractive. Just like a wolf is made to kill, it's like that," and then Butch said that Bodine wasn't too bad at killing either.

Right now, Bodine was missing Butch. The man complained less than Shitty Mitty and he was just overall better company. A man you could have a laugh with, instead of at. He was wondering about Butch. It wasn't like him to just up and leave. But Butch had been acting different before he disappeared. Keeping secrets. That had pissed Bodine off.

Pissed him off enough to have words with Butch, even a bit of a dust up. He felt bad about that now, but Butch had been acting like some smug sonofabitch. Bodine figured he was well within his rights to take a round out of him. Fellas would back him up on that. But Tommy wouldn't like the looks of it. Bodine figured he'd better find Butch and set things straight before Tommy got to Cobalt.

Bodine felt Shitty Mitty pushing back, bony elbow poking into his spine, didn't like the feel of that, said "Calm down Shitty, I was just getting comfortable, that's all," and he used his own elbows to push off of Shitty Mitty, digging them in good, giving the guy a taste of his own medicine, then laughing, saying, "So tell us all about your big day hauling that stinking nag up and down the centre of town."

Before Shitty Mitty could squirm around to face the group of men and tell his story, one of them said, "I heard it split open before you even got past the Prospect Hotel."

"Made two of them ladies standing outside the hardware store vomit into their little, perfumed gloves," another fella said, and then the men were laughing and drifting away in groups of two or three, a few of them taking their drinks and moving to the nearby tables along the wall.

The bar was narrow, dirty and ill-lit. It had windows, but that didn't matter much. Buildings had gone up so fast around it that there wasn't anything to see except the backside view of the rough lumber buildings on either side. No one complained though, just glad to have a place a man could get a drink, the authorities wanting to keep up the appearance that the mining camp was dry, keep the men going to work day in and day out without any trouble, dependable. So there weren't too many places in town to drink, and fewer still the police left alone.

Shitty Mitty turned himself sideways to see Bodine. He was going to explain how it wasn't like that at all, how he'd wrap the chains around the horse no problem, but Bill wasn't interested, saying to Shitty, "Get me another bottle, all these freeloaders drained mine."

"So, what's going on Bill, what are we up to tomorrow?" Saying it a little too loud, Shitty reminding the other guys that he ran with Bill.

Bodine grinned, downed his whiskey, said, "Not interested in tomorrow, interested in tonight. Grab that bottle Shitty, come on, let's have ourselves a game."

"Give us a bottle Frank," Shitty Mitty said, rapping the bar with his knuckles, looking over and seeing Bill settling at a table, already a few guys drifting towards him, Shitty worried about losing his spot, yelling down at Frank, "Come on, what's taking so long?"

Frank, shaking his head, said, "Shitty, you got to stand up for yourself. You don't even know most of these freeloaders. Might as well just hand over all your money now, it's all going to be gone by the end of the night anyway. Bodine will make sure of that."

"Best you be minding your own business," Shitty Mitty said, tossing a few coins down on the bar, "just keep a proper list and give it to me later, I'll settle up what's owing, but I want it in writing." And he grabbed the bottle and headed over to where Bodine was sitting, hurrying to grab a chair before the fat-faced fella that was hanging around stole his spot. The man was shorter but wider than Shitty and was trying to get Bodine to pay attention to what he was saying, Bodine saying to him, "Move along."

Shitty set down the bottle and the fat-faced man reached for it, but Bodine's hand got to it first, holding it down on the table, saying to the man, "I said move along, you're talking nothing but bullshit."

The man shook his head, kept his eyes on the bottle, said, "Just saying what I heard, thought you'd want to know, heard you'd been asking around after Butch. Seemed like the least I could do."

"Whatcha heard?" asked Shitty Mitty, feeling uneasy, noticing that the man's hat was too small for his head, and his head, large as it was, too small for his body. The man leaned in close like he was telling secrets, not seeming to notice that Bodine was now wearing a dark expression, started, "Butch was working out by Kerr Lake…"

Bodine said, "It's none of your fucking business, Shitty," but the fat-faced man wanted to tell his secret, so he said, half whispering, like out of respect for Bodine, "They say that monster, it lies down and waits at the bottom of the trenches, out there where Butch was working. Some of the fellas think that's what happened."

Shitty wasn't sure what he thought of all the talk of the monster that had started up a few weeks or so ago, but the rumours were starting to fly fast and steady. A group of prospectors up from Colorado who were working out near Kerr Lake said they'd heard a monster shrieking at night, another one said he saw a demon out in the treetops when there was a full moon. No one had actually seen it in daylight, not really. Only caught glimpses of it, but Bodine said they were probably drunk, saw the back side of some big old bear, said those kind of fellas, they were just greenhorns, scared of the dark.

Bodine was getting agitated about what the man was saying, Shitty not surprised when Bodine finally jumped up, taking hold of the man by his shirt collar and talking low but mad like, "You saying those fellas you've been talking to know something about Butch?"

The man said, "Hey Bill, whoa, no need for that, just trying to be helpful."

"Well, you're not. You tell your friends to keep their fucking mouths shut 'less they got something useful to say, understand, now get out of here."

The man, straightening his collar, said he was sorry for bothering Bodine, then backed up a few steps before turning to leave – everyone knew you had to be careful turning your back on him.

Shitty watched as Bodine sat back down, brooding now, grabbing the bottle and taking a long pull before banging it back down on the table, saying nothing.

Shitty thought maybe he could still salvage the evening, tried, "Hey Bill, you wanna deal?"

"Not playing cards, not tonight."

"Thought you said we would."

"Never you mind 'bout what I said before, what I'm telling you now is that we're not playing."

"You going to visit that little lady you got?"

"Shut your mouth Shitty, just shut it and mind your own fucking business. What I get up to is none of your concern."

"Sure, Bill. Sorry." And then Shitty shut up, knew better than to say too much when Bodine was getting snarly. He filled the two glasses on the table. Willing to wait.

Bodine downed the shot, sat for a while staring but not really looking at anything, Shitty getting restless but trying to be patient, knowing the man couldn't go too long without the sound of his own voice. Finally, Bodine said, "An old friend's coming to town."

"Yeah? Who's that?"

"It's Tommy."

"That Coffin fella you told me about?"

Bodine had told him that this big shot, Tommy Coffin, had bankrolled him and sent him up to Cobalt to lay the groundwork for some big operations. Shitty found that hard to believe. When Bodine first got to town he'd head out every now and again, said he was taking care of business and didn't feel inclined to tell Shitty what he was up to. But lately Bodine didn't seem to get up too much, except running a few girls and drinking. And the cards. The man could gamble, just wasn't very good at it. And Shitty could tell Bodine had been some pissed off when that fella Butch had shown up a few months later, and Shitty always suspected he'd been sent by that Coffin fella to check up on Bodine.

"Yeah, that's right, Tommy Coffin."

"When you first got here, he was all you used to talk about …"

"Shut up Shitty, try listening."

"Sorry Bill, was just thinking …"

"Don't bother doing no thinking either, just listen would you?"

"Why are you bringing this up now?"

"Jesus Shit, you can't just listen, can you? Now I found out today he's coming sooner than I thought, so we got to get things in order. Listening to that sonofabitch gabbing about Butch reminded me I got to take care of some things, and fast."

"This here fella Coffin, he a prospector?"

Bodine smiled, "He's whatever he wants to be Shitty, Tommy's something else. Been everywhere and done everything."

"That right?" Shitty Mitty said, feeling annoyed, didn't know this Coffin, didn't want some new fellow coming and upsetting things. Shitty had a good thing going, between the horses and the odd job thrown his way, he was doing alright. He'd been right wrung out by the other fellas in town before Bodine came along, all thought themselves big shots out looking for their motherlode, and him just dragging away the dead horses. But now at least most fellas in town let him be since he started running with Bodine. That could all change because of this Coffin.

Shitty asked, "How long is he sticking around for?"

Bill laughed, said, "Don't you worry your shit-filled little head about Tommy. And instead of flapping your gums at me, you can get out there and start looking into where Butch might be. Tommy will be wanting to know."

"How long you know Butch and this Tommy fella?"

"We're all Butte boys, grew up together."

"Like since you were little kids?"

Bill seemed annoyed by the question, poured himself another shot and kept the bottle close by, Shitty wanted another drink himself but wasn't sure what to do, wasn't going to reach across the table and grab it, said, "Thirsty myself, pass over that bottle," but Bill ignored him and said, "Shut up Shitty, I'm trying to think. Got a lot on my mind."

Shitty Mitty knew how to shut up if he had to, had lots of experience at that. But things were different with Bill. The man might talk mean, but he gave Shitty responsibility, let him come along during his dealings, like he was Bill's back up. No doubt about it, his luck had changed the day Bill Bodine came to Cobalt.

It had been pouring rain and cold that day, Bodine pushing his way off the train, starting to make his way through the crowd, and Shitty Mitty spotting him right away, yelling over to him, "Got a place to stay mister?" A few men looked up hopefully, but Bodine had ignored Shitty and kept moving. Then Shitty noticed the fine pair of six guns strapped to the big man's belt.

Shitty Mitty slipped through the crush of bodies to catch up to the man, took hold his arm and said, "You best hide those Mister, Constable up there going to take them away from you." Bodine had looked around, asked, "Where is he?" and Shitty nodded to the man close to the far end of the train, said "He waits there to greet everyone coming to town, takes away their guns so as to avoid trouble," then he added, "Some fellas say they don't get 'em back." Shitty saw the change in Bodine's expression and asked,

"You got a place to stay?" Bodine had said, "I was told to get set up at the American Palace," and Shitty said, "Follow me, I'll get you there without going past the Constable."

And he had gotten him into town with his guns still under his long coat and since then Bill had kept Shitty around, and that's how Shitty liked it.

Bodine said, "I gotta figure out where Butch is."

"Ain't seen hide nor hair of that fella in a few weeks, you know that."

"Not asking you about what you don't know or haven't seen. Maybe he's up and left, but I gotta know that, understand? Ask around the camp. Maybe you can figure out if he caught a train on out of here. Butch was still running schemes up Montreal way, on the side."

"What kind of schemes?"

"Ain't none of your concern Shitty."

"Well, maybe if we knew what he was up to, we'd know why he was missing."

Bodine shrugged. "Butch kept to himself. Don't know about his latest side deals, something maybe to do with the railway, but some other things too. Know he was laying some groundwork for Tommy."

"Groundwork for what?"

"It's big money. Railway. Mining. We're going to be men of this new century, Shitty, you can get on board or get out of the way."

"Hey no, didn't mean anything by it, Bill." Shitty didn't like the sounds of this, hadn't taken much of a liking to Butch. He was a mean sonofabitch. So he wasn't sure he wanted this Tommy Coffin around either, didn't sound too smart. Cobalt was jammed packed with fellas thinking they were going to be millionaires and ended up heading out of town, dead broke and used up. Or worse. Some fellas just disappeared, their wives turning up at the train station looking for them. Them women never had much luck. If the bush had taken their men it was done and over, no one was going to stop looking for silver to go searching. So why did he have to look for Butch?

"I know a bit about mining," Shitty said, "not too sure about this railway work though."

"Don't need you to know anything, just need you to do what I tell you, understand?"

"Yeah, alright Bill, okay, I'll ask around about Butch. Maybe get that new detective in town to look into it."

"One of them Thiel sonsofbitches?"

"I don't think this new fella's a Thiel or a Pinkerton operator. More like an independent. O'Brien's his name."

"With the mine?"

"No, up from Butte."

"Butte? Well, ain't that a coincidence."

Shitty shrugged. "Lots of American fellas up here."

"What you say his name was?"

"Got himself a right peculiar name. Modesto O'Brien."

Bill, absent-mindedly scratching under his arm, not looking at Shitty Mitty but saying, "Modesto? Seems to me I know that name, kind of name that sticks with you, but can't quite place it." Bill thinking on it now, frowning, said, "Yeah, why not, see what he can scrape up for us, don't mention my name though. Until I can place the man. And find out more about him."

"You think you know the fella?"

"I didn't say that Shit, would you pay attention. I said his name was familiar. So stop standing around gawping and get on over and visit that friend of yours."

"Ain't no friend of mine, Bill."

"That's right, I forgot Shitty," Bill said, shoving a slip of paper into Shitty Mitty's hand, "you ain't got no friends." Heading for the door, he added without looking back, "Go get me the things on that list I just gave you, over at Devlin's drugstore. And settle up the bill."

CHAPTER SEVEN

S he was on time. Perhaps she was more interested, more intrigued, than she had let on. The thought pleased him, though he wasn't sure why. Since Biddy died he'd kept to himself, didn't seek out the company or comfort of other human beings. But then this was a strange place, this mining town that asserted itself in the middle of the deep forest, no one pausing to worry or wonder about what had been here before men had started busting open the ground. Puncturing holes in the bottom of the old lake, stirring its glacial secrets, draining it like a bathtub and leaving piles of fish, enough to send the seagulls mad with screeching and feasting. And the men, young and old, charging off into the bush, piling onto the rivers, nose to nose in their canoes, heading off after the scent of silver like a pack of bloodhounds off leash. In such a strange place, it was easy to lose one's moorings.

Her rap at his door had been light and she hadn't waited, turned the handle, and slipped inside.

"So pleased to see you this evening, Miss Bow."

"I do believe you will be more pleased to see your liquor if I'm not mistaken," she said, presenting him with the bottle.

"It was, I assure you, your company I was seeking," he said, drawing the blind down on the door and crossing the room, "The libations simply add to the charm of the evening. Now come, make yourself comfortable."

He placed the bottle on the table next to his chair and reached for two small glasses he'd left waiting at the edge of his desk. He placed them carefully beside the bottle then sat, looked at her expectantly. He found himself nervous, glad of the comforting bottle next to him.

She remained standing, placing her coat carefully over the back of the chair. The energy around her was hard to read, a stillness in the dim room, the far corners dissolving into darkness. Modesto gestured for her to sit across from him at the small table. There was a lace cloth draped over it and a few candles at its centre.

"Please, take your seat. You've participated in evenings such as this before, so you need not make strange. I am quite anxious to begin."

The rustle of her dress as she sat, candlelight across her face. She said, "No Ouija board, Mr. O'Brien? Crystal ball?"

He smiled, "I do believe you are mocking me."

"I am just wondering where the tools of your trade are. You do promise to tell fortunes after all."

"Perhaps we could consider that more of a catchall phrase. Now shall we begin?" he asked, but found himself simply watching her, wondering about this woman so possessed by such beauty, her clothes well cared for but worn, the frayed sleeves of her dress. The same dress she wore yesterday. The small case she carried. The scarred and reddened hands.

Why the scars, and why had this woman not found herself married, settled in an ample brick house with soft chairs, whiling away the afternoon playing cards? Picturing her now, still in the mauve dress but seated at a small card table with other ladies, but then the slippage and she is out of the confines his mind's eye, out of frame, joined by tall and misshapen shadows taking the other chairs, settling in, then a dark, thin hand reaching for the deck of cards at the centre of the table.

"Mr. O'Brien!"

He pulled himself back into the room. "Sorry, I was distracted by your shadows."

"Perhaps I should be going."

"No please, indulge me, Miss Bow," Modesto said, now reaching for the bottle of whiskey, saying as he poured, "I really do feel that this session might be able to help us. It is a way for me to focus my thoughts, reach pathways of possibility that are, in the light of day, elusive. Just sit with me here, let your mind go, see where it takes you ..."

"Mr. O'Brien, really, this ..."

"Perhaps closing your eyes will help. Shut out the distractions."

Lily sighed impatiently but closed her eyes. Modesto took a deep breath himself, steadying himself. It was, however, impossible not to continue to look at her. He was surprised that he could see the faint blue lines in her eyelids, how was that possible, her skin so thin and translucent, like ice, found himself still staring, and then the eyes were open and looking back at him, such a pale shimmering blue, and she said, "Mr. O'Brien, clearly it isn't myself who is troubled by distractions, could you please focus on your business of spectres and table-knocking or else see me to the door?"

"I do apologize, but you must know that you are really quite bewitching."

She stared at him for several seconds, Modesto feeling frozen in that hard gaze, like the hare noticing the wolf not a few feet away. No, maybe not that grim, maybe more as if mesmerized. He'd seen mesmerism done, but never experienced it himself. Perhaps this was it?

"Here, a quick drink perhaps before we begin," and he slid the glass towards her and she asked, "Is this part of your technique?"

"It can help with relaxation."

"Fine, let's begin, anything to find Lucy." She closed her eyes, something very resolved about her tone when she said, "Go ahead then, work your magic."

Now unsettled, Modesto poured himself another glass, wondering over her expression for a moment, and the glass she wasn't touching, keeping her eyes closed as if resting. He was troubled though, this woman had strange edges, a vagueness to how her physical presence met the world. It was hard to focus on a subject that seemed to be dissolving and then reconstituting herself, she seemed in flux. But it was also tantalizing.

So he began. The drifting.

When his Gran had first taught him to reach out to the other side, Modesto accepted it like he accepted everything Biddy Savage had told him, as simple basic truth. She said she'd learned it from her mother, who'd leaned from her mother before.

Modesto had asked, is it only for mams and Grannies

Usually, but I can see you have been touched, I can teach you

How do you know

By the whites of your eyes, but come now, we have to go

Where

To the betwixt and the between

Where's that

It's where the other ones are, it's where you mama was born, on that big ship in the middle of the ocean, neither here nor there, neither home nor this place

Who are the other ones

They're the voices from home, from the sand down by the water, and the trees along its shore, from under the ground where you walk and don't see them

But you're not at home anymore Gran

Not to worry, I brought them along with me in my pocket

And then they had sat in the dark together and drifted.

O'Brien always started his own drifting in that same dark room that Biddy had conjured the first time he had sat with her, sent his mind to circle around the dark room, to get oriented, and then back to this room in which he now sat with this woman who had crossed his path in the here and now. He was looking for images, sights and sounds that might show him something of what was brewing, but his mind kept slipping. Something about the combination of this woman and the burning liquor she had brought with her. It was making it difficult to concentrate.

Breathing slowly, letting his mind wander, hoping to connect with the threads and lines and waterways that flowed through him as he found his way towards the other side. From the first time he'd tried it he'd thought of it as a kind of drifting, a small boat at sea, carried by the rise and fall of the waves, going where they wanted. That what it was like. His grandmother had warned his mother often, watch that boy, keep him tethered and close by, you'll lose him—and his mother would say, 'Lose him? How on God's sweet earth would that be possible, sure he's always underfoot!' And he was, never too far away from that tiny kitchen, from the chickens roosting in the lilac trees, from his mother. Or Biddy Savage—he loved her more than anything.

Drifting now, though the lines and threads that were too hard to see, too faint, in the distance. She must be a cautious one, this Lily Nail.

He said, "I feel like you are resisting."

"Don't be ridiculous, there is nothing to resist. If you insist on carrying on like this perhaps you could have the decency to provide me with another whiskey?"

"Of course," he said, sliding her glass beside his, filling them again and then wondering when had she drunk it? That was odd, he really was distracted. He slid the glass back, her reaching for it before he'd let go, brushing his fingers with hers. It was like being hit. Or bitten? Snapped at. A sharp, sudden sensation, so cold, stinging. O'Brien pulling his hand back quickly without thinking, instinct, and now it felt like perhaps someone had held his hand to ice, a lingering searing cold. Then it was gone.

She slowly took her drink to her lips, a sip, looked satisfied, said, "I am a little weary of this."

"Is that what you are? No, that isn't what I am sensing, I think you are afraid. But there is nothing to be afraid of here."

"You're wrong. I'm hardly frightened of you, but I am frightened for my sister."

"This man we're searching for, he frightens you?"

She drained her glass, said, "Don't worry, Mr. O'Brien, by the time this is all over, he'll frighten you too."

Modesto was quiet for a moment, then closed his eyes again, sought the dark room, waited, breathing, waiting still, then seeing in his mind's eye the threads of light, pale purples and blues, moving in the room, hovering, they were so beautiful, so he followed, further and further, but then they began to thin out until they were only vapors that seemed to slip away and dissolve, leaving nothing for him to follow, to hold onto. Severed, all of it.

That had never happened to him before. For a moment he panicked, where was he now, stranded? But his eyes could open, he could see it now, the glow of candlelight, the small table, her at it, staring at him. Everything just as he had left it.

And she said, "You see what happens to promises made? To the promises of moonlight cruises on the lake, of sidewalks made of violet glass? Beautiful music and candlelight. You see now? They just vanish."

There was nothing to be said to that, to the sureness in her voice. Had she too seen the violet tremors in the air around her swirl then vanish?

Unsure now of this woman, Modesto asked, "Why did you come this evening?"

Lily sighed, said, "To see what kind of a man you are, Mr. O'Brien. After all, I am placing a good deal of trust in you."

Modesto doused the candles, said, "I wonder if you haven't bewitched me."

"A witch? Is that what I am?"

She was smiling, but he said, "Maybe. I don't know."

"I am certainly not a witch. Don't be ridiculous."

"My head is spinning."

"And that's my fault? Not the liquor's?"

"Yes," hesitating, trying to settle the torrent in his head, said, "no, well maybe not. I don't know what it is but there is something in my mind."

"I think you may be having some sort of fit. Would you like water?"

He was cold, very cold, the north wind blowing around him, loud in his ears. He glanced about for the open window or door, but the room was sealed up tight and the sky outside was merely the same grimy, bleached grey. He saw that Lily's knuckles were white from gripping hard at the edge of the table as if she were holding herself in place, but her eyes were calm.

He stared into the violet eyes, amethyst. From the earth maybe. But hadn't they been blue eyes? And then he wondered, about things changing, first his sign, now her eyes. Was it him? But others too could see. Maybe everything was not quite what it seemed. But everyone always seemed so sure of what they saw. He felt now he wasn't sure of anything. Except that he very much liked the unsettling company of Miss Lily Nail.

He said, "I'm going to tell you why I'm here."

"In Cobalt?"

"Yes."

"Alright, tell me. Though I suspect I have a general notion. Hell bent on revenge?"

"Yes, actually. Why would you think that?"

"What other reason, besides greed, would bring a man to a hell like this?"

"Love perhaps?"

"There is none of that about you."

"How sad, but yes, I suppose you are right."

"And who is it you are pursuing?"

"A small gang of men from Butte."

"What did they do to you?"

"It is an odd story." He hesitated, then started, "I was ten. In school. There was this older boy, our neighbour, Kit Murphy. Maybe a few years old than me. He was beautiful. And kind. A different sort of boy. And my Gran had such a soft spot for him. She was always filling his head with stories from the old country, tales of ghosts and highwaymen. He'd come by every now and again, and she'd pull out her clippings about Billy the Kid, said that he had been a good son of Ireland. Kit loved the stories, think he fancied himself some sort of wild west outlaw or mountain man. Tried to look the part too, as much as any boy could, even stopped cutting his blonde hair."

"In Butte?"

"Yes. In Butte, that tender town."

"What happened to this boy with the long blonde hair?"

Telling the story suddenly seemed impossible. Modesto felt the black inching its way up along the inside of his skull, heard his Gran say,

It's alright, go on, tell her, this one is familiar to me

How do you know her

I'm not sure, it is hard to see past all of the old yet new of her

But she is familiar

Yes, familiar, but strange as well

Lily interrupted, broke the spell, said, "I want to know how the story ends."

Modesto said, "Yes, of course, it is just sometimes difficult, the event still fresh in my mind after all these years."

"Were you friends with this boy?"

"In a way. He was older, but I worshipped him. I was steeped in the stories too of course, imagining myself joining Kit's gang one day, riding the trails ..."

"And your own long hair?"

"Yes, I suppose it is sort of a belated gesture of loyalty. At the time there was a group of boys, not quite so kind ..."

"There always are, aren't there?"

"Disheartening as it is, yes. And one of these took a disliking to Kit. Teased him endlessly, mostly about his hair. But Kit wouldn't cut it. Likely his parents were unaware of the relentlessness of the teasing. I know Gran tried to tell them, but they were quiet people, thought it would pass, you know, boys will be boys, and Gran threatened to go to the school herself, but Kit wouldn't have it. Thought it would just make things worse. But I know it was hard on him, so he just escaped further and further into his own world. Waiting to be somewhere else."

"Did he have a chance to be somewhere else?"

"No, one warm, sunny day in May those boys dragged him out into the dust of the school yard, held him down, and cut his hair off. Then just left him there crying, in front of us all. It was terrible. The teacher, all the students, everyone, including myself, just watching. Most of them were laughing though, high sport I guess," Modesto paused, saw the black circling, circling, circling the sun on that day.

"How dreadful."

"It was. When he ran away from the school, we went looking for him, his parents, my Gran and Ma and me. I found him, slumped over in the corner of a little shed at the back of his garden. Killed himself, carbolic acid. He wasn't so beautiful then."

Lily was quiet. It was a while before she managed, "What happened to the boys that cut his hair?"

"Nothing of course. They were out of school for a few days, kept home maybe until things settled down. They were back to setting cats on fire before you knew it."

"Your Gran must have been heartbroken."

"She was, and none of us were ever quite the same after Kit died."

"And these boys, now grown to men, they're here now?"

O'Brien sighed, "Why wouldn't they be? I have followed their trail to many places, but always have missed them. I've tracked them and lost them. But I ended up in Toronto and heard there that they were developing business interests in the north. Following the lure of easy money. So I came here to look and, if need be, wait."

"Maybe we're all drawn here, desperate for something."

"Perhaps," Modesto said, "these places of disturbances seem to have a powerful pull on predator and prey alike. There is no end to the likes of swindlers and liars in this place. Mrs. Shay, the landlady at the boarding home I intend on moving you to, she herself bought stock in the illustrious Queen Cleopatra mine, where the silver flowed like the Nile River itself. Out of pocket her month's earnings. Nothing but gombeen men here, opportunists."

"I suppose. But false stock is not worrying me, it's something worse. There's something much darker that fraud or thievery here."

Yes, Modesto had sensed it, sensed the promise of wealth flowing like the sewage into every crevice and depression, following every thin channel carved through the rock, seducing every hopeless optimist and greasy speculator and sending them all out into the bush to scratch and sniff and pray to the rock to yield up some silver. Yes, the strangeness here was dark.

"It could just be that great temptation of wealth," he said, "but there is something else here, you are right, it's like a weight when you step out your door. Tries to follow you, attach itself to you, slips around you at night. I will be glad to see the end of this place."

"Are you thinking of leaving?"

"Not until I find my men."

"It was a childhood brutality. You've nursed it for many years."

Modesto smiled, "What is the point of a good grudge if you can't hold on to it, and it to you?"

"I'll grant that there is a place for a good grudge," she said.

"And yours? Would you tell me of your reasons for being here?"

"That is a story for another day, Mr. O'Brien. I think our time together tonight is finished."

He glanced at the bottle, and she said, "Don't worry, I'll leave it."

"I should see you to Mrs. Shay's."

"I'm sure I can find it, or another place. I could stay at the Prospect Hotel, it seems a popular spot."

"No, too much of a gathering place. And the walls are no more than an inch thick. There are no secrets there. And you arriving without luggage? That would draw attention."

"Fine, but I was tripping over boarding houses on my way here, I am sure I can find a discrete one."

"No, I'd like you to stay with Mrs. Shay. It's down in Finn Town. As the houses go, it is not completely dreadful, and she is a decent woman."

Modesto followed her out, taking her arm. "I will spend tomorrow trying to determine your sister's whereabouts. Keep to your room, perhaps take your meals there as well if possible. A lady such as yourself will be noticed, and it is possible you might be recognized. I will see if Mrs. Shay can find out some suitable attire. I will let you know when we are to leave."

"If you are to get an early start in the morning you best be measured in your drinking tonight."

"Not to worry, Miss Bow," he said, "I've learned the hard way to leave enough for breakfast."

CHAPTER EIGHT

The gossip concerning the detective who'd shot the horse right in the middle of town couldn't hold the town's attention for very long. Even the sun, offering a lustrous silver gleam overhead, had been unable to capture the attention of the men toiling below. Why look up when there was the hope of real silver below? So the sun had finished its dejected slide towards the western horizon when startling news spread along the jumble of streets, alleyways and trails: a prospector, working very early in the morning out near Kerr Lake, had seen *it*. And worse still, the men had whispered to one another, *it* had seen the man. That got their attention.

Now they were all gathered in the Bucket of Blood Saloon and John Moberly was starting to tell his story, one hand clasped onto the bar as if to steady himself. The bar was packed, every prospector, mining man, and layabout was there, and every table was taken, some men standing on chairs to see over the crowd that kept pushing in.

"It was dark this morning when I left the camp," Moberly was saying, but someone interrupted just as the story was starting, saying loudly, for the benefit of the crowd, "Heading out in the dark, course you're going to see a boogeyman," and the man sort of laughed, a couple of guys joined in the snickering but most were quiet, wanting to hear the story.

Moberly stretched his neck a bit, trying to see who had spoken but it was a blur of faces staring at him, and he said, "We all do it, try to keep our business to ourselves. Not one of you here haven't tried to sneak out of camp while the fellas in the tent next to you are still sleeping."

But feeling the eyes of the room on him made him feel something close to shame, and worry. As if they all knew what had happened before, before the monster. Not that he'd done what other men hadn't thought of doing, him and Butch just had the gumption to actually do it.

The day they had watched the young man setting off, shiny new shovel hanging off his backpack, it had been sticky with the spring heat, the snow melting fast along the creek. Butch and him had hid as they'd watched. Moberly had been busting rock for months and finding nothing—then this fella turns up, coming off his trapline out near Kerr Lake, doesn't know the first goddamn thing about prospecting, and has the nerve to come into town bragging that he was picking silver right up off the ground like it was nothing special. And that didn't seem fair.

So they'd caught up with him, just as he was putting in the first marker, Butch offering him some water, all friendly like, as Moberly had skirted around and came up from behind. No one had even missed him, or had gone looking. That was over a month ago. But this thing with the monster had happened today. He told himself they had nothing to do with each other. But he was having trouble keeping the guilt and the fear away from each other.

"John!" someone yelled, "Com'on, whaddya see?"

Moberly gulped down a mouthful of whiskey, said, "I went out to start back at my trench, got a little turned around, some of my markers seemed missing, not sure, but I knew I was close. I just came into a clearing and finally had my bearings, then, at the edge of the woods just ahead, well…" he paused, stared past everyone, like he was seeing it all over again, "Didn't believe it at first. Thought maybe it was the light, but it was as clear as anything when it straightened itself out." Took a deep breath, drained his glass, "Just dropped my shovel and ran. Didn't look back."

• • •

By the time Modesto arrived at the Bucket of Blood the crowd was crammed in the doorway and pouring out onto the sidewalk, men jostling for position so they could hear Moberly better. Modesto had seen the crowd and decided to see what was happening. He was keeping his search quiet, hoping to come across the men he was tracking without having to ask too many questions. Didn't want to scare them off. He was tired of trailing along after them. It was going to finish here.

He slipped around the back and came in through the kitchen just in time to hear the man who was holding everyone's attention say, "I think I surprised it," the man pushing his glass towards the barkeep who was ready, the liquor sloshing in and spilling over the rim, Moberly then grabbing it and taking a quick gulp as every man waited for the story to pick up again, "but I can tell you for sure I lit on outta there as fast as I could. Didn't even really look where I was going. Just ran."

Wasn't hard to believe looking at the man, his face all torn up from the branches slapping and cutting him all the way back to town.

But it was the faces of the men hanging on Moberly's every word that interested Modesto. Rapt faces, their expressions vivid with all that they had been dreaming and fearing and conjuring, this beast. Every morning the men emerged from their cheap rooms or tents to stumble down to the town square, find each other and talk over the numerous rumours and sightings and accusations. Men had started to go out in pairs, and some mine owners were talking about getting security. Just to control the workers of course, not that they believed in this monster. And now, after all of the pale hints and ghosts of information, a man who had seen it, had a story to tell.

Moberly wasn't a fine-looking man, but now there was something almost obscene about him, the streaks of dried blood under the sweat on his face, the way he clawed at his collar as if he had some strange pox that was causing him to burn up. It was hard to look at him or look away. Moberly himself seemed unaware of the reaction of the crowd to his words, more like he was telling the story to himself, like he couldn't believe it, saying, "Just as I laid eyes on that, that, thing, it seen me, and I saw that it was sort of bent over something, someone, a body."

Men weren't even drinking anymore, they were leaning forward, waiting and repulsed, and Moberly said, "Pretty sure it was the body of a man but couldn't swear on a Bible to it, it looked long dead, but that thing, at first it was hunched up over it, making some, some godawful noise, snarling, like it was guarding it, like a dog with a bone. Never heard or seen nuthin' like that in my whole life."

There was quiet for a bit as the men digested what they had just been told. Then a younger man, flushed in the face, clothes threadbare, said, "But it was early, Mr. Moberly, real early right? Might have been in the light, maybe a bear or something?" saying it like he wanted it to be the case.

"Just said I'd seen the damn thing, didn't I, Clem? I seen with my own eyes."

The young lad was shaking his head at Moberly's certainty, said, "You know that's just a ways further on from the claim I'm working. We been out there together. Can't tell one tree from the next when its dawn like that, the light and all, it's impossible."

A big man, moustached and with a dark beard, leaning on the bar close to Moberly, interrupted, "What'd it look like John? The boy's right, it could a been a bear."

Moberly asked, "Why the hell are youse asking all these fucking questions for anyway?"

The big man said, "Chrissake John, you saw it, we want to know what it is!"

Moberly was now rubbing his forehead, said, "Didn't ask to see it, did I?"

"Well, Moberly," said Bill Bodine, leaning back in his chair at a table close to the bar, smiling, the men in front of him moving back as much as possible to allow Moberly to see Bodine, "I think if you come in here yelling like some schoolgirl that you seen a monster, I think we need to know exactly what it was that you think you saw. Right fellas?" Bodine drunk now and playing to the crowd, men nodding at him, the bearded man saying, "Yeah, that's right Bill."

Right fellas? Modesto knew that voice, that drawl, so slow and sure and mean, knew that taunting tone, could see the expression that went with it. Like it was yesterday. He tried to see the source, but too many bodies were blocking his line of vision. But he didn't really need to see, knew at that moment he'd been right to follow his instincts to this town, knew too that Bill Bodine hadn't changed much as he'd grown from boy to man.

Modesto slid along the wall until he could finally see Bodine, sitting there grinning and waiting to see how things would play out, shaking his head as if the monster story was the most foolish thing he'd ever heard.

"Mr. Moberly," Clem said, trying to placate the man, "we're just curious about the whole thing, that's all. No offense meant."

Bodine said, "You said there was a body. That's not something we can just ignore."

"Said I thought it was a body."

"Well for chrissake," Bodine said, "you know what a body looks like!"

Moberly turned to the crowd, eyes red, snarled, "You want to know what I saw? I startled it, and it took hold of that corpse like it was some, some ragdoll ... and this thing, it was tall and thin, I don't even know how to describe it, it moved like it was sort of hunched over, and she looked back at me, and those eyes..."

"She!" Bill exclaimed, "Oh Moberly, why didn't you say?" laughing now, other men's faces starting to relax a bit, looking to Bodine now as he said, "you got yourself some big ugly girl-friend stashed out in the woods," laughing now, and other men joining in. Modesto could see the relief on their faces, glad to have some other way of thinking about the thing, glad too that this Bill had a knack at making things seem small. Modesto knew all about that.

Moberly said, "You fucker, Bodine," and Clem tried to grab hold of Moberly's arm as he pushed himself off the bar, but there was too much force in the man's body to be able to slow him down as he lunged for Bodine who was still sitting tipped back in his chair, so the whole thing, man and chair and Moberly, came crashing down together.

Moberly, enraged but drunk too, yelling at Bodine, "You fucking son of a bitch!" Bodine was cursing too, trying to untangle himself, looking embarrassed as the chair caught his leg and tripped him as he tried to pull himself up.

Two men had hold of Moberly's arms, were trying to pull him off Bodine and get him back on his feet, still holding him when Bodine wound up and punched Moberly hard, in the neck, the force almost knocking over the two men holding Moberly's arms, one of them saying as Bodine wound up for another, "Hey Bill, enough," but Bodine slammed his fist into the man's face. Moberly's head snapped back and stayed lolling backwards.

Bodine spat, said, "Get him out of my sight," and the two men dragged Moberly towards the door as the crowd parted and watched, a couple of men murmuring that he didn't look so good, lousy claim jumper that he was, wasn't as though everyone hadn't heard the rumours.

Modesto left the way he'd come in, taking the alleyway and coming around to the front of the building just as the two men heaved Moberly's limp body off the sidewalk, not even waiting to hear the heavy thud as it hit the hardened mud before heading back in. A few men were heading down the worn path that led to the cluster of tents at the far end of the main street, but nobody seemed to pay any mind to old John Moberly.

The man was flat on his back, face red and slack, eyes open but vacant.

Haul the man up to the doctor's office? Not worth it. It was a good two blocks away, the terrain pitted and muddy. Modesto doubted he would be able to carry him, and dragging him just seemed unbearable. Although he wasn't one of the men Modesto was looking for, there was a grim rankness to the man, he made Modesto feel mean, inclined to just keep kicking the man until the job was done, until once and for all, done for John Moberly. But the meanness scared him, didn't like it crawling around inside his thoughts.

So no, not tonight. He stood, straightened his coat, stepped over the body, and headed for his office.

CHAPTER NINE

He was still thinking of Moberly when he turned the corner and saw that someone was waiting outside his office door. He slowed, concerned that perhaps the men he was hunting might possibly be hunting him, but then was oddly pleased when he saw that it was her, face deep into the shadows, leaning into his doorway, trying, he assumed, to make herself as invisible as possible. Still, the paleness of her skin, her eyes shining. The scent of violets. It was her.

"This is the second time I find you outside my door unexpectedly," he said.

"You kept me waiting a frightful length of time, Mr. O'Brien."

"I was unaware we were to meet. And this is a dangerous time for a young lady to be out on the streets. Hadn't I suggested you stay to your room?"

"Never mind that, you're needed, over at the boarding house. A terrible thing has happened."

"At Mrs. Shay's?"

"Yes, do come along."

"Is this to do with our case?"

"No, no, nothing to do with that, but please, do come along."

Modesto hesitated. If it was not to do with Lucy, or his business in town, then why involve himself? He could risk drawing attention to himself. The incident with the horses had already caused too much commotion.

"You are irritating me, by delaying like this. Now, please, just come along, I've been waiting too long as it is."

"What has you so agitated, if I am allowed to ask?"

Lily whispered when she said, "There's a young woman, dead, in her room. Mrs. Shay found her not an hour ago."

"Did she notify the Constable?" Modesto asked, but Lily was already walking away, just an outline in the dark now, saying, "Mr. O'Brien, come along."

So he did, catching up with her and walking quietly beside her until they reached John Moberly, nothing but a big lump of dark still lying in the street, and she just shook her head, said, "This town."

Modesto said, "Yes indeed, a town crawling with the worst of our species."

She stopped, turned to him, said, "Oh no, that scoundrel is not the worst, not by far. You remember that. There are far worse men in this town."

They stepped around Moberly, made their way past jumbles of lumber, crates, barrels, and rock, navigating along a deep trench stinking of garbage. Crossing on skinny planks, they moved down along the sloping side street, away from the lights of the town centre, the darkness now thick around them.

Modesto said, "Please, take my arm, it is impossible to see in this light."

"I can see fine enough, thank you," she said, and then added, "There, up ahead," and there indeed was the small white sign, barely visible, 'Shay's – Boarding.'

The door was opened before they could knock, and they were ushered in, Mrs. Shay saying, "Get in with you both before someone sees."

Once in the narrow hall entrance Modesto said, "Now, Miss Bow has explained what has occurred but if you could tell me yourself Mrs. Shay."

"Just come along, come along to the room," she said, making her way up the stairs and then down a narrow hallway, wood creaking underneath their feet. The woman was small, white haired and walking with a slight limp. Modesto had stayed in the boarding house for a few days when he first arrived, Mrs. Shay saying she preferred to rent to the young ladies, sometimes a married couple, had even had a few squalling babies once or twice, but the men caused trouble. With the drink. Modesto had assured her he would not be drinking, and his stay would be short. A series of further questions revealed that his people were from Ireland, and Mrs. Shay pressed until she determined it was in fact Kerry, as were hers. She made an exception.

They stopped outside a door, the wood still unfinished, Mrs. Shay apologizing, "I'm after getting a coat of paint on the place, but just can't find the time what with the cooking and cleaning and laundry. Sure the day's never long enough and good help is as scarce as hen's teeth."

She fished about in her apron pocket for the key, hand shaking as she tried to slip the key into the lock, Modesto touching her on the shoulder, gently took the keys out of her hand. "There, there, Mrs. Shay, I'll do it."

"I can't bear to see her again, can't bear it!"

"That's fine, that's fine," he said, asked, "were you close with her?"

The landlady shook her head, said, "She'd just been here two weeks. Cute as a button she was. We exchanged a few pleasantries, this and that, but she kept to herself for the most part. But this, it's so dreadful. And her all alone in there like that."

"She came to Cobalt on her own?"

"I don't know about that, I only know that when she came here there was a man with her, paid for her room for the week. I didn't ask any questions, not my business. But I kept an eye on her, and until today she gave me no cause to worry myself."

"And how did you come to discover her this evening?"

"I was just coming to tell her she had to pay up for the second week. I hated to do it, mind, a young woman like that here on her own..." then Mrs. Shay started to cry, adding between sniffles, "... I mean I can't let the rooms for free. There's other young ladies needing places, every day I'm turning away the likes of some young one, just the other day a nurse, desperate for lodgings, and God knows this town needs them, so what can I do?"

"Yes of course, of course. So you were coming up to get the rent?"

"Yes, I knocked, and waited, but no answer and I knew she was in there, thought to myself, enough of these shenanigans, her in there pretending to be asleep."

"What made you think she wasn't asleep?"

"I'd heard some moving around earlier, these walls, as thin as a priest's wallet they are. That's what made me think she was still up, and I could go and ask after the rent, telling myself I have to eat too, running around town all day, carrying home the groceries myself, worn out I am. I think I was feeling a bit hard done by about the money owing."

"And so you knocked, there was no answer, and then did you just go in?"

"I knocked a few times, not too loud so as not to disturb the other guests, but there was no reply, so I decided to just go on in, thinking maybe even she was hiding someone in there with her."

"Because of the noise you'd heard earlier?"

"Yes. And because she didn't answer."

"And did you hear anyone leave the house?"

"From my room I hear what's over me, but not always what's in other parts of the house."

"Alright, so then?"

"I called out for her but there was no answer, I listened for a few seconds but hearing nothing, that set me to worrying. I thought maybe she had already slipped out without paying. I lit the lamp and went on in. Sure nearly dropped it seeing the girl like that, oh Mr. O'Brien ...."

"And then?"

"I backed out of the room quickly, locked the door right quick, left the lamp behind even, wasn't in my right mind. Then I thought of sending Miss Bow here to collect you since you were acquainted with one another. I didn't know what else to do. And may God never weaken your hand, Miss Bow, for being so kind, it was a frightful thing to involve you with."

Lily said, "Of course Mrs. Shay, anything to help."

"The young woman's name?" Modesto asked.

"Hattie. Hattie Boyle."

Modesto could tell Mrs. Shay was working herself up into a good cry, said, "Why don't you wait downstairs, Miss Bow will stay with me. We'll have a look and then perhaps we should consider calling the police, this could get complicated."

"It'll be bad for business, Mr. O'Brien, to have a corpse found in my establishment, you know how folks are. This could be the ruin of me."

"Alright, for now go on down and why not make us some tea. We'll be down shortly and perhaps we can come up with some way of dealing with this matter that is discrete."

Modesto waited until he heard her steps on the stairs then slipped the key in, the door opening, the room still lit. Modesto felt Lily freeze beside him, her hand up to her mouth, murmuring, "Oh no."

But Modesto could say nothing. Just stare at the young woman, slumped oddly over in the bed, her body going one way, her head seeming to go the other, and her face, half covered in red inflamed patches, her the eyes dull blue and flat.

"My god, Mr. O'Brien, what happened to her?"

Modesto found he was having trouble moving, trouble thinking. It was just too similar, the burns, the same terrible twisted, convulsed head, he could still hear his mother crying and his Gran saying, "Poor young man, like his head is trying to get away from his body," and the afternoon was hot, and his Gran had taken his hand and led him out and told his Ma to go get the police. She had taken him inside and made him tea. Let him have his tea in her single, perfect cream-coloured teacup made to look like a basket with shamrocks dancing on it.

"Mr. O'Brien?" Lily now turning to him, her hand lightly on his arm, "Mr. O'Brien, please, you look as if you are about to faint. If it was fainting Mrs. Shay needed, I could have provided that myself."

Modesto tried to drag his mind's eye away from that hot May afternoon, away from the shed at the back of the yard.

Modesto said, "He had been such a beautiful boy."

"I need you here and now for this poor woman, please!"

And then he was back in the stuffy room with the crooked young woman and her burnt face. She was in her night dress. The acid had burnt holes in that too. Half her face a crusty red mess. Blueness around her lips. "I would say this young woman took carbolic acid, spilled some on herself in the doing so, perhaps a shaking and uncertain hand. It isn't always an easy thing to take your own life."

"Suicide—but, she's so young!" Lily now distressed, "And why, why this way, it seems so painful, why wouldn't she have just taken laudanum? Surely it would be so much less violent. Oh the poor dear."

"Not everyone has access to laudanum. You can get carbolic acid at any drugstore."

"She would have had some."

"Laudanum?"

"Yes, why wouldn't she? There's lots of girls like Hattie here in Cobalt, brought here, half the time under false pretences, lied to and bullied until they'll work in one of the brothels. She'd need something to dull the pain of it all."

Modesto moved closer to the body, then saw the bruising on the neck, her arm. Heard a scuffing sound behind her head, mice behind the wallpaper? The wallpaper was also bruised, stained and faded, as if the room was absorbing the decline of young Hattie Boyle. Mice behind the walls, mice behind the walls, "Do you hear that?"

"What?"

"The mice, what are they trying to say? Crying maybe? Sure, they're crying."

Lily said nothing. He could see the wariness in her eyes, said, "Don't mind me, don't mind me at all," his eyes now with tears, and he said, "Please, check then, her belongings, see if there is laudanum here."

He glanced around the room, the small washstand, a single dress, a coat.

"Yes, here, on the nightstand," said Lily.

A different story then, about what happened in this room. Not another desperate young woman taking her own life, but something else. Exactly what was unclear though. He took another look at Hattie Boyle, said to Lily, "Perhaps now we should have a few words with Mrs. Shay."

"Yes, I suppose, oh this room, so small and the smell in here, so sickly sweet ..."

"That is the acid. Time to get you out of here, Miss Bow, please, come along," he said, taking her arm and leading her out the doorway, closing it quietly behind them and then heading down the hallway, turned to see the pallor on Lily's face, asked, "Are you faint?"

"No," she said, "Angry."

"Yes, angry."

"Ruin and abuse, Mr. O'Brien, ruin and abuse. It's all that tawdry places like this have to offer."

They found Mrs. Shay downstairs in the parlour.

"It is a terrible matter Mrs. Shay," said Modesto, "just terrible. I was wondering, if you are able, if you could answer a few questions for me?"

"If I know the answers I will."

"When was the last you saw her?"

"Sure as I told Miss Bow here, she done come into the kitchen, all in a state. Must have been around seven o'clock."

"Did she have many visitors while she was here?"

"No, hardly a soul."

"Are you sure no one could have come inside, tonight, to visit her?"

"As I told you, I heard some moving around, but sure I don't sit outside of the girls' rooms guarding them, do I? I was in my room in the back though, minding my own, not much need to check, this is a quiet bunch I have here. Mind, I might have dozed off, tired as I was from all my errands today. But what does it matter if the poor girl had a caller, some fool broke her heart, doesn't matter now …."

"Mrs. Shay, I must tell you that I believe that Miss Boyle may have been murdered."

Mrs. Shay stopped dabbing at her eyes. "What did you say, Mr. O'Brien?"

"There is a chance that your lodger's death is suspicious. Perhaps she was murdered."

"Murder under my own roof!"

"It will be difficult not to have the police involved…."

The landlady had her hankie out and was crying into it, shaking her head, wailing through her tears, "The police won't be after doing anything about this poor thing, surely not at this time of night either, all sleeping off their drink. When that working girl was shot down by the train station, they couldn't be bothered to even rouse the doctor, just sent that despicable scrap man to collect her. And those police had been chumming around with that scoundrel that shot her, said she'd brought the tragedy on herself, by walking out on him."

"Well, it is possibly a crime that has occurred here, and we at least owe it to Miss Boyle, and other young women in this house…"

This brought another wail from Mrs. Shay, "Surely you don't think the rest of them are in danger? Lord Almighty in Heaven, I am to be ruined. What if word of this gets out to the other girls?"

"Perhaps the good doctor can help us in this case, contact the authorities himself. Miss Bow," O'Brien said, seeing her in the doorway, just a shadow now, "would you be able to assist me in moving Hattie to Doctor Saunders' office?"

"Lord help us," said Mrs. Shay, "the good doctor might not be pleased to be woken up for a patient that can't be helped."

"Not sure he needs to know the state of our poor Hattie beforehand…But we should act quickly, we want to do this before light, the town is busy enough at dark, it is sheer madness during the day. This way the police don't need to come barging in here tonight."

"This is a terrible business. And as surely as the sun follows the moon I'll be out the money for the burial as well."

"I could assist with that," Modesto said.

Mrs. Shay managed a smile, "If you don't mind me saying, Mr. O'Brien, you are generous for a man still owing money," she said, then softened, added, "Oh don't you mind me, like they say, if I'm not complaining, I'm not breathing. And as for the money you owe me, find out what happened to this poor young thing. I'll take care of sending her back to her people, they came from Tralee you know. The poor dear."

"Was she straight from Ireland, Mrs. Shay?" asked Lily.

"Oh no, poor thing had come up from America."

Modesto felt the pause in the room, almost hoped she didn't ask, but Lily did. "Where in the states, do you know?"

"Surely I do, the same place that Mr. O'Brien hails from, Butte, Montana."

There it was, another tangle. Modesto hesitated, said, "That is very kind of you Mrs. Shay, on all counts, to forgive my debt. I was planning on heading out of town soon on another matter for a few days, but a brief delay should not trouble me too much. I'll find out what happened to Miss Boyle. Might be most efficient to start with the man who dropped her off here, would you know who he was?"

"I believe I do. I didn't like him, not from the first time I laid eyes on him. I had the feeling she didn't care for him too much either, not that I pried. Sure he had something to do with this terrible mess. A man like that and a poor wee thing like Hattie. I believe his name is Bodine. Find him, Mr. O'Brien."

Not a surprise. The tangles now seemed all around him, binding him tighter, binding him to the men he had been following for these past number of years. Was he tied to them by the yarns of the Fates? That storied trio of goddesses, spinning, measuring and cutting, was he caught up by their threads? And the ones his Gran had spoken of, different and darker, what had they been called? Had she once told him not to speak their names, not to call or conjure them?

Too late Moddie, they're here, the Morrigan, they're here

Where Biddy? I can feel them, but where

Not to worry now, they will do their work, you must do yours

He turned to Lily, her standing stone-faced in the doorway, asked, "You familiar with this man?"

She hesitated, said, "No, why would I be?"

Another lie. Strange woman, this Lily Nail, with her rage and her secrets, lying when he saw no need for her lie. Did she want

him to answer her question, to say to her that she must know
Bodine because she and her sister were now bound to the fate of
Modesto O'Brien, and, accordingly, to the fate of Bill Bodine,
Butch Daly and Tommy Coffin. That seemed very clear to him
now. "Just curious, Miss Bow. And not to worry Mrs. Shay, I'll
find Bodine."

"And to the devil with him when you do," she said.

"There is little doubt about that Mrs. Shay."

• • •

The doctor took some rousing, but Lily persisted in knocking
until he appeared, groggy and annoyed, "What is it at this infer-
nal hour?"

"There's been a terrible poisoning," Modesto said, the body of
Hattie wrapped in a sheet and in his arms.

Lily didn't want for the doctor's reply but pushed the door
wider and entered, Modesto close behind her, crossing the room
to set Hattie down on a table.

The doctor glanced at the small form, the sheet covering her
face. "What's this?"

"A fatal poisoning."

"Then why bring her here? I'm a doctor, not a miracle worker."

"The land lady was very distraught, and as I believe an in-
vestigation is warranted, and did not want to send the entire
household into hysterics by hauling in the police, relocating her
here seemed wise. The cause of death will need to be determined
for the police ..."

"That would have been up to the police to decide. You said it
was poisoning. An accident then? No need for police or investiga-
tion," he pulled back the sheet, "Good god!"

"I should think accident is out of the question."

"A suicide! God have mercy!"

"I'm not so sure."

The doctor frowned, looked to Hattie's face, saw the burns and the lividness. "Carbolic acid."

"Yes, likely. What is less clear is whether it was self-administered or forced upon her."

"Forced? What are you talking about?"

"There are signs of violence on the body."

The annoyance returned. "Explain yourself man, who are you, and this woman, here with you, who is she?"

"I am Modesto O'Brien, a detective, new in town. This is Miss Bow, a resident at the same boarding house as our victim and was pressed by the landlady into assisting me."

"What is your connection with the deceased?"

O'Brien shrugged, "None. I was known to Mrs. Shay, the landlady, and, in her panic and distress, sent for me to attend to poor Miss Boyle."

"It would seem common sense to contact the police directly in such a situation. Finding a deceased individual in a boarding house."

"Perhaps. But here we are. I will escort Miss Bow back to the boarding house. I leave Miss Boyle in your care, to contact the police. And please do mention the possibility of wrongdoing."

"You know, Mr. O'Brien, a young woman like this, on her own, it is not hard to imagine the depredation that might have overtaken her. I have encountered this before, these young girls taking their own lives. It is not surprising, after all, that in their shame they might see fit to take such drastic measures?"

"This poor young woman was restrained and forced to ingest carbolic acid. There's no shame on her, none at all."

CHAPTER
TEN

There was a commotion out on the street, but Modesto was trying his best to ignore it. He was concentrating on the train schedule. He was about to close the window facing the street, to shut out the noise, when a red-faced boy burst into his office, out of breath, sputtering a jumble of mayhem and gore. An accident down at the station, he had to come, and come quick.

Modesto, pulling on his green coat and straightening his plum-coloured tie, asked why the boy had come to him, the boy saying he knew all about detectives solving crime, but that they should hurry.

"Hurry to what?"

"The train, I was down at the train, everyone …"

"Yes, so?"

"The mist, it was so thick, laying over the lake. A fella in the crowd said it was the steam from the sewage…"

Modesto could already feel the focus of his work drifting away, absorbed by Lily, her sister, this crowd of characters with their drills and dynamite and silver. "What did you see boy, for God's sakes, out with it?"

"A man, run over by the southbound train."

"An accident! Why are you fetching me?"

"The body was laying on the tracks, sir. And it had no head."

• • •

Getting down to the train station hadn't been easy. A dense crowd was pushing down through every alleyway and horse trail to get to the train once the main road became too congested, but the boy grew into his role, shouting 'Make way, police," as he forced his way through the crowd to make a path for Modesto.

As they cleared the last row of bystanders, the boy charged ahead towards the body lying at the north end of the train, but Modesto paused, taking in the sea of men now gathered near the train, the sombreness of their dark clothing interrupted only occasionally by the lightness of a woman's hat. Between the crowd and the train were some recently debarked passengers looking disoriented and some outright frightened. Two women, each with a few children clinging to them, the children crying, the women struck dumb by the huge and unsettled crowd. Clearly not the welcome party they had expected.

Modesto turned to the crowd, yelled, "Alright now, everyone to move back, let's not crowd the train. Everyone back."

The crowd responded to his efficiency. Some of them recognized him from the incident with the horse, but all of them wanted a role in the town's latest drama, telling themselves and each other there was no other place like this, a place where a man could become a millionaire overnight, where a man could shoot another man's horse in broad daylight and simply walk away. A place where there were silver nuggets the size of cannonballs and headless men to be found on the railway tracks.

Modesto began to assign duties to those nearest him, each man wearing an expression that said, choose me, choose me, let me get closer to this abomination of a headless man. A young man was dispatched to the hotel for sheets, another to the hospital for a stretcher, one of the few women present was set to herding the newly arrived women and children away from the station.

The mist was moving, swirling and lifting as the slight wind blew in from the east, drifting away from the railway tracks. The boy, such a tiny sentinel, looked relieved to see the detective headed his way.

"Here he is sir, the man," the boy said.

"Yes, I can see that," Modesto said.

"Bad corner sir."

"That bend just past the bridge?"

"Yes sir, just last week another man was killed, right down there. Must've stepped away from the tracks right by that coal shack there, see? And well, as the train raced by, if the force of it didn't pull the doors of the coal shack open. Those doors shoved that poor fella right into the train. Some folks think them trains come into town too darn fast."

"Yes, the train is clearly a factor, but why was this man here in the first place. Do you recognize him at all?"

"Without his face?"

Modesto smiled, a fair question. "Maybe his clothes, boots?"

"Dressed like all the men."

"So a miner?"

The boy shrugged, "Maybe. Or a teamster. Could be a builder, not a blacksmith …"

"I see," Modesto said, cutting off the boy before he listed every occupation in the mining camp, "And is this the usual time for the train?"

"Yes sir."

Modesto glanced up towards the station, then stepped past the body to the other side of the tracks. The train tracks followed a gentle curve, running between the edge of the lake and the train station. The train now sat, belching and shuddering, with its engine car just beyond the station. It was possible that the engineer hadn't even noticed the man, stopping at the usual spot.

Then he saw what he assumed was the head.

A small roundish object resting just beside the tracks, well past the front end of the train.

Train as guillotine. Wrenched onto the railbed by the force of the train, the upper part of the body crushed and bleeding and sunken down between the tracks, the head severed and sent bouncing down the track. Remarkable. Remarkable too that so far no one had noticed the head. Just as well, could spark a degree of hysteria that could go very badly given the size of the crowd.

He asked the boy to stay put, said he'd return with the sheet to cover the body. At the train station the crowd seemed to have doubled, some people now taking to the hotel balcony across from the train station to get a better view. All around him was chatter, the whispering, everyone offering opinions to his neighbour about who or what was responsible for this calamity.

Modesto found the hotel proprietor with the sheets, beckoned the ashen-faced engineer and brakeman to follow him. When they hesitated, he said, "Come along gentlemen, this mechanical beast is, after all, your responsibility."

The mist was heavy. Impossible to see the lake, though now there wasn't much to see, just a soggy bed of puddles and gouges. There were gulls calling, but he couldn't see them either, just heard their cries and the sound of their wings overhead. Everything below wore a dirty, dull grey pallor, making the body even more startling, the faded blue of the man's trousers and then the livid reds.

Modesto shook out the sheet and draped it over the body, said, "Stay here until the Constable arrives, the police will want to speak with you."

"I don't know if I can, the body ..." the engineer stammered, staring at the small patch of red as it appeared, already soaking through the white of the sheet, then added, "I thought you were the police."

And then a shriek. A loud one, followed by yelling, and more shrieks. Modesto turned towards the station and the crowd was suddenly both withdrawing and expanding, moving forward, arms waving and pointing, men yelling "Get the women back," but no one really moving as the rumble of alarm travelled from one end of the crowd to the other, everyone shouting, "Did you see it? Did you see that? It was the monster, look at it!"

And then, "It's coming back, its coming back for its prey!"

Modesto scanned the fog, could see nothing, glanced back at the crowd. They were all looking and pointing in different directions.

But then there was a new burst of shouting and pointing as the boy, engineer and brakeman came running back towards the crowd, the brakeman yelling, "It's here, behind the train, we heard it. Everyone get back."

"No, it's there, gone onto the lake!"

"Wait, no see, up there on the rocks!"

Modesto ignored the voices, hurrying up along the tracks to where the head lay stranded, more interested in it than any monster conjured by a bit of death and fog.

And yes, it was the head he had spotted. Now up close, it was small and odd, the shock of reddish muck at the end of its neck, face down and settled against the outside metal rail. Modesto nudged the head gently with his foot. He was surprised, heavier than he thought it would be. He crouched and rolled the head over, the face wearing a look of resignation.

He was startled by a loud cry from down the tracks, "Protect the body. Don't leave the body to the monster, the monster."

Modesto stepped away from the head to cross back over the tracks in order to see the crowd. There were several men accosting the brakeman who was trying to push his way through the crowd, others taking hold of the engineer who was looking completely bewildered, staring first one way then the other. The engineer began yelling, "Let go of me, it's out there, let go," but they hauled him along with the brakeman, the crowd now bunching up behind it all, emboldened by each other, by the spectacle of confrontation.

What monster though? Must be just the mist and high blood. But it was escalating, and high blood frightened him. Hard to decide whether to stay put or return to the crowd and try and restore some civility. Or just go back to his office and leave the bloody mess to the local police.

Modesto sighed, decided to deal with the head before it started another surge of madness from the crowd. But what to do with it?

He hesitated, reluctant to cover the head with his prized green coat, but the shouting was loud and blood thirsty from the other end of the train. Cursing, he began removing his coat when he felt a puff of frigid air against the back of his neck. The icy sensation touched his collar, seemed to penetrate right through his coat, seemed to hold him in place. The faint odour of, what? Rotted flowers? Maybe. The cold was taking on an almost corporeal form, like it was pressing against him, so he exhaled slowly, reluctant though to turn around just yet, not really prepared to see it, and he was so cold, so he just stood and it was as if everything was frozen and then the cold seemed to past right through him, perhaps the ghost coming back for its head, but then he was jarred, jostled by an ill wind as the creature sloped past him, bending to take hold of the head, feeling the brush of the grab against his boot.

And then it was past him, disappearing into the morning's mist, an arm but not an arm, rangy and thin, swinging as it seemed to lope and dematerialize at the same time, how could that be, not like a ghost, but a real arm but with almost no substance, but at the end of it, in the clutch of the long claws, John Moberly's head.

• • •

Remarkably, consumed by the uproar over the cowardly engineer, not another soul had seen the thing grab the head and disappear into the morning's fog. Modesto stared into the fog for a minute or so, then turned to walk slowly back towards the other end of the train. Deal with the body now that the head was gone.

He could hear the engineer protesting, pleading, "It was just your eyes playing tricks on you, now let me be and get back to my train," and then a deep bellow saying, "Clear the way, clear the way gentlemen, Police Constable Calder coming through, move aside."

The crowd parted to make way for the Constable, Modesto hearing someone mutter, "It's about bloody time."

"What's all of this mayhem about?" the Constable, shouting over the voices, "A train accident?"

That sent the crowd into an uproar. "That engineer, drove right over that man," yelled a voice from the back and that set off a variety of accusations, most of them focused on the beleaguered engineer who stood twisting his cap in his hands.

"Now, now, everyone, settle down, back up, and quiet down."

"Calm down?" shouted a man standing close to the engineer, "Better string this man up, its murder. We all saw it."

"The brakeman too!"

"Are you all blind, the monster, we all saw it!"

Calder surveyed the scene, turned on the engineer, "Can you tell me what the hell is going on down here?"

"Oh sir, Constable, I think that's best done by Mr. O'Brien here."

Calder was annoyed, looked around through the crowd, "And who the hell is that?"

His eyes landed on Modesto, standing calmly beside the engineer, his coat turned a deep evergreen by the gloom of the skies, an expectant look on his face. Calder barked, "You O'Brien?"

"Indeed, I am sir."

"And why the hell should I be talking to you?" Mad at not knowing what was going on, looking foolish in front of the crowd.

"A young lad came to fetch me, just my bad luck I guess. New detective in town, but I have some experience working with the law, thought I might be of use. Just tried to keep things calm until you could get down here."

"Seems to me you've done a hell of a job of it."

"It's true that the crowd has gotten itself quite worked up. But the crowd is not really the problem. The problem is the man on the tracks."

"On the tracks?"

"Yes, a man who appears to have lied down on the tracks at some point before the train arrived and is now dead. Because of the train running over him. He's without his head."

The Constable stared at Modesto, then said, "I see. Anyone see him before the accident. Why the hell would he lie down? Was anyone able to say who it might be," he then paused, added, "I mean, seeing he's without... well, hard to identify."

"Why not come down and see for yourself Constable, I am sure you will be able to ascertain how long the man might have been there. Could even have been late last night."

"Why would you say that?"

"Someone suggested that the body might be a John Moberly?"

Calder was scowling. "Who said that?"

Modesto made to scan the crowd, shrugged, and delivered the story that needed telling. "Not sure sir, there was a lot of shouting of opinions and rumours and being new here myself, I am not sure I can attribute it to any one person, but I did hear that a John Moberly was drunk and angry last night when he left a saloon, the Bucket, and that someone named Bodine had his boys toss this fellow out onto the street, dead drunk. And that was the last that anyone had seen of this Moberly fellow."

"Billy Bodine?"

"I believe that was the name."

They began walking, Modesto and Calder, the engineer and brakeman trailing along reluctantly. Calder occasionally saying to the various groups of men they were passing, "Alright, let's break this up. I want everyone to move on, lets clear the area."

Some of the crowd began to disperse but much of it remained rooted to the spot. Mutterings of, "You don't know what happened," and "You don't know the half of it," were heard, the crowd belligerent now about the fate of the body. Calder stopped in front of a half dozen or so prospectors, asked, "Any of you know a John Moberly?"

The men glanced at each other, shrugged or shook their heads, one asking, "That the dead man?"

"Not sure as of right now..." Calder started, but was interrupted by a voice shouting from somewhere behind him, "John Moberly? Is that Moberly? He seen the monster! The monster, must've come back for him!"

Calder turned on Modesto. "What is he talking about? You didn't mention a monster."

"It didn't seem all that relevant sir, assumed it was just a matter of group hysteria. I know nothing about this Moberly and the monster."

"I see." Unsatisfied.

They reached the body, Calder sighing, said, "This is some mess we got here. What in darnation could have led this man to lie down here like this?"

"I suppose if there is any truth to the claim that Mr. Moberly was hallucinating, seeing a monster, then it could indicate a certain degree of mental instability. And someone also mentioned that Moberly was having trouble with his mining claim. I'm sure it isn't the first suicide you've had to deal with ..."

Calder recovered himself, saw the picture as it was drawn for him, the desperate prospector, run ragged, sleep deprived, time running out, too much drinking. "Yes, of course. I see." He had a story now he could understand and believe, that made sense to him.

Questions about what the police were going to do, about the dead man, the monster, the brakeman and the train—now terribly behind schedule—were persisting, the crowd not budging, so Calder turned to the crowd, squared his shoulders and said, "You all know what a man will do when pushed to desperation. This fella probably dragged himself down here to put an end to it. Hard to say exactly what happened here, but seems to me that the most logical explanation is one of drunkenness and depression. Now unless anyone has any information that I don't already know, let's get back to work so we can get things here cleaned up and get the train running again."

"What about his head?" a young man asked, Modesto recognizing him from the saloon as the prospector who was working near Moberly's claim.

Calder pushed his Stetson back off his forehead, then striking what he clearly thought was a respectful tone, said, "It is unlikely we will ever recover it now."

"Well, geez, I think we should try."

"Not sure what you think will be left …"

"But…"

"But nothing," the Calder said, testy, "you go on back to whatever you've been doing and leave this to me. A train runs over a man when he's lying there with his head on the track. Where do you think that head is? It's under the train son, and unless you want to crawl under that train yourself and scrape him off it, then I suggest you and everyone else here get this goddam town back to work."

The young man looked a bit hurt at the sharp tone, but pulled himself away from the scene and began his walk up the hill. Here and there groups of men followed suite, still talking, still looking back, but the energy was leaving, the crowd becoming deflated, surly.

Modesto himself headed up the hill before Calder had more questions for him. He was thinking about the head, wondering about the thing that had carried it off, whether he had really seen it or not.

Wondering too why the head of Mr. John Moberly had a bullet hole through its forehead.

CHAPTER ELEVEN

*I*t was the ship that Biddy had sailed away from Ireland on, and the water was cold and stormy all around it. The Atlantic, yes, the crossing of the Atlantic. The rough waters tossing the ship, it lurching one way then another. But it was the scraping sound of the scuttling up along the outside of the ship's body that had all the passengers huddled together, watching as the inky claws came up over the edge of the ship, and then the things hauling up their shadows, hauling them up and over like you would a big fish, except they were black and hunched and fluttering all along the deck and the edges of the ship. And he was a child on that ship, watching the panicked expressions on the faces of the adults, but then there was just him and Biddy.

She had a tight hold on his hand

She said, them there, they're the Morrigans

Who are they

Birth and death, our fate, that's who they are

Why are they here

They're coming aboard for us, laying claim to us

Can they do that

Once they're summoned, they do as they please

Did we summon them Gran
Maybe the ship did
How
With its smell of death
He and Biddy watched the Morrigans come, one after another,
their long hair streaming behind them like creatures unto themselves
and the air was heavy with their scent
And he asked Biddy, what is that smell
That's the stink of men and death
Why do they smell like that
It isn't the hags, they've followed the scent to the ship
Then he said he didn't mind the smell, it was sweet, like flowers,
and he looked up at her and saw the hand he was holding wasn't
Biddy's, but belonged to one of the Morrigans, her dark claw on his
small, pale hand, and he looked right up into her face even though he
thought he should be afraid, and she was looking back at him with
pale lilac eyes and then he was climbing the masts behind her, and
the winds, the winds were so strong and the Morrigan hissed, don't let
them blow you away little boy...

A voice nearby pulled him into the daylight, saying, "If you insist on passing out, I'm not sure you will be helpful in finding Lucy," and then he was waking, finding himself with his face flat against his desk, parched and disoriented.

Lily was leaning over him, dressed all in black, and she said, "Mr. O'Brien, here please, wake up, have some water, you look a fright."

He pulled himself upright and smoothed his rumpled shirt, took the glass of water, thirsty now, draining the glass as he tried to sort himself out and let his mind catch up.

He asked, "What brings you in here today in your mourning clothes?"

"Mrs. Shay loaned the dress to me, for Hattie. She is sending her off today. I said I'd go with her."

Modesto rubbed his eyes. "The train station?"

"Yes. A sad business."

"Give me a minute Miss Nail, I'll be right with you."

He went to the small room in the back of his office with its blue wash basin. Splashed his face with the chilled water.

Lily called out to him, "Are you alright?"

He straightened his shirt, pulled on his vest. "In a manner of speaking," he said as he returned to join her, "though I am still in the thrall of my nightmare, I'm afraid. Some mornings are worse than others."

"I will leave you then to sort yourself out, but I thought you would want to know about Hattie."

"Of course. I will try and make it down, though keep in mind there was quite a commotion there this morning, the matter of the body on the tracks. I suggest you do not overstay your time there."

"I understand."

"I will be in touch soon about our travel plans. I have a few things to review here for now but will do my best to join you."

Lily turned to leave just as the door swung open, Shitty Mitty standing uncertainly in the doorway, another man peering in behind him, both men's eyes falling on Lily Nail even as Shitty Mitty said to Modesto, "Didn't know you was busy, otherwise would have come another time, but I ran into Mr. Cooley here, brought you some new business ... "

Lily smiled, said "Not at all, please do come in gentlemen, I was just finishing my business with Mr. O'Brien."

Shitty Mitty sort of bowed, seemed not sure how to behave, but stayed put in the doorway, trapping Lily inside. While staring at Lily, he said to Modesto, "Was down at the livery and Mr. Cooley here came in an' tells me that someone has gone and taken his cows, all of them, and one of those cows was going to be calving."

"She's my favourite," Cooley said from the doorway, so Modesto said, "Please, do come in Mr. Cooley," and so the man did, stepping past Shitty and into the office carefully, as if crossing a hidden threshold, stopping just inside the door and saying, "Thank you, Mr. O'Brien, and do excuse my manners," removing his cap, a small-framed man. He extended his hand, "Mr. Patrick Cooley, pleased to meet you."

"And how might I be of assistance?"

Mr. Cooley glanced over at Lily. "I don't mean to be interrupting."

"No, not at all Mr. Cooley. This is Miss Bow," Modesto said, "in town with the theatre. She was just taking some respite from the sun. Now, what is on your mind?"

"Well sir, and begging your pardon, Miss Bow, for interrupting your rest, but I think I might be needing the services of a detective Mr. O'Brien. Never thought I would hear myself saying that, but there it is."

"I told him," Shitty said, "you could maybe git his cows back."

"And the calf," said Mr. Cooley, "don't forget that."

"Yup, that's right, that's what I told him."

Mr. Cooley said, "I let 'em wander a bit, you know, choose their own spots for the day, but they always come home as evening sets in. But they've all just up and gone."

"Might they be wandering in any of your neighbours' field?" Modesto asked.

"I had a look, but there aren't too many folks living out my way. I been there only a few months myself. I said to myself, those cows kept in town are a sick looking bunch, they keep them packed in there, got sick hogs running around with them, no way to treat a cow. And your milk would be no darn good. And the water can't be trusted. So, I said to myself, well, I'll keep a small herd and do a milk run into the town. Now I had trouble with the creek running near my place, poisoned it was! Sent two of my cows floating downstream, all bloated up like. So I moved them up to higher ground, left 'em grazing up there for, oh, maybe a few days before

I went to check on them. Well, I'll be damned if I couldn't find hide nor hair of them."

When Mr. Cooley finished his story he was red in the face, as if worn out from the telling.

"And you searched I presume?" Modesto asked.

"I looked for two days, dawn till dark, found some trampling in the underbrush, tracked them a ways, looked like they ended up down at the road, near the railway landing there, but couldn't say for sure they was my cows. But that's what got me to thinking I best come to town and ask around."

"I see, and did your asking around bear any fruit Mr. Cooley?"

"That is just the thing, Mr. O'Brien, that is just the thing! So I was down in the square talking with a couple of fellows, and now this is second or third hand ..."

"That's fine."

"If I may speak plainly then, Mr. O'Brien, I believe my cows may have been stolen, then loaded into a railcar at the landing."

"And once the cows were on the railcar?"

"That's what got me to thinking see? Those fellas I mentioned, the ones down in the square, well they were talking about some railway crew working up there at end of rail line, end of steel they called it, said there were some real bad outfits operating north of here, said there were men working up there pretty much held as prisoners, men locked in railcars, even had boys working out there in the bush, imagine that? Now, I wouldn't had paid much attention except one of the fellas mentioned that they were feeding the workers rotten meat half the time. That's what got my attention, Mr. O'Brien, and made me think, I should go and get myself a detective."

"That is indeed a considerable amount of information you have there Mr. Cooley."

"You think them railway fellas might have taken them?"

"Hard to say Mr. Cooley, hard to say. There is no direct evidence linking your cows to the railway, but there is a certain logic to your suspicions. Give me a day or so to ask around, see what I can find out. How many cattle are we talking about here?"

"There's just three of them sir."

"Oh, not so many at all. And colour, markings, something that might help me identify them?"

"They're all dun coloured, Mr. O'Brien. Gentle beasts. I hate to think of them out there in that wilderness. The bush ain't no place for a cow"

"Quite right Mr. Cooley, quite right. I will do my best."

"I much appreciate your looking into this Mr. O'Brien, and I ain't a rich man but I will pay you for your efforts."

"Yes, of course Mr. Cooley. And I must thank Milton for bringing me the business."

Shitty Mitty said, "Not saying anything about what you do or don't do, Mr. O'Brien, I just know'd you was a detective, and when Mr. Cooley here mentioned that there might be some gunplay up there in those camps, well I thought a man with your experience might be just the ticket, know what I mean?"

"I'm not so sure about that ..." O'Brien started, but Lily spoke up, said, "Oh, Mr. O'Brien has assured me he is no ruffian."

"I think his sign speaks for itself, don't you, Miss Bow?" Shitty said.

The troublesome sign. Modesto steered the conversation elsewhere, asked, "That scar, Milton, on your neck?"

Shitty Mitty's hand went to his throat. "What about it?"

"It's quite impressive. Seems like you may have had quite an experience yourself."

Shitty rubbed at the ridge of red that sliced across the front of his throat, curving up at each end slightly. "Usually keep it covered up, folks don't like looking at it, but I was some warm today. It's something eh? Got it as a boy. My dad was laid up, so he had my brother and I out cutting trees. I was fourteen, my brother just eleven, old enough to know better. There he was, chopping away, and then let that axe fly right out of his hand and into my throat. Had to travel over 20 miles to town. It was forty below too."

"Goodness," Lily said, "you must have been half froze, and the pain!"

"Hadn't been cold I woulda bled out like a stuck pig," he said, fingering the scar again, "so I reckon I was lucky it was winter. Sure did leave me with an ugly mess though, didn't it, Miss Bow?"

Lily said, "Well, no, not really, it almost looks like a smile."

Shitty stared at her for a second, said, "Well, it ain't."

CHAPTER TWELVE

Mr. Cooley left with Shitty Mitty, but not before thanking Modesto again and saying his cows meant the world to him and he would be forever grateful. Modesto then turned his attention to Lily but with just a curt nod she was gone too. It felt to Modesto as if she had just vanished, he couldn't even be sure whether he had actually seen her leave, and he wondered about his mind, whether he could trust it. But if not his own mind, then whose?

He crossed to his desk and withdrew from the top drawer the drawing he had made when he had gotten back from the train station. Smoothed out the sheet of paper, sat and stared. The wraith stared back.

He had made the drawing as soon as he was able to get away from Constable Calder. Although he doubted he would ever forget the image of John Moberly's head disappearing into the fog, he felt it was best to capture the strange vision to the best of his memory. Looking at it now, he wondered if it was even possible: it was tall, thin, and he had drawn the edges of it very lightly because he had a hard time, with the fog and the strangeness of it all, to tell where the creature began and ended, changing shape as it moved maybe? The thing was like something from the stories that Biddy had filled his mind with, goddesses and wraiths, demons and talking trees. It seemed as if lately there was room for little else in his thinking.

The long thin arm. Now remembering the palest of mauve that coloured the veins or bones or skeleton that the creature seemed to be draped over. He sighed. It was, he now thought, quite beautiful, but still something to be feared. He carefully folded the paper and tucked it into his coat pocket.

Time to clear his mind. He had just returned from the train station and a young woman, several months pregnant, had knocked on his door, could he find her husband, the man having come up to Cobalt three months ago to go prospecting but still no word from him. No one could remember meeting or seeing him. He told her to come back with a personal item of her husband's. Another older fellow came by with a map, asked Modesto to show where there might be silver, would cut him in on any findings. Modesto told him to leave. A young widow came by, her man had fallen to his death in one of the mines. Could Modesto talk to him, assure her that in his last moments he hadn't suffered, tell him that she loved and missed him. He needed some fresh air before more lost souls were washed up on his shore.

As soon as he stepped out onto the street the energy of the scene was almost unbearable. He was tempted to head back inside. Everything seemed to be moving, men, wagons, horses, moving in every direction, even the roads seemed to be moving, the pitch of things high and excited. Modesto closed his eyes, hoping when he opened them things might be standing still, quieted, but no, it was still frantic, even the sky was churning overhead, colours of coal and mud.

He started towards the town square and then Shitty Mitty appeared beside him, starting right in, "Well, what do you think of that Mr. Detective, quite the morning so far, everybody's quite riled up. Apparently, we got ourselves another fella striking it rich, and another one of them there suicides! Some young woman."

Modesto wondered about that sentiment, as if both the riches and the deaths belonged to the entire town.

Shitty Mitty kept going, saying, "And everyone's also talking a lot about you, Mr. O'Brien. And the monster. It was one crazy morning. Well, I wouldn't be surprised if you didn't see it for yourself. Folks said you were down at the far end of the train. Maybe you saw it eh?"

"Do you believe in the monster?"

"Folks are saying it was some strange business, Moberly saying he saw the monster and then the monster showing up when he was found dead."

"But nobody actually saw the monster, did they?" he said, picturing the wraith like arm, the swinging of the head, "They only saw an impression of it, an idea of it. I would imagine that everyone who said they saw it would have described something completely different."

"You saying folks making things up?"

Modesto had to stop quickly to avoid being struck by a large cart loaded with barrels and crates, Shitty saying, "Hear them fresh apples are forty cents a basket! Forty cents, that's a lot of money for a few old apples."

There had been a small apple tree in their yard in Butte, near the back gate. Modesto had loved that tree. Biddy had planted little flowers beneath the tree, tiny purple, white and yellow ones, said they were violas, she said they were good for the heart. It occurred to him that he could use them now, feeling suddenly tired of the perpetual motion around him. It was dizzying. A few more steps and again they were brought up short, a water trough placed to block one of the main trails that snaked out to the main street through a series of back alleys. Modesto promptly sat down on it. Shitty hesitated, then sat down beside him.

Modesto sighed, taking in the mud that was now caked up around his boots, and noticed that at the base of the water trough there was a pair of large leaves, crushed into the mud, only the large ends sticking out. Large and thickish and turning to brown, the burdock leaves had the appearance of leathered wings—could it fly away if it weren't bogged down by the crust of mud and the weight of the trough? Could it take off like a big moth? He sat waiting, staring, as the leaves became a moth, Modesto now sure he could see large furry antennae at one end, thick bulb bottom at the other. Leaf to moth. Perhaps he too could become something else, transform into some other kind of thing. Fly off.

Shitty prodded, "You don't believe those folks are telling the truth about that monster?"

The moth, gone. "It's just that often we don't really see what we think we're seeing."

"Well, if you can't trust your own eyes, then what can you trust?"

"I rarely trust my own eyes."

"You say some damnable things, Mr. O'Brien, got yourself some strange ideas."

"Yes, perhaps."

"Not sure ideas like that are going to help you in this town."

"You are probably right about that as well. But what would help me, Milton, is getting to the livery, but it seems to me each time I try to make my way over there the street has moved, or a new building in going up, or I get waylaid so many times I lose my way. Do you have advice on the least treacherous path to the livery?"

Shitty Mitty seemed pleased by the question, liked to be thought of as a man who knew a thing or two about the town, said, "You are right about that, things changing here every darn minute. If I were you, I wouldn't go anywhere near Silver street, some lady got knocked right off her feet by a big piece of rock no more than an hour ago, came flying right off that ore bucket, been swinging back and forth across the lake all morning."

"Alright then, guess I will brave the muck of Swamp Street."

"Going to see that horse of yours?"

"As a matter of fact, yes. I try and get her out for a walk each day, will help her strength come back. Keep her spirits up."

Modesto rose, Shitty along with him. He was unsure as to why Shitty Mitty continued to dog him, but the man jogged along beside Modesto until he could barely stand it, feeling hounded and harried by the constant chattering about silver, monsters and the rising price of bottled water in the camp. Modesto paused to get his bearings once they reached the Square, said, "It was good seeing you, Milton. Think I can find my way from here."

"Maybe I'll just head over there myself, might have some business with Mr. Carr."

"Is there something on your mind?"

"Well no," Shitty said, "I just …. well, I was just being friendly is all. You think I need something from you? Sonofabitch like I do."

O'Brien felt a sudden closeness, as if this man, with his crooked mouth and watchful eyes, was leeching onto him, too close, too close, and the mud was then on the hem of his coat and he could only stop and stare down at it, trying to get himself under control before he was unable to stop himself from taking hold of Shitty's face and burying it in the mud.

"No offense intended, Milton," he managed, "it is most often the case that I am coming to you to find out what is happening in this town, it is unlikely that there would be anything I would know that you did not. My apologies."

Shitty Mitty seemed confused by the apology, confused too by Modesto's pallor. "You look right peaked there, Mr. O'Brien. You alright?"

"Yes, fine I suppose. Just the noise."

"The noise! Well, goddammit, if noise makes you feel particular, then you are in the wrong town."

"Yes, I am quite aware of that, Milton."

CHAPTER THIRTEEN

"Get up you lazy sonsofwhores, there's work to get done."
Lucy lay still, wondered at first if she was dreaming, but then the man was walking between the row of bunkbeds, banging on the edges with the butt end of his rifle, sometimes hitting the bunk, sometimes the man in it. She saw JoeBo as he passed by, giving her bunk a sharp jab. This was their first morning waking up in the railway workcamp, arriving the night before to the shabby, disorganized cluster of makeshift buildings surrounded by a ring of pock-marked mud and bush.

The worker the others called Antoni swung down from his bunk, drew himself to his full height, said to JoeBo, "Are you the man in charge?"

JoeBo said, "My gun says I am. Around here, the gun is the law, and the law says you work."

A few of the men started grumbling so JoeBo said, "You fellas best not be getting too big for your britches now."

"You cannot keep us here against our will," said Antoni, "some of us are leaving today, maybe all of us."

"I don't think you'll be going anywheres. Last bunch that tried
to run out on their obligations got hunted down like dogs, hauled
back here by some of our fine detectives and ended up on bread
and water for a few weeks. That what you want?"

"You cannot put men in jail without a trial!"

"He got a trial alright, right here in this bunkhouse by a
fine and upstanding lawman. And he was one of the lucky ones.
Another fella up and ran out, now we tried to find him and bring
back to safety, but we lost him in the woods. If he didn't turn up
dead a few days later, just up the trail a ways."

Antoni was shaking his head, said, "We did not agree to this.
We thought we were working lumber camp, further north."

"Don't matter what you thought, we got the law on our side.
You are legally obligated to fulfill your work contracts," he said,
patting his coat pocket.

Lucy figured they were just plain old pieces of paper, but the
rifle was what the men were watching, and they started to move
off their bunks, reach for their clothes.

An older man, sitting on the ground as he pulled on his boots,
said, "You treat us like galley slaves."

"You treat us like galley slaves," mimicked JoeBo, grabbing
hold of the older man's hair with his left hand, yanking back his
head until the man winched, "what a pack of goddamn whiners
I got here. Think you need to understand how lucky you are to
even have a job. You gotta learn, when a man finds himself in
Driftwood City, he no longer belongs to himself. You got that?"

The man nodded as best he could with JoeBo's hand holding
him still. JoeBo pushed the man's head as he released him, saying,
"Greasy bastard."

Lucy joined the other men in the line-up, pulled down her hat
and then covered the lower part of her face with her bandana to
keep off the flies, asked as she passed JoeBo, "So who do we belong
to when we're in Driftwood City?"

"Well, boy, you belong to Mr. Tommy Coffin, and don't you ever forget it."

Jesus H Christ. She really was in deep trouble.

CHAPTER
FOURTEEN

He named the dapple-grey horse he had bought from the teamster Molly, and she was doing him a world of good. She was a fine creature and was recovering nicely. Heading back from his visit to the livery, he was almost enjoying the warmth of the spring sun on his back when he heard the uproar. Couple of men jogged past him, laughing, seeming to be headed towards the Prospect Hotel.

"You're going to miss the excitement," Shitty Mitty said, hopping down from the wooden sidewalk, "I'll wait if you got business and we could head to Jamieson's grocery together."

Modesto couldn't believe it, in a town of thousands of men, at every turn he stumbled over Shitty Mitty. "Whatever is occurring over at the grocery store, I don't have much interest. I've had enough drama for a while."

"I was just wandering around when all the fellas started running past, said there was a bear down at Jamieson's. Wasn't looking for no bear. Sometimes, I look for the pigs, but only if I need the money real bad. Like to stick to horses, don't like dealing with the pigs."

"Why is that?

"The cholera. I figure they all got the cholera. Dirty animals. Don't want to get no cholera."

"If I'm not mistaken, pigs have their own form of cholera, not sure people can get it from them. People get cholera from bad water."

"Why now you're a medical man."

"My Gran had stories about cholera outbreaks, from when she was young."

"In Butte?"

"No, the west of Ireland."

Shitty nodded like he knew where that might be, but asked, "Thought you was from Butte."

"I am. My Gran went over to America as a very young woman. Her stories of cholera outbreak were always very vivid though."

"Was it like a plague?"

"I suppose. It is a bacteria that infects people and then it is spread through dirty water or food cooked with dirty water. My Gran said her family listened with dread to reports as the disease spread all across Europe. By the time it reached Ireland, people were maddened with fear. People weren't sure what was causing it. There was all kinds of madness and fear. Turned people into monsters."

"What do you mean by that? Monsters?"

"She said that people became crazed. Would attack each other. And the healthy ones would persecute and hound the one's that got sick, hound them out of their homes, their towns. At times they would bury the living too soon, out of fear or ignorance. So people thought the dead were getting up out of their graves."

"You got lots of peculiar stories, Mr. O'Brien."

"Yes, I suppose I do. But they can be instructive, don't you think, Milton? Push us to consider things in a different light. I have always thought, since hearing her stories about that moment of slippage, you know, from living to dead, that occupying that space is a very tricky place."

"I don't follow a lot of your gibberish, Mr. O'Brien, think your Granny filled your head with nonsense."

"Perhaps."

"Like about the cholera. Ain't never heard anything about a sickness turning people into monsters," he paused, then said, smirking, "Hey, maybe that's what happened to that there monster out there," he said, nodding towards the scraggly line of trees that lined the horizon, "maybe it got the cholera from the pigs. Was just a normal man before the sickness."

"I doubt pigs created your monster."

"Ain't my monster, no sir-ee, I stick to dead animals."

"Well, I prefer my animals alive, Milton. And I can't help but wondering, now that I've been in this dreadful town for a month now, walked through it, around it, past it and back, and I've seen the horses, a few dogs, and the cows and hogs of course, but where are the creatures? I haven't even heard a bird singing."

"Maybe can't hear them over all the commotion and blasting. Fella hears gulls often enough though."

"Yes, there are the gulls, I like their cries, but still, I do miss the sound of a blackbird singing. It's as if this place has erased the natural world in few short years. Unbelievable."

"It ain't all that bad. I heard Mr. Bilskey has a wolf cub. Might be getting a zoo too. And then there's that bear I've been trying to tell you about, it's getting drunk over in the basement of Jamieson's store. They'll probably need to shoot it."

"Shoot it? But why?"

"It's down there drinking all of Mr. Jamieson's beer and they can't get it out! Those fellas said they're going use it for target practice."

A huge pile of waste rock was slumped against Jamieson's Meat & Groceries store. Looked ready to devour the place whole. There was a number of men crowded around the door of the wood-framed building, laughter and shouting coming from inside.

Shitty Mitty pointed to the thin man pacing in front of the store, said to Modesto, "That there is Mr. Jamieson."

The store owner glanced at Shitty as they approached him, said, "Don't need no hangers on, got enough inside. Best you keep moving, Shitty."

Shitty Mitty hesitated, his mouth working, embarrassed, but unable to find the words. Modesto could hear another roar of laughter coming from inside the building. He addressed Mr. Jamieson directly, asked, "Is the store open for business?"

"Of course not," annoyed at the question, "can't get in there myself, must be twenty, I don't know, maybe thirty men inside...." And then the sound of breaking glass coming from inside the store, and he shook his head and said, "making a mess of the place. As if I don't have enough troubles."

"Mr. Jamieson, let me introduce myself," Modesto said, extending his hand, "I'm Modesto O'Brien, detective, new in town. I happen to know a bit about bears and, if it is your wish, am willing to remove the bear from your store. And the men. Is that something you would find amenable to your needs?"

Jamieson looked to Shitty, "You know this man?"

"He's the fella that shot Werner's horse."

"Right, yes, I heard about that. Alright then, what was the name? O'Brien?"

"That's right."

"Are you going to shoot the bear?"

"No, that is hardly necessary."

"Don't care if you do, don't care if you don't" said Jamieson, "but I got to warn you, some of those fellas are armed in there, been taking a few pot shots just to keep things entertaining I suppose. I tried to get them out, but they threatened me, and my boy too."

"Are they drinking?" Modesto asked.

Jamieson glanced at Shitty, "This ain't a new liquor inspector you're bringing around? Got enough trouble as it is."

"Not to worry, Mr. Jamieson," said Modesto, "I have no position on the prohibition of drinking in the camp, I'm only interested in resolving the situation. Now have the men inside been drinking?"

"They're all cranked up, drunken fools! Got into my whiskey, the beer! Taking bets right now, how many shots to drop the bear without hitting another keg. They already put a bullet in two of the kegs, just keeps the bear down there. Shooting like that, just as likely to hit each other as the bear."

"And you haven't summoned the Constable because of the kegs?"

"I can't see how this is a police matter," Jamieson said, then putting on his shopkeeper's face, asked, "How much is this going to cost me anyway?"

"How about one of those bottles, if I can get it done before they're all broken or drained."

Jamieson said, "Alright then, I'm a fair man, you get them out of there and you can have your pick of what's left. You want Shitty to go in with you?"

"No, that won't be necessary."

Modesto pushed his way through the men in the doorway. It was hard to see where the door to the basement was, the store thick with men's bodies, cartons knocked over, apples trampled underfoot. Men helping themselves to Jamieson's stock. The store was small, crowded, but in total Modesto thought there were likely only twenty or so men inside.

"Alright gentlemen, coming through," he said, moving slowly through the crush of men as he made his way to the top of the narrow staircase that led down to the basement, the scent shifting from whiskey and sweat to beer and bear.

A few men were blocking the doorway. Just below them were a couple of men at the top of the stairs, joking about the loud slurping and moaning of the bear below.

"Clear the stairs now gentlemen, please, in an orderly fashion, make your way back up into the store," Modesto said, and as he was talking he was looking for pistols, saw one hanging loosely in the hand of a young prospector, an apple in the other, and a stupefied look on the man's face. Modesto had the gun out of the young man's hand before he was able to protest.

The doorway cleared, Modesto was able to move down the stairs, the bear now in view, sitting back on its haunches surrounded by a few kegs that were shattered and battered, the floor wet and the bear wet too. That half-rotted smell of bear, the sour yeast odour of the beer. The bear was on the smaller side, maybe just under two hundred pounds, good thing too because the space the beast had managed to get itself into was more of a cellar than a basement.

Louder this time, moving back into the room, Modesto said, "Everyone back up, Mr. Jamieson needs his store back and doesn't want to have to get the authorities involved, after all it was all just good fun in here, right boys?" He took the arm of the prospector closest to him and gently turned him and then said to the man next to him, "Help him the rest of the way would you," and the man did because he was asked, and Modesto proceeded to slowly herd the men further into the store.

As they crowded into the main part of the store, trampling a soggy array of vegetables underfoot, he said, "No harm done boys, but please, keep moving, out to the street now. Mr. Jamieson has engaged me to remove the bear. He is aware that many of you may or may not be partaking of alcoholic beverages, and due to his good nature, he wants to avoid involving the authorities. Might be wise under the circumstances," he then glanced at the man closest to him, spoke directly into his bloodshot and wary eyes, said, "to kindly leave the premises."

Modesto waited as the last few stragglers exited though the store's front door. He closed it and retraced his steps into the basement, the sludge of trampled vegetables, mixed with liquor, making the floors slick. He descended partway down the stairs, the bear still sitting but seemed wobbly now, drunk and disoriented, making small sounds somewhere between a grunt and a sob.

"Yes, I know the feeling well good friend, know it well."

He approached the bear, the bear swinging its big head towards him, the grunt stronger now, maybe agitated, but Modesto said, "Now, now there, let's get you up and out of here, the fresh air will do you wonders."

• • •

Mr. Jamieson was just opening the front door to peek in when bear and man emerged from the top of the basement stairs, Modesto half carrying, half dragging, the bear, its front legs dangling, back legs seemingly propelled by his escort. Modesto said, "Mr. Jamieson if you could show us a clear path out behind your building."

"Look at this mess," the shopkeeper said, surveying the muddied mix of broken glass, vegetables and tools, "goddammit. Now what am I supposed to do?"

"Yes, it is quite the trouble you've been caused but if I may, a discrete exit for the bear, he isn't big, but he is getting heavy."

"There's a door right there, just to your left. Will take you out behind there, but watch your step, one of those companies is sinking a shaft right goddam there in the middle of town, that's what the rock pile is about," the shopkeeper said, crossing the shop to open the door but moving backwards quickly as the bear neared, saying, "Think that there is Bilskey's bear though, keeps him down at the mine. You pay a nickel and you can feed it ice cream, best return it there," but it was as if Modesto had not heard him, so he repeated, but less sure now, "Think that is Mr. Bilskey's bear," and Modesto said, "I think this fellow is in need of some fresh air, a wild creature like this is unpredictable, best to keep him away from town for now, after all, we don't want anyone to get hurt now do we?"

And Mr. Jamieson nodded his head in agreement as the man and bear moved past him, the bear's small eyes unfocused and roving as Modesto half carried, half dragged the drunken creature through the mud, up over the wooden sidewalk, and onto the street.

There was hooting and laughter once the pair came into view of the men waiting outside. They watched as the pair continued towards where the sparse bush began, Modesto then setting the bear down on all fours and removing the chain from around the bear's neck. The group grew quiet, their exuberance waning as Modesto helped the bear back up onto its feet, the creature wobbling a bit, then its thick, shaggy arm draped itself across Modesto's back and the two turned off the trail towards the woods, and the men just watched until one of them said, "That's a strange fellow there. Where's he from?"

And another said, "Something not quite right about him. He a friend of yours Shitty?"

And Shitty Mitty could feel the mood turning surly, said, "No sir. Just had some dealings with him is all."

CHAPTER FIFTEEN

"So this is the fucking Cobalt I've been hearing all about."

The swagger was as much in his voice as his body, but that wasn't the first thing Shitty noticed about Tommy Coffin. The first thing Shitty Mitty noticed was that Tommy Coffin wasn't very big, but he was some terrible looking, lean and powerful built around the shoulders, his hair a bleached out looking reddish-blonde, his eyes such a pale blue they almost looked white with the sun now shinning in the man's eyes. Shitty was having a hard time pinning it down, but it was a strange sensation. He was both handsome and ugly at the same time, almost looked wrong somehow, now saying loudly, "You can feel it boyos, the money in the ground. Like a pulse." And he laughed, rows of perfect white teeth.

"I told ya," said Bodine, "this place is going to make us rich."

Coffin, looking around, asked, "Where's Butch?"

"Haven't seen hide nor hair of him in a while."

"What? He knew I was coming. You told him it was today?"

"Hasn't been around to tell or I would'a. By the time I heard from you he seemed to have already lit out. Didn't leave word."

"That's not like Butch. You look for him?"

"'Course I did. Asked around. You know how he can be though, Butch goes his own way. He'll show up once he hears that you're in town."

Coffin slapped Bodine in the chest, said, "He damn well better! Now let's get us a drink. That fucking train ride left me parched."

It wasn't until Shitty put the bottle down on the table, and then sat down, that Coffin even seemed to notice him, asked Bodine, "Who's this?"

"Milton Steam, I'm a friend of Bill's," Shitty said fast, trying to get his own version of himself in before Bodine could, but then Bodine said, "Name's Shitty Mitty, hangs around a fair bit, don't ya now Shit, but he can be of use. Knows everything about this town, been around here since before they even found the silver."

"Alright then, Shitty," Coffin asked, leaning back in his chair and putting his hands behind his head, muscles against the white shirt, "what do I need to know about this town? What kind of money are fellas making here?"

"There's fellas getting rich here, lots of fellas, but there's fellas getting poor too. And there ain't a darn inch of land in this here camp that ain't been dug, claimed or built on! They're draining the lakes too, to git to the silver below. Silver lining every bit of this place. Further north too." Shitty, excited by Coffin's attention, kept talking, "And something that might interest you, there was a bear getting drunk this morning! I mean they say this town is dry but no sir-ee, and the drink makes everything crazy, there's fellas blowing themselves up to get at the silver, these greenhorns not knowing that dynamite and whiskey don't mix too good! One of 'em even set part of the town on fire, can you believe it?" Shitty smiling, pleased with himself.

There was a small silence, and then Tommy leaned forward, finger pointed at Shitty, "I'll tell you something right here and now, Milton, about what might interest me and what might not.

When I was a young man, I happened to be passing by a string of warehouses, down by the railway yards in Butte, it was dark out and cold, just a few weeks after Christmas, and I saw a fire, the firemen already hard at battling the flames. So I went down, and joined a bunch of fellas there watching this happen, and there was all manner of stuff in these warehouses see? Iron bars, gas pipe, iron wheelbarrows, you get the idea, don't you?" pausing until Shitty nodded, "Good. And so maybe the firemen knew there was dynamite in there or maybe they didn't, but it didn't take long for one of those fucking warehouses to blow up, the roof went straight up, hundred feet in the fucking air, and came down on everyone, along with the metal pipes and the wheelbarrows, and then the other warehouses went up too and you can just see it, can't you?"

Yes, Shitty thought, he could, but he was feeling uncomfortable, those bleached eyes of Coffin fixed on his own. Shitty managed a muted 'Yes.'

"Good, glad you're keeping up here. Good for you. Now when the first blast went off, I happened to be standing behind a few of the horses that had been blanketed, waiting for the fire truck. The impact blasted that horse right off its feet, caught me as it went down, I was crushed underneath, broke my leg like. And you know what laying on the ground all around me, Shitty?"

"Well, I guess some dead fellas …"

Coffin interrupted, "Yes that's correct. Dozens and dozens of them. Bits and pieces of them too, they had to collect some of them in baskets. So, you can see Shitty, after witnessing that, and surviving it, at such an impressionable age, I might not be very interested in some dumb bastard blowing himself up or some bear getting drunk. But can you think about what that taught me and what I might be interested in?"

Coffin didn't wait for Shitty to answer, said, "I learned nothing mattered more than being the right fella at the right time and in the right place. Understand? I was all of those things that time. I could have been elsewhere, and never witnessed such a spectacular thing, or I could have been on the other side of the horse and been in a basket myself, you see? So, what I'm interested in knowing, from you, and ol' Billy boy here, is whether I'm correct in following my instincts, that I'm going to be the right man at the right time in the right place in this town of yours?"

Shitty wasn't sure what the answer to the question was so he looked to Bodine, the man perking up at the mention of his name, saying, "I guarantee it Tommy, we're going to be rich men by the time we say good-bye to this town."

"You're planning on leaving?" asked Shitty, but Coffin said, "That's what I wanted to hear boyo," now smiling, turned his attention back to Shitty, said, "why don't you go fetch us another bottle like a good man?"

Shitty didn't want to leave, wanted an answer to his question, worried about the future, but Bodine nodded his head, said, "Go on, git. And not the cheap stuff."

Pushing his way to the bar, Shitty was worried. If they left, would they take him with them? And if not, what would he do, would he be enough, enough what he wasn't sure, but he knew he needed to be more than what he had been before, so he didn't have to go back to just pulling the honey wagon and chaining and dragging dead horses. Said to Frank, "A bottle of the good stuff," then added, "we're celebrating."

"That right Shitty? And what are you celebrating?"

"That ain't any of your concern."

"Then why did you tell me you stupid sonofabitch?"

And since Shitty had no way of explaining that he'd told him so that other men would think he was important, hanging out with this big shot from Butte, he just said, "The bottle, alright?"

Frank shrugged, passed him the bottle.

By the time he got back to the table, Bodine and Coffin were smiling, looked like they were deep into the trading of stories, and

Bodine was saying, "Remember the time we found that wee slip of a thing, and she was thinking we couldn't hear her down there, trying to steal your horse …"

The ending of the story was lost in laughing and then Bodine poured them a round and told another story just like the first one, and then another, and both men were laughing at everything the other one said, and then Bodine slapped Shitty on the back, said, "Pour us another round."

Shitty was reaching for the bottle but Coffin pushed back his chair and waved his hand, "That's it for me gentlemen, that's it for me."

Bodine protested but Coffin said, "Needs be fit and fiddle for the morning boyos, we got ourselves some hunting to do. First thing in the morning we'll be having to round up Butch, find out what whorehouse or jail he's ended up in. Now, why don't you tell me where I can find that bit of woman I had shipped up here a few weeks back and I'll be off."

Shitty saw Bodine suddenly looking uncomfortable, hands still clasped around the empty bottle, like maybe he was steadying himself with it, and he said, "She's not really here anymore Tommy."

Coffin's eyebrows going up, "That so? She get away on you?"

Bodine shook his head, trying for something that looked like sorrow but really just looked guilty, Shitty wondering if he was going to now see the famous Tommy Coffin in action, lowering the boom, like Bodine said he did, wondering too if that was Coffin's woman or just another one of those girls Bodine brought to town to work the boarding houses.

Bodine said, "No, no, nothing like that. She up and went and poisoned herself."

"Did she now? And why would she have done something like that Billyboy?"

Bodine struggled to come up with the right story in the right way. "She was sore Tommy, real sore, said she was promised all kinds of things, she was going on and on about fancy hotels and purple lit sidewalks and all kinds of crazy talk. Said she was going to have a baby, that she was in love with you. Couldn't get her to shut up."

Bodine paused, but Tommy said nothing, half-drunk now but paying attention, so Bodine said, "So what could I do? Had to settle her down somehow, told her I'd get her something to get rid of the baby. Told her she had one more chance, we'd fix her but then she had to get back to work, start covering her costs. But couldn't talk sense to her. She said she could keep the baby, that you'd come for her. See? I didn't have any choice," added, "knew you wouldn't want any trouble, word getting out, about the girls I mean."

Tommy said, "There wouldn't have been any trouble if you knew how to handle things."

Shitty Mitty was interested to see how Bill would react, usually didn't take any backtalk from anyone, wondering too if the things he'd gotten at the drugstore was for the woman, if he could get blamed for anything, but Bodine just said, "I did handle things. And now there's no trouble."

"And exactly how did you handle it?" Coffin asked.

"I told her that was fine, that I'd put her on the train myself, but said you weren't going to want any baby. Told her the carbolic acid would do the trick."

"Carbolic? She believed you?"

Bodine shrugged. "She took it. Needed a bit of encouraging, but she took it. Then I left her alone."

There was silence for a few seconds as Coffin stared at Bodine. Then he burst out laughing, shaking his head, said, "Jesus to Christ! Well, find me another one, doesn't make much difference in the end, a whore's a whore."

Shitty was disappointed. He figured the girl they were talking about was the one over at Shay's Boarding house. The one who killed herself. Shitty had liked the story of the two suicides. Now this girl who died, well, that didn't sound like no suicide. Not exactly anyhow. Bodine was laughing though, and Shitty thought maybe tricking the girl like that was funny after all, it just wasn't a story he could tell anyone, not just yet anyway, until he knew whether he could get in trouble or not. Bodine said, "Get us that bottle Shitty", and he had to go beg Frank for a third bottle, promising him he'd pay up soon as he could, and wasn't he a man of his word?

CHAPTER
SIXTEEN

"Don't care if you're getting wet," JoeBo said, "keep shovelling."

She was up to her knees in water, they all were, the trees too, the muskegs swollen from the winter run-off and wet spring. "Can't shovel, the muck just slides off the shovel," she complained, but JoeBo said, "Use your fucking hands, I don't care, just clear this swamp."

Lucy was trying to situate herself from what she was hearing around her, chatter among the guards, the camp cook's gossip. They'd passed a few prospectors, some heading up to a place called Larder Lake, listened to them shooting the shit about conditions on the river and the goddamn bugs sending more than a few of their companions back out of the bush. From what she could tell, her crew were working near where three rivers, the Black, Driftwood and the mighty Abitibi, met up. She didn't know too much about the area but already knew it was remote. Lily might have a hard time finding her.

Maybe it would be better to take her chances and head off into the bush, follow the Black River south and hope she ended up somewhere near a settlement. But it was hard to think straight what with the squelching of the murky swamp as her shovel tried to find a full load of muck, then hauling it up through the turgid water, each shovelful conjuring a legion of bugs, it taking all of her concentration to try and shut out the feeling of them crawling along her hairline, making their way down the back of her neck.

It was the shouting and the deafening cracking sound that pulled her from her focus. She straightened up in time to see the tree top finish its mighty flop onto the ground, a spray of cones and branches and then men were shouting and running towards the tree. Its massive crown was on the ground, the tree cut part way up, the thick trunk snapped and uneven. Lucy knew as she moved slowly towards the tree that the bad thing she had felt earlier had happened.

JoeBo was striding over to where a group of men were yelling, trying to lift and move the huge tree. He pulled a few men away from the scene, one man wailing and JoeBo striking him, telling him to back off and shut the fuck up, and then Lucy heard him say, "Goddammit, this is just what I needed. This cursed fucking job."

The body was barely visible beneath the thick dark green branches.

JoeBo turned on the huddle of men. "What happened?"

Several men began to talk at once, some trying in English, most just speaking in their own language, gesturing to help explain, but JoeBo shouted, "Shut your mouths!" Then pointing to Antonio, "Did you see what happened?"

"Yes, I was here. We had clump of trees to clear, three trees, sharing one stump. We cut the two, me and Martin. And then we notched the third, I checked, checked to the east where it was to fall, cleared everyone, but it twisted, hit this tree here and broke it, just smashed it," pointing then to the tree and man, "sending its branches down, he was a far away, but this tree hit him, we yelled, he began to run, but it caught him."

"Did you check him, see if he's dead?"

Antonio glanced to the two men closest to him, and one said, "Dead."

JoeBo grunted, spat, and looked out towards where the sun was high in the sky. "Alright, you two, get over there, start digging. We're burying this sonofabitch and getting back to work."

"Burying him here?" Antonio asked, "Here in the middle of nowhere? No, no, we must take him back with us, send his body home."

"This here muskeg is going to be his home now, and I ain't losing any more time over this. Get him out from under the tree and bury him."

"But, the body, but..." Antonio stammering, "we must prepare the body, look at him...."

JoeBo said, "Don't think he's going to mind. Now get him in the ground. And none of this six-feet-under, just enough so no bear comes along and digs him up for dinner. A few feet will do just fine."

The men looked at each other, glanced over at where the relative of the young man was bent over, head in hands, Antonio saying, "Please, the uncle ..."

But JoeBo just patted the gun in his holster.

Antonio stared at the gun for a moment but then slowly moved away, turned his attention to the clearing of the mess of branches and limbs of the mighty tree. Two of his countrymen picked up shovels, moved past the grieving uncle, one resting his hand on the man's shoulder for a moment, and then they started digging.

Antoni looked over at JoeBo, said, "We need to mark his grave, with a stone or cross."

"Whatever you say pops," JoeBo said, "Take off his boots, stick 'em on one of those branches. That'll be his cross."

So they took the boots, set them atop the shallow mound of dirt once the body was laid to rest, and got the fuck back to work like they were supposed to.

CHAPTER
SEVENTEEN

"Will I be seeing you tonight, Tommy?"

He was sitting on the edge of the bed, feet planted firmly on the floor.

"Tommy?"

Tommy pulled on his boots, snapped, "Jesus woman, would you shut up. Can't you see I'm thinking?"

"Sorry Tommy."

"Jesus Christ. Just get out."

He couldn't be bothered to look up her, her making those small sounds of hurt they made, all the fucking same, trying to make you feel guilt. He could hear the rustle of her dressing, still some of those small sounds. "Hurry up. I got business to get to."

She paused on her way to the door, said, "Well, thanks Tommy, if you want to see me, just ask downstairs for Miriam. My name is Miriam."

He glanced up at her, held out his hand, said, "Come here."

Smiling, she reached for him, his hand clamping onto her wrist, he said, "I don't give a fuck what your name is, but you better fucking remember that you call me Mr. Coffin," he kept squeezing her wrist until her eyes were watering. He pushed her hand away, said, "Leave the door open, and send Bill up."

• • •

Tommy was drumming his fingers on the small table when Bodine walked in, not giving the man a chance to even sit down before asking, "Remember when we were back in Butte, the night we were down at the Dumas, the night that sonofabitch Carter went for me? Remember that?"

Bodine couldn't remember anyone called Carter, but he sure remembered the Dumas Hotel, they had some fine times there, the pack of them, headed down on a Saturday night. "Yeah, not really Tommy."

Tommy raised his eyebrows, "Really? You have no recollection of us dragging that fucker into the alleyway and kicking him until he was crying for his mother?"

"No, don't recall. Not sure how you can tell all those fellas apart Tommy, there's been quite a few over the years," grinning now, "that we took into one alleyway or another."

"Carter, from the mine, he hired us on as guards. Didn't want to pay up what was owed us, remember, he caught you and Butch drinking on the job."

Bodine said, "Oh yeah, right, I remember."

"You don't, you fucking daft bastard. But never mind. I told you, told you that night, that there would come a day when we'd put the likes of Carter in his place. Show them all."

"Yeah? Guess we did that by leaving him to die like a dog in the alley…"

"You listening Bill? I'm telling you, I can feel that this is it. Billyboy, you, me and Butch, we're going to be leaving here rich men."

"Sounds good to me. Maybe head out to California afterwards!"

"Anywhere we want Billy, anywhere we want. First thing is to get ourselves out of that fucking railroading shit. Nothings coming of this railway subcontracting, think it's time to cut our losses, take what we've got coming to us upfront and then get out. We'll be needing cash to get ourselves known up here, to get in on the game."

"Been some trouble up there in that workcamp. I got the sonofbitches that hired us bellyaching about making our deadlines, and then the crew we subcontracted out to bellyaching about the weather and the workers. More trouble than it's worth if you ask me."

"That's what I'm saying, Billy, I want you to get up there and handle things. Get things settled down and get in touch with that contractor, Chandy's his name, and get the rest of our money."

"Won't be much left over. Got to pay those lazy sonofbitch workers. We still owe for the supplies and grub too. I'm trying to keep costs down but I'm telling you, Tommy, sure ain't getting rich running greasers for the railway."

Tommy was shaking his head and said, "You aren't listening. We're leaving the railway bullshit behind us. Its silver, silver is going to make us rich. So just pay your man out there, what's his name?"

"JoeBo."

"Yeah, so pay him to keep him up there for now, tell him whatever you need to, but they gotta keep at it till we hear back from Chandy and get the rest of the money. Throw a few bucks JoeBo's way and then we're out."

Bodine said, "Completely?"

"We're washing our hands of that two-bit operation. We can use the cash from Chandy to keep us going here until everything falls into place."

"Well, they're ain't working if they don't get paid Tommy."

"Sure they will Bill, you'll figure out a way."

"Yeah, alright," Bodine said, "I'll figure it out. Sure do hate going up there, you wouldn't believe this Driftwood City, in the middle of fucking nowhere, just bugs and bush. Christ almighty."

"Don't you worry Billyboy, I'm going to round up some fellas to back you up, case there's any trouble. Then I can focus on getting our silver and getting out of here."

"But where are we going to get the silver?"

"We're going to take it."

"Like rob the train?"

"No, we're going get ourselves a real, in the ground, rich fucking vein of silver."

"We don't even got a claim."

"No, but other fellas do, Bill," he paused, added, "That's why we gotta find Butch. I heard from him, few weeks before I headed up, said he was onto something. Something big."

"Butch didn't say nothing to me about it."

"Sent me a telegram, that's why I came up earlier then I planned. Said he had a line on a sure thing," Tommy paused, added, "Said we were going to have ourselves one of the richest silver mines in the camp."

"Why wouldn't he have said anything to me about it?"

"All he told me was that he was working some scheme, that it was going to get messy and he was trying to keep things quiet."

"Pretty much impossible to keep things quiet here. Place is a rumour mill, just grinds out the bullshit by the ton. Was he working with anyone?"

"Man named Moberly."

"Moberly!" Bodine was surprised.

"You know him?"

"You could say that."

"So it shouldn't be too hard to find him."

"Might be.

"Why's that Billy?"

"Moberly's dead."

"Dead? When?"

"Just the other night."

"Think this silver business could have gotten him killed?"

Bodine shrugged, "Doubt it. Moberly was in the Bucket of Blood, going on, hysterical about that there monster that's got everyone talking. Man was nothing but a goddam fool."

"What happened to him?"

"He got run over by the train."

"Run over by the fucking train? Drunk?"

Bodine was slow to answer, so Tommy said, "You have a hand in it? You tell me right now Billy, don't want to be hearing it from some other fellas."

"He had me right riled up all night, found him passed out drunk. I put him on the tracks, just seemed like the thing to do."

"Who else knows?"

"No one. I was on my own."

"Jesus Christ. This Moberly could have told us about Butch."

"Then Butch should've told me. Not right, after all these years, not trusting me."

"You and Butch have a falling out?"

"No, nothing like that. But he was keeping to himself. Took trips out of town without letting me know, talking to other fellas, like Moberly I guess, things like that. I didn't know what was up with him, and he sure as shit wasn't helping out up at Driftwood."

Coffin nodded but didn't say anything. Bodine hated it when Tommy was quiet, so he said, "You know how he could be sometimes Tommy, get in those moods, keep to himself. And Moberly? The man was half mad. Why was Butch partnering up with the likes of him anyway?"

"Well, we're going to find out, Bill, you're going to find out. Sure there's a good reason Butch was partnering up with this Moberly."

"Moberly's dead and Butch is missing, maybe dead himself. Don't see how we can figure this one out."

"Butch dead?"

"Not saying that, just thinking, fella doesn't just vanish."

Coffin leaned forward, said, "You're right about that, so now you're going to get out there and find Butch. You're going to do everything you can. And tell that Shitty Mitty to keep his mouth shut. I don't want our business being chewed on by every prospector and greenhorn up here. And I don't want any more fucking surprises. Understand?"

"Yeah, 'course Tommy. I'll handle it."

"But you're not handling things, Bill. You're not thinking things through. Just leaving Moberly on the tracks, that's risky. Man might not have been so drunk, might've come to, might've known you dragged him there. Not finishing the job. That's your problem, don't make it mine."

"I did finish it Tommy, I shot him. Made sure he ended up dead."

"Shot him? Not worried about the law?"

"You don't have to worry Tommy. I shot him in the head, but then that train came along and took his head right off, it must be smeared all over the belly of that train."

Tommy stared at him for a few long seconds, then laughed, "You got the luck of a fucking paddy, you know that?"

CHAPTER
EIGHTEEN

There was no time between the knock on the door and the man coming through it. Once in the room, he settled himself on the chair, surveying the room as if buying it.

Modesto felt the skin across his head tighten, mouth go dry, had no time to think or speak, Coffin saying, "Name's Tom Coffin. I'm in need of a few men, detectives like, to help me out with some, what would you say, some reluctant workers, men trying to get out of their legal obligations to me. I've got the two Thiel agency men in town, couple of my own, but I could use a few more. I'll have a man drop by with your train ticket, someone will meet you at the end of the line, take you on up to my camp. It's up the Abitibi, someplace called Driftwood City, wherever the fuck that is."

He paused, waiting for Modesto to answer, but Modesto was looking past the man's shoulder, unable to look at him, seeing instead the memory of Coffin as he dug his thick hands into Kit's shoulder and yanked him out of his chair in the classroom, dragging him out into the hard sun of the schoolyard, the other boys cheering him on. It was a long time ago, but it felt so recent, still so raw. Modesto had worried that somehow, that after all the years,

Coffin would be able to recognize him, but no, of course not.

Coffin's pale eyes narrowed, he asked, "You up for the work, man? Sitting there like a statue. You are the detective, aren't you?"

"Yes," Modesto finally said, "I am a detective."

"Fine, I'll send a man by. He'll give you the details."

Leaving, Tommy glanced up at the sign, *Gunman & Fortune-teller*, turned back to Modesto and said, "Get your own sign up there boyo, so people know you're in business, too much confusion in this fucking place, tried to find tobacco and ended up in the fucking butcher's."

"I'm sure you found something there to your liking."

Coffin eyed him. "That's right."

O'Brien said nothing, and Coffin just stood in the doorway staring up at the sign. He scratched his chin, asked, "That a mistake?"

"Oh," sighed Modesto, "probably."

"What's wrong with you man? Just answer the question, do you read fortunes?"

"Is that what the sign says today?"

The red gathering at the top of the man's ears, sticking out from his head like hard handles. "Are you fucking with me?"

Modesto said, "Sorry, an attempt at levity I suppose, perhaps it was inappropriate."

"You're fucking right there."

"Won't happen again, I can assure you. And yes, I read fortunes."

"Why do you say 'read' like? Says up there you *tell* people their fortunes. Fortune-teller. What are you reading?"

"The person."

Tommy stared at him, asked, "What does that mean?"

"It means that who you are, and what you've done, is written all over you, plain as day."

"Then why would I need you? Why can't any damn fella tell me what's going to happen?"

"Because they can't see it."

"And you can?"

"That's right."

"Why? Something you were taught?"

"Sort of. Passed on in the family you could say."

"You call out the dead?"

That was an interesting question. "Sometimes they call me."

"What does that mean? Speak straight man, I'm losing patience."

"Yes, at times I talk to the spirit world. It's not impossible, if one pays attention."

Tommy took a quick survey of the office, the disorder and half-finished unpacking, said, "I might be back. And you better be here when me or my man shows up, seems to me you can't make up your fucking mind whether you're staying or going."

"There are a lot of things I can't make my mind up about. But heading up the Abitibi River isn't one of them. I'll wait for your man. And I'll wait for you, should you decide there is a spirit that is wanting your attention."

Tommy smiled, said, "I'm wanting *his* attention. Best he show up."

"I'm sure no man, dead or alive, would keep Tom Coffin waiting."

CHAPTER NINETEEN

What a pair. Coffin sitting stiff, upright, arms crossed. Bodine squirming, shifting in the hard-backed chair, feet moving around. Modesto got them seated at the table, lit the few candles in the room, one on the table, the others perched up on a windowsill beside and behind the men.

"I don't want any of that knocking table bullshit. Invisible writing bullshit. None of that."

"That isn't really my approach," Modesto said. He could feel his own heart pounding, mouth dry.

"Fine."

"This was a friend of yours, the man you're seeking?" Modesto asked.

"That's right."

"Do you have anything of his, personal belonging of some sort? It helps."

"Shitty told me you might be asking for something," Coffin said, reaching down and retrieving a small hatchet. Placed it on the table. "It's all we got. He used this for marking his claims, blazing trees like."

The metal head of the axe picked up the flicker of the candle. Modesto suddenly felt reluctant to pick it up, it lying there between them. Could feel Coffin's eyes on him.

Coffin said, "Go on, let's get started. Pick it up man, don't sit there gawking like a fool."

"Mr. Coffin, I ask for your patience and sensitivity this evening. I am not a fairground performer. So please, silence on your part and concentrate on your deceased friend."

"I never said he was dead."

"If your friend isn't dead, why are you here?"

"A test."

"A test? Of what Mr. Coffin?"

"My associate here thinks perhaps our friend could be dead. If you call him, he comes, he's dead. If he doesn't, he's alive. Simple. A test."

Modesto sighed, intrigued by the man's faith in the process but glad he had a reason not to follow through on the reading. The dark energy in the room, Coffin's and his own, was rising like bile in the air, stinking, oppressive.

"Mr. Coffin, the effort and energy it takes to reach out to the departed is tremendous and not to be trifled with. Rousing the dead as a test is a sure-fire way to anger the spirits, and I'm afraid I am not willing to do so. I'm afraid under the circumstances I cannot be of assistance."

"Are you fucking kidding me?"

"No sir, I am not. My deepest apologies but I cannot help you."

Coffin's face reddened, his blood up, Bodine stood, muttering *fucking bullshit* under his breath, but Coffin wasn't budging, saying, "I'm going to ask you once more to do the reading."

"Mr. Coffin. You can threaten me, certainly, but don't insult the spirits. It's simply not in your best interest."

With that, Modesto pushed himself back from the table, but Bodine was there, grabbing Modesto's shoulder as if to push him

back down in the chair, said, "Sit down and show some respect."
The hand on the shoulder, seeping its vile nature onto Modesto,
uncontainable.

*To the black room, no choice but to go there, but still, that sickly
sweet smell*

   It's sticking to this one Biddy, it's on his hands

   *Yes, this one is drawn to it, likes the thrill of it, even the scent. He
likes to see it over and over, likes to mark himself with it, hear himself
saying to her, it won't even hurt, it will just take the baby, take the
baby away, poor Hattie Boyle, no time for shock once the burning
started on her lips, mouth, throat. Poor Hattie. Him leaving her just
like that, closing the door so quiet, he had a smile on his face*

A rigidity overcame Modesto, preventing him from crumpling under Bodine's strength, instead he tipped sideways then
staggered backwards, hands to face, and he could hear Bodine
say, "The man's mad."

The room seemed to be moving around Modesto, hard to stay
upright, but god knows what a beating he might take if he went down.
The boots of Tommy Coffin up and down his spine. But to stay upright took enormous efforts, he felt the big hand of Bodine take hold
of him, sensing a new wave of nausea washing over Biddy and himself,

*Oh Moddie, there's the buzzing and stinging, then a beating, such
a beating, who's that there in the room with the stench of this one?
Wait, look, it's her, the one you've been searching for, that you've been
wondering about, and she's taken it on the chin, hasn't she, with the
smell of soil and the chittering of tiny black bugs*

And the smell of the soil and sweat were overpowering, gag-
ging, and then Coffin, sounding alarmed, said, "Get the man into
a chair, get him into the chair."

But Bodine didn't move. "I'm not touching him, look at him."

"Goddammit," Coffin shouting now, "get him in the chair."

And Modesto felt the hands on him, pulling him forwards,
him unable to find his legs, where were they now? And felt his

body bend stiffly, pushed back into the chair and Bodine saying, "Look at him Tommy, Christ man, he looks like he's seen a ghost."

Tommy now moving towards him, Modesto wishing he could move, get away from this man, but he felt the thick hands on the lapels on his green coat, the coat Biddy bought for him, a proper coat she'd said, one he could become himself in, and here he was, with the man's hands grabbing hold and shaking him, and Modesto could feel the snakes under the man's skin, coiling like muscle, or was it the other way around, were his sinewy muscle coiling like snakes?

Modesto's eyes rolled back in his head, scanning the black room for signs, for help, for any kind of help, didn't see the hard slap coming, sending his head snapping back and Modesto, saying it from the deep of the black room,

Do you think I don't know who you are

"Is he talking to Butch?"

Bodine, sounding panicked, said, "I don't know Tommy, let's just leave him."

"I need to know about Butch." And grabbing hold of Modesto again, shaking him hard, leaning into him, "Is it Butch, are you seeing him? Is he there?"

Then another slap, Modesto thinking the next one would be with the fist closed, the man's temper sounding all around the room, and Coffin was saying, "You tell me what you see?"

But the last slap was enough to pull Modesto out of the black room, feeling, like always, that it was too soon. If he could only wait, Biddy would be able to tell him what to do, how to be himself, how to fill the green coat. Tommy was leaning over him, hands still sunk into the lapels, the knuckles white except for two red scars across them, trophies perhaps from the last beating he'd delivered.

"You can let go of me now."

Coffin seemed thrown by the change in Modesto's demeanor, stepped back, bumping into Bodine and cussing, turning to the other man and saying, "For Christ's sake, give me some room here," then turning back to Modesto said, "You tell me right now, did you see Butch?"

"I'd like you both to take your belongings and leave."

"Not until you tell me what you saw. Was it Butch, Butch Daly?"

"I'll not be charging you for the sitting, but I insist you both leave immediately."

Then Tommy laughed, Modesto seeing the change in the man's face, from uncertainly and fear to cocksure.

Tommy said, "You fucker. Won't charge me! Good Christ to Mary you have a lot of nerve man. Now you listen to me, if you saw anything, you tell me now."

Modesto, impatient, not thinking, grabbed for the hatchet that sat on the table to pass it to Coffin. It was like being thrown across the room.

The blackness and the boiling bloods and tangled tree roots and shouting, and the hatchet in the back of the head, matted hair coming away on it and the hand of the man who held the hatchet sliding it off then wiping it clean with a fistful of grass and then blackness

Biddy saying, my god it's the man himself and his man you've got there with you, you've roused it now

And ravens were screaming and soaring, bumping into the very matter of his brain and then nothing but cold, pure searing cold. And then the blackness

And he wanted to stay but the silence was troubling him, the silence all around him, like he'd lost his hearing, he couldn't even hear the breathing of the men in the room, and when air finally came back into Modesto's lungs, he could tell whatever had transpired had frightened both men. Tommy had backed up several feet and the cocksure look was gone again. The axe was on the floor at his feet.

"What the fuck happened there?"

Modesto tried to slow his breathing, managed, "Pick up the axe and be on your way gentlemen."

Coffin stared down at the object for a few seconds, hesitated, glanced over at Bodine then bent and picked it up. Hefted it in his hands as if he half expected something might happen. Seemed relieved, stared at Modesto, said, "Shitty said your people are from Kerry."

"That's right."

"Yeah, well, they're all a strange lot down there, the wild west and all."

"If you don't mind, its good evening to you gentlemen."

Coffin said, "Tell me, for the love of god, did you see Butch?"

"I'm not sure what I saw. I can only tell you that when it comes to the dead, it's standing room only around the likes of you two."

• • •

Neither Coffin nor Bodine said anything as they left, Coffin taking one last look back, seeing the tall, thin man smoothing down the lapels of his coat, then pushing the long hair out of his face. And meeting Tommy's gaze with his flat, green eyes.

Once up the road, Bodine said, "I sure don't know about you, but that was one of the damn craziest things I've ever seen."

"A madman."

"What now? Seems like it was another dead end."

"You never liked Butch."

Bodine glanced quickly at Coffin. "What's that mean?"

"Well do you?"

"Known Butch since I was a kid, you know that."

"Not what I asked you Bodine."

Bodine. Coffin was serious, calling him that. "Butch and I got on just fine."

There was silence for a few moments, and Coffin asked, "When did you last see him?"

"Butch? I told you Tommy, saw him down at the Bucket of Blood. Said he was heading out in the morning."

"You didn't go with him?"

"He didn't ask me to. You know Butch. He kept secrets. Wasn't going to tell me."

"Worried you'd tell every sod buster in town."

Bodine wasn't sure if Coffin was joking, said, "Butch said his business was his business. When I'd ask he'd just say he was going to set it straight first. Then he'd let me know."

"What'd that mean?"

Bodine shrugged, "I figured he was after a claim. Maybe wanted to make it legal, come into town with proof of staking."

"You staked any claims yourself?"

"What? No! I been too busy up the line, taking care of your business up there."

"From what I hear you been busy down at the Bucket of Blood with the bottle."

"Look Tommy, I don't know what folks are saying, or if Shitty is filling your head with lies, but I been nothing but loyal. I've been up the line to check on things up there, ask JoeBo, and I took care of that girl, kept you out of the picture. You got no cause to question my loyalty."

Coffin sullen, the pair walking in silence up Swamp Street until Coffin stopped. "What did you say that fella's name was?"

"Some peculiar name, can't quite recall. Began with a 'm' I think, and it wasn't fucking Michael that's for sure."

Coffin, shaking his head, laughing now, but sounding mean, "That's it. I knew I'd seen that fella before. Little Moddie fucking O'Brien. Jesus Christ."

CHAPTER TWENTY

When he heard the door opening, he froze. Damn his carelessness, he should keep it locked. This was no time to let down his guard. Coffin could remember him at any time.

So when he saw Lily slipping in and closing the door behind her, he was relieved, but said, "You shouldn't come here. It isn't safe."

"I am trying to be as discrete, as you requested. But I've hired you to find my sister. I would like an update on your progress. I don't feel time is on our side."

"I have a good idea of where your sister might be. Just waiting to be sure. You should be prepared to leave soon. We'll be heading north of here."

Lily shook her head. "Why can't we leave now? What exactly are you waiting on, Mr. O'Brien? You don't seem to be out searching, or investigating, or doing whatever it is you should be doing!"

"I have every confidence that I'll locate Lucy soon, very soon, but I don't go around chasing clues like a bloodhound."

"How then? How can you possibly find her if you never leave your office? I half think you're afraid to step out of this very building."

"Well, of course I'm afraid, have you seen this town?"

"Then for goodness sake how will you ever find her? You can't even find out who killed poor Hattie, what kind of detective are you anyway?"

"Bill Bodine killed Hattie. Told her the carbolic acid was to take away the baby."

"She was pregnant?"

"Yes."

"Oh god, how dreadful. But how do you know that Bodine killed her?"

"I saw him."

"What do you mean you saw him? You're not suggesting that he attended one of your ghost calling sessions?"

"As a matter of fact, he did. Not willingly though. He was hauled in by Tommy Coffin. He was looking for his friend Butch Daly."

Modesto didn't have to ask if she knew them, could see it in those hard eyes. She stared, skin unbelievably pale.

"Please, do have a seat," he said, and he poured out two glasses, hand shaking so they spilled over the top. She sat, reached for the drink, licked away the spilt alcohol around the rim and then looked to Modesto expectantly.

He said, "So you do know Butch Daly?"

"Yes," she said.

"May I ask how you know him?"

"I knew him in Butte."

Modesto sighed, "So it occurs to me that you are familiar with these three men: Tommy Coffin, Bill Bodine, and Butch Daly. At this point, Miss Nail, we should be pooling our knowledge. Perhaps it is time you told me how it is that your path is tangled with these men."

"Daly was on the train with me. I was in the wrong place at the wrong time I suppose. I was coming to meet Lucy, and there he was. When he approached me, I didn't know what to expect but he was surprisingly pleasant, said he would get me a wagon when we arrived, that the town was impossibly crowded and that I would need help as a young woman. I was worried, but I was surrounded by people on the train, so I felt safe enough. When we arrived in Cobalt, I looked out into the sea of men, everyone pushing and shoving, it was frightening, and Daly took off his coat, threw it over me, tore off my hat and dumped his dirty cowboy hat on my head and literally dragged me off the train, told me to keep my head down as we headed for a man that was waiting for him with a wagon. Daly told the driver there was a change in plans, that he should take me to the Castle, that Daly would make his own way there later."

"The Castle?"

"Apparently one of the local bordellos," said Lily, "Daly told me the man would make sure I was kept nice and safe until Tommy Coffin arrived in town, and wouldn't I be a nice surprise. Then he told the man to keep his hands off of me but to watch me closely, that I was a nasty little bitch. Talked as if I wasn't even there. It all happened very fast. There were so many people everywhere, I tried calling out, I tried to get off the wagon, but the crowds and noise just drowned me out. Then we headed straight out of town, and there was bush everywhere, it was very disorienting so I decided to try and get away later. He took me to a little settlement and hauled me into some shabby makeshift cabin, locked the door and left. I waited until dark, managed to dislodge the door with the fire poker and decided to take my chances in the bush. I ran and ran, the bush was impossibly thick and I crawled when I had to, just to put distance between him and I. It took me three days to find my way out of there."

"Three days in the bush? You didn't run across any prospectors who could have helped you?"

"I saw a few groups, but I hid from them. Why would I trust them?"

"It is remarkable you made it out."

"I was very frightened at first. It was cold. And dark. The howling of wolves at night. But by light I followed animal trails, drank from the streams they drank from, even curled up in their shelters at night. Once I found Cobalt, I was able to clean myself up enough to get a hotel room. I had the impression they had seen worse than me stumbling in through their doors."

"So you knew Tommy Coffin well enough to take your chances with the wolves?"

She paused to finish her whiskey, then said, "Wouldn't you?"

"Indeed. And is that how you acquired all your scratches?"

She glanced down at her hands, the thin red lines now fading. "I prefer not to talk about my time in the woods. But I will tell you about Tommy Coffin."

"Please do."

"I was a different person then, you should know that. Too young, naive. When I first laid eyes on him I thought he was beautiful. Everyone did, always praising him as so handsome, so strong. Capable. Men and women, they all loved Tommy Coffin. I had only seen him in the flesh a few times, passing him in the street, felt his eyes on me. I am ashamed now to admit I was flattered. How could I not be, he was the talk of the town. The Prince of Dublin Gulch."

"I must confess I find that baffling."

"Perhaps you saw him as he really was, but for most of us his name was like a spark to the imagination. To imagining another way of being in the world. Not worried all of the time, like Lucy and I, or any young woman in the Gulch. I was able to do some housekeeping, but the pay was poor and the men of the households were often dreadful. It was hard to keep steady work. And the stealing that we did had us living in constant fear. So it was hard not to dream of a man like Tommy Coffin making everything alright."

"Didn't he frighten you? Extortion, robbery, beatings, always violence at his heels."

"Not at first. I only saw the money he had, the way people treated him. I confused fear with respect I suppose. But once Lucy and I started our readings, things got better for us and I no longer thought too much about Tommy Coffin. We started to feel like maybe we could make a go of it, save up, get a small farm, a few cows. And there were times when Lucy was actually able to help people during the readings, a lost horse or a missing child found. She was proud of that. But by then it was too late. He'd seen me looking his way. And once Lucy and I started to get a name for ourselves, I think that intrigued him as well."

"Did Lucy use her second sight during the readings?"

"Sometimes. It's not like Lucy could put it on like a suit of clothes, it came to her when it came to her. The rest of the time we just did our best. We had the debunkers, of course, but you only needed to have Lucy's second sight work once or twice and word travelled. Believers didn't care what the debunkers had to say, they cared what the Nail sisters had to say."

"Did Coffin come for a reading?"

"I'm not sure if he wanted a reading but one evening he just showed up. We were having a good night, lots of customers. We worked from a small table on the back porch of this apartment we were renting up on Ash Street, some people made appointments, but a lot just showed up, especially on warmer nights. They'd just line up along the fence of the small yard in the back. It was dusk, and I happened to glance up to see how many people were left waiting and my god, I was looking straight into the eyes of Tommy Coffin. He was right outside the porch, not in the lineup, but just staring at me."

She glanced at her glass. Modesto filled it. "I nudged Lucy under the table, we were in the middle of a reading, some miner from the Kelly Mine asking about his mother back home. Coffin moved up a bit, so he was right by the door, still watching me, bold, even the miner we were reading for felt it, looked over his shoulder towards Coffin, and that seemed to sort of break the spell and then Coffin stepped inside the porch, just jerked his head at the man, telling him to move."

"And did he?"

"No, to his credit, the miner hesitated, looked to me to resolve the situation. I wasn't able to actually look at Coffin, I could feel the heat rising in my cheeks, to be under the gaze of this man I had once been longing for, but I managed to say that if he wanted a reading he could take a place in line and wait with the other good people. And that we needed to finish the reading we were doing."

"I imagine he didn't like that."

"No, he looked very angry at first, both Lucy and I holding our breath, but then he laughed, said he'd do just that, slapped the miner on his back, and said he hoped he got good news from the old sod, but as he was turning away, for some reason, he reached down and tapped one of the cards on the table, then picked it up and sort of tossed it towards Lucy, said he wanted a better card when it was his turn. When she reached for it she sort of bumped his hand. It startled her, but worse, she saw him."

She paused, slight shake of her head, and Modesto asked, "Is that how she reads, through contact, touch?"

"Not usually, most often she simply sees things, often unbidden."

"That is often the way with second sight. But if a person is sensitive, if they take in energy, and the other person gives off strong energy, then it is quite possible to see much of that person. Lucy is likely very porous."

"Is that what you are, porous?"

"A veritable sieve," he said smiling.

She smiled too, said, "As you say, he must have had very strong energy because Lucy yelped like she'd been burnt, and then went into such a trance, I'd never seen her like that, her eyes rolling up, her shaking, babbling. The poor miner thought it was about his mother, and he jumped up too, clutching his hat, saying no, no, no, me Ma, and I said to the miner that his ma was fine but he needed to leave and go home to her."

"And Coffin?"

"It was so chaotic," she said, her colour heightened, as if she were right back there on that warm summer's night, "Lucy was still in her chair, her face buried in her hands, rocking back and forth, yelling about the devil and his fire. I tried to get her up, pulling her to get her inside. I almost had her inside, when she went rigid, her arm flying up as if it was being controlled by a puppeteer or something, so odd and unnatural, and she pointed at Coffin, he had backed off the porch and was standing in the yard, and every-one was watching, and she said something like get away from us, you're the devil, you're the devil himself, and I saw him, he looked furious. I just pulled Lucy inside, and locked the door, got her calmed down a bit. But I had to go back out to get our cards and lock up the porch."

"Had everyone left?"

"No, I'm not sure if they thought we'd be coming back out or were just completely captivated by this drama involving Tommy Coffin himself. It was getting dark too, and I thought I could just slip out and gather up the cards. I was pulling the screen door shut and his hand slipped over mine, said he'd come back for his reading. I was shocked that he'd waited there, and I tried to pull free, told him my sister had taken a turn for the worse. He said he couldn't wait, then one of the men at the back of the yard called out, are you open or not? And I said no, that we were closing for the evening, my sister was ill. And I told Coffin to let go of me. He was whispering by then, said if I wasn't working I could go out for a walk with him, and I said I had to take care of my sister and he said that I didn't, and he pulled on me, pulled me off balance and I stumbled down the little step, and I heard Lucy call my name and then she was out on the porch and I told her everything was fine, to go on back inside, and by then everyone was just watching as he started to drag me across the yard and his grip was so strong, I was telling him to let me go and he just kept pulling on me."

"No one stepped in to help you?"

"No, no one. They just stood watching, and then," she shook her head, "I can see it so clearly, Lucy came flying out the door and across that yard, went right up to him, she spat right into his face, yelling, 'Your name is Tommy Coffin and you're nothing but a whore monger' and she cursed him to hell. He was so shocked he let go of me, and I grabbed Lucy and we both ran into the house and all those people were then watching Tommy Coffin as he stood in the middle of our yard, empty handed, wiping the spit off his face."

"A suitable comeuppance?"

"You could say so, but he certainly didn't take it very well. He came back later that night. We were sleeping by then, but Lucy woke up, saw them in the yard. Through the little window, Bill Bodine, Butch Daly, and Tommy Coffin. They were setting fire to the house. We escaped out the cellar door. They burnt the place to the ground, the fire spread, took the boarding house next door, along with poor old Joe O'Sullivan and his cat up on the third floor.

CHAPTER
TWENTY-ONE

"This here is one of them that tried to run Mr. Bodine."

Bodine was sitting at a small table in the centre of the room. He didn't say a word, just kept looking down at the ledger. Letting everyone know he wasn't interested in them, was interested in the money.

"I didn't run, I up and quit, there's a difference," Lucy said. After a single day of working on the railbed, Lucy decided she wasn't sticking around, no matter what. Especially after that boy died and they buried him right there in the mud.

Neither man spoke. JoeBo stood behind the crate she was sitting on, ready to grab her if she bolted again. He needn't bother, she was too tired right now to do anything but sit. She'd been caught packing up her bedroll, JoeBo not wasting any time hauling her into the shabby tent that passed as an office, saying to her, "Time for you to see the boss, he came up to check on the work and he aint' in too good a mood right now."

When she saw Bodine she was just relieved it wasn't Coffin, not too worried that the big lug of a man would recognize her. Bodine looked up, said, "This here accounting of everything tells me none of these men are working hard enough. They's eating more and costing more, all of this, bedding, shelter, transportation, well seems to me that we're just giving these here fellas a free ride and some of them don't seem very appreciative of that. That how you see it JoeBo?"

"That's about right."

"Be happy to stop costing you money," Lucy said.

Bill Bodine shifted his gaze from JoeBo to Lucy. "You got quite the mouth on you young fella. But you don't seem like no foreigner? What are you doing in with this bunch?"

Lucy shrugged. "Didn't sign up for this. But I'm going to change that by heading on outta here. Your man here though is holding me against my will."

"Is that right JoeBo, did this young fella not sign up? Pretty damn sure we got a contract with his name on it."

"Sure do."

"Right here in this pile?" Bodine asked, and JoeBo nodded. Bodine, without even looking through the papers, picked the top one, waved it around, said, "This here's your contract."

"Didn't sign no contract. And you're paying these people slave wages. Sinking down into that clay and muskeg, for that you pay 'em a measly fifteen cents an hour? A man can make three dollars a day down in Cobalt."

"That right boy? I suppose that's too bad for you then, see, since you signed a contract, can't just up and head off to Cobalt. We got to protect ourselves from unreliable workers such as yourself."

"I'm leaving."

"You can leave, but first you need to pay me the money you owe me. If you have it, you can just walk on out of here."

Lucy frowned, "Don't owe you no money."

"You most certainly do. JoeBo, what's on this little bastard's ticket."

"Train fare is fifteen dollars and sixty cents, food on the way up, that's another five dollars and fifty cents, blankets are another six dollars and twenty-five cents, and then there's the doctor and mail services on top of that for another dollar and twenty-five cents. Now that isn't including his room and board once he got to camp, we ain't added that into the ledger yet. Way I see it Mr. Bodine, this young fella is owing you almost thirty dollars."

"Thirty dollars!"

"That's right boy. Now you gotta understand, I have costs too, besides feeding and lodging you, I got to buy supplies, tools, I had to travel up here on account of the trouble you cause, so you gotta pay up if you want to head on out. That's just plain fair. Do you have thirty dollars?"

Lucy was thinking, hard, when Bodine said, "Search him."

JoeBo grabbed hold of Lucy, ran his hands over her coat, then yanked it off, patted the pockets, "Nothing. Scrawny fucking pollack, shows up without a cent."

Lucy exhaled slowly, hadn't noticed she'd been holding her breath but feeling the man's hands on her, couldn't be bothered to breath, getting ready to fight, if they found out she was a girl maybe they would have raped her right then and there. Then thrown her in some trash heap out back more than likely.

Bodine said, " I'm going to do you a favour boy, going to teach you a lesson. You know you deserve to be jailed for planning on running away and not paying the money you owe, so that's exactly what is going to happen here. Seven days, bread and water. Give you lots of time to remember how much you like to work. Now, just to make sure you don't get any big ideas on the way to your new accommodations, take off your boots."

She didn't move, just stared at Bodine, unsure of what to do. Didn't want to lose her boots. It'd be almost impossible to get out of there without them.

JoeBo kicked her foot, "You heard the man, take them off."

She shook her head. "I'll be needing my boots."

"Are you saying no?" Bodine sounding almost incredulous. Then said, "Did you hear that JoeBo, he said no?"

"Maybe he didn't hear you."

Bill said, "Boy, now I asked you nicely to take off your boots, you have trouble hearing me?"

Lucy didn't answer, there was no point. Rarely did a man ask a question he actually wanted an answer to, and never men like these two. So why waste her breath. It was going to come anyway, she could already see the man's fist clenching, probably glad she talked back, give him something to hit.

"Time for this young lad to be taught a lesson," Bodine said.

With that he stood, came over quick and yanked her right off the crate, it flying out from underneath her. He dragged her out into the yard, throwing her down, and tore the boots from her feet, gave her a few hard kicks and then dragged her by one leg across the yard while the men who did not speak her language stood, watching the boy dragged like a sack, limp and not fighting, staring up at the sky.

Bodine was dragging her towards the squat building set off to the far side of the camp, saying, "Christ you fucking foreigners stink to high heaven" then wheezing a bit because she was getting heavy, he said, "You fucking sack of spuds," dropping her foot and said, "Crawl," and she did, not even thinking about it, listening too hard to what the bird was saying in the blur of green and light and song above her, and she kept listening as she entered the small structure that smelt of men and fear and had iron bars over the window, Bill giving her a final hard kick as she scuttled through the door, her yelping as he did so, and the song of the bird was gone.

CHAPTER
TWENTY-TWO

"We're working railway contracts now," Coffin said, "but it's the mining that's caught our eye."

The man sitting across from Tommy Coffin smiled slightly. He was a stout man, neatly trimmed moustache, tidy clothing. Lauchlin Campbell prided himself on his orderliness and business sense. No silver fever for him. Practical and knowledgeable, eventually anyone looking to invest in the Cobalt mining camp showed up at his office. Campbell said, "You're certainly not the only one."

"No," Tommy said, leaning onto the table a bit, "but as far as you're concerned, I'm the only one of interest to you. Lots of fellas out there don't know what they're looking for, don't know how to get it. Once they have it, they don't know what it's worth. I do."

"You're a mining man?"

"Butte born and raised."

"That's copper. You'll be hunting for silver here."

Coffin said, "Copper, silver, gold, it's all the same."

Campbell shifted in his chair, said, "Not exactly, Mr. Coffin, now the geology of the Cobalt Mining camp..."

"I don't need a geology lesson. I was told that fellas were picking silver up off the ground. You saying that was a lie?"

"Not at all, it was the spectacular surface silver that launched the rush. But now the ground has been heavily prospected, anyone hoping to make a strike is trenching. And even those endeavors are now quite advanced. My recommendation would be to go further afield..."

"I'm after any unclaimed properties, or under worked properties. Or properties that could be had by a man who knows what he wants. Can you help or not?"

"Mr. Coffin, I feel it is my responsibility to warn you that setting out to prospect without a knowledge of the geology of this camp is a sure-fire way to get yourself..."

"You're quite right mister, I don't know too much about geology, but I do know about money, and what I know about money is that it's always the other fella who has it, and not some hard-working bastard like myself. That's going to change here. You understand me?"

Campbell took a few seconds to appraise the man in front of him. There was nothing of the mining man or prospector about him. "Perhaps your wisest course of action is to grubstake some of the prospectors heading out to Elk City, there is enormous promise out there..."

"Not interested in giving my money to some other fella to find silver," Coffin interrupted, shaking his head, "I want to find it myself. Now where is this Elk City?"

"It is north of here, up the Montreal River, but you would need to move quickly, there are at least a couple of dozen canoes leaving from Latchford every day."

"Canoes! I'm not bloody Lewis and Clark man, I'm thinking of something closer."

Mr. Campbell was frowning now, said, "I'm sure you've been told that the Cobalt camp itself is claimed and staked to the high heavens. There is not a sliver of land that is not being worked. Gilles Limit, where the forest preserve is, it might be opening up soon, but it is not available right now."

"Any derelict properties. Or those with a fella not too vigilant?"

"I'm not quite sure what you are asking for, Mr. Coffin. Given the incidence of claim jumping in the early days of the camp, most prospectors, and their investors, have become very careful men."

"What about out at Kerr Lake?"

Campbell looked surprised. Everyone knew Kerr Lake was claimed, and then claimed twice over. "I'm afraid Kerr Lake is staked right out. If there was any chance someone might sell, it vanished when they found that vein near the shoreline, almost a foot wide of solid silver."

"Now listen to me, I am well aware that Kerr Lake is staked. I know all about it. It's staked because it is prime ground. The reason I'm engaging your services is to save time, my time, in identifying the most promising claims there. Then you can leave the rest up to me."

"All the ground is proving out. It's a rich area."

"A name, Campbell. A name. You come back to me with a name and location for what is looking to be the best ground out there."

"It will be a pretty penny, I can guarantee you that! To convince a man to part with one of those Kerr Lake claims you'd have to have quite the powers of persuasion. And access to substantial capital ..."

"You don't have to worry about my powers of persuasion."

"As you wish, Mr. Coffin, you can try your luck. There's a man by the name of Jowsy working out there, on the north end of the lake. Had four claims, got in early on. Some British investors had grubstaked him, sunk a fair amount into a couple of the properties. Now next to them is an interesting patch, staked by one of those fellas from across Lake Temiskaming, but there was a problem with his paperwork, and then some sort of accident. The claim was then picked up by a couple of prospectors, but one of the partners seems to have left town, and the other partner was the poor fellow hit by the train. Jowsy was down at the Mining Recorder's office before that train pulled out of Cobalt. There are many rumours about that claim, and it is quite possible it is going to be tied up in the courts, but Jowsy will know. I could look into it on your behalf if you wish."

"You do that. Come back with a map of the claim area and where I can find this Jowsy. But understand that Tommy Coffin doesn't want his name spread from one end of town to the other."

"Of course, always discretion in matters of money, Mr. Coffin. I should mention, in interests of full disclosure, that there is some talk of that ground being cursed. There's been some, I'm not even sure what to call it, disturbances out there? They're accidents, of course, but there are also accounts of prospectors hearing strange sounds, now all this talk of the monster. You know how these prospectors can be, a superstitious lot. It is possible that Jowsy, or even a few of the fellas with adjacent claims, might not be as keen to be working that ground anymore. But keep in mind that the men out there will still know the value of what they've got, it won't be cheap."

"I told you, Campbell. Let me worry about making the deal with this Jowsy. I can be very persuasive."

Mr. Campbell said, "Yes, of course you can."

CHAPTER TWENTY-THREE

They kept the fire small. After a walk of a half hour or so up a mucky trail, through swamp and scrub, they stopped to build camp, Lily saying her feet were soaked through, she wanted to dry out her boots, make some coffee.

It had been Molly and a wagon as far as Mill Creek, then they caught a comfortable train at the flag station there that carried them north. The sheer number of people coming and going in the town of Englehart meant that Modesto and Lily were able to travel without attracting much attention.

The train that left for the end of line at McDougall Chutes the following morning was not quite as comfortable. The passengers sat on wooden benches along either side of what seemed like a single caboose, the other cars reserved for supplies needed to construct the railway: building materials, tools, provisions, even horses and canoes. The prospectors and railway men sitting across from Lily and Modesto didn't have too much to say to them, but when leaving the train, one paused, said, "I seen lady prospectors before, but I ain't seen one as fine looking as you," eyeing her tall boots and breeches. Lily edged past him, replied, "I've seen a few prospectors myself, and you might be one of the homeliest." At that point Modesto suggested it would be best if they camped away from the small settlement of boarding houses and stores, keep to themselves. That had been fine by Lily, and when they found a secluded spot, she got right to setting camp.

"You set a quick camp," Modesto said.

"Lucy and I have spent our fair share of time on the trail," Lily said, then removed her boots and socks, feet bare and lit orange by the fire. She leaned in and fanned the embers, and Modesto thought of Biddy bent over the hearth, blowing onto the embers on those cold mornings saying, "I'm blowing on this fire like the angel Gabriel blows on his horn." Modesto wondered about that, about her mixed-up jumble of saints and angels, monsters and warriors, all tumbling around her, tumbling, jumbling. Were they there beside that fire, were they with them now?

Lily was quiet for a few minutes, staring into the fire as Modesto got the stew heating and then poured her a cup of coffee. She said, "What do you think is going to happen?"

"I won't really know until I get there."

"Are you sure I shouldn't come along?"

"I think one of us needs to stay back, just in case."

"Just in case of what?"

"I don't come back. You'll have to try then."

"Are you basing your trepidation on your psychic ramblings or do you have some harder evidence? We could be wasting valuable time if Lucy is not out here."

"But I am fairly certain she is."

"Based on?"

"The evidence. This railway outfit working up near Driftwood City, both Bodine and Coffin are involved. And a young worker, an Englishman, turned up in Cobalt claiming to have been forced into a railcar at gunpoint in Montreal and then taken up here work on the railway."

"You are suggesting Lucy was somehow mixed up with one of these work gangs?"

"It's possible. If you were late getting here, and there was no word left, she might have headed to Montreal to search for you there. How she might have gotten involved with these labourers is unclear, but you did say she had a way of finding trouble. And Mr. Cooley said he'd heard there were young men, even boys, who are reported to be at this work camp up at Driftwood. Lucy could be one of them?"

"She is often taken for a boy, yes."

"After that it is simply a feeling. I think I may have sensed her, from Bodine, during my encounter with him and Coffin."

"Was she alright?"

"Alive. That much I could tell."

"That could mean anything."

"It could. And given that it is unclear exactly how much difficulty we may be encountering, I would like you to keep this with you," Modesto said, unholstering one of his revolvers and passing it to Lily.

She hefted it, ran her fingers over the pearl handle, said, "It's pretty."

"Gift from my Gran. She told me it was the same kind that Billy the Kid carried."

"Of course," Lily said, and passed the gun back towards Modesto, "thank you but I don't like guns."

"I could show you how to use it, if you aren't comfortable."

Lily smiled. "Both my sister and I are familiar with guns, grew up around them. Lucy is actually a very good shot. And we have had to use them occasionally, usually to persuade upstanding mining men to part with their earnings."

"You might need to be doing more than persuading with Coffin, you know that better than anyone."

"Keep your gun. Let Lucy have it, she'll make better use of it. The truth is, Mr. O'Brien, I simply don't need it."

Modesto saw her across the fire, calm, unreadable. "Yes, you're probably right. But I'm just not sure why."

Lily knelt close to the fire and stirred the embers with a thick branch, the fire flaring up. Then a slight rustling in some leaves close by, Modesto tensed, but then saw the hare, its ears lit by the fire and glowing.

Modesto said, "Join us by the fire, little one."

The hare hopped closer, sat, its fur turned orange by the fire.

Modesto said, "I've never seen an orange hare before."

Lily stared at him, said, "Surely you know it is just turned that way because it is near the fire."

"But it is orange. It looks orange to me. Turned a colour by light, isn't that what all colour is?"

"Don't be silly, Mr. O'Brien."

"I often fear that my coat turns black at night. That would bother me. I like it green."

"You worry me, Mr. O'Brien, I certainly hope I haven't made a mistake in trusting you."

"Not to worry about me, Miss Nail, I've made it this far. And I am very keen to meet your sister."

"And why's that?"

"To encounter a like-minded individual. I'm quite certain from what you've told me that your sister would agree that this little hare is indeed very orange.

Lily sighed, unrolled her blanket, and said, "She most certainly would."

CHAPTER
TWENTY-FOUR

She half thought for a moment she'd been buried alive. Taste of dirt in her mouth, the air close. There was a disorienting feeling of heaviness against her chest, and the sharp pain in her arms hurt enough to make her think they had been pulled right off her body.

Lucy tried to move her hands, sinking her nails like claws into the ground, it was hard packed, so she scratched at it, and someone whispered something she couldn't understand, a scuffling in the darkness, she couldn't even tell where it was coming from in order to shrink away from it, realizing now she was lying on her stomach, arms stretched out over her head, bound, the rope rough. Her wrists hurt.

The voice was closer now, whisper like a puff of dank air across her cheek, but she didn't understand him, then more scuttling and another voice, rough, asked, "You alive boy?"

She thought she was, tried to raise her head to speak but then her arms hurt too much, sharp pain and her face dropped, mouth still tasting dirt.

"He moved," the man said, "come here, help me."

She could feel hands moving along her, first on her back, patting as if searching, then at her elbows and the voice saying, "The ropes, get the ropes."

And everything was hurting, burning pain as the hands fumbled and tugged on the ropes, not seeming to make much progress, hearing cursing and muttering and wondering why they wouldn't turn her over, her face sore and stinging from the hard dirt, and then her hands were free and someone was saying, "Careful, turn him slow," and there was a hand under her arms and a pair along her back as they rolled her over and then she was sputtering, then yelped in pain as her arms were dropped and then a thick hand was over her mouth and the whisper turned to a hiss, "Want to get us killed?"

No, she certainly did not want that.

She could feel them withdraw from her, scuttling back, some muffled talk. Seemed like there were maybe three or four men, probably men from the work crew. She slowly moved her arms down to her sides. In doing so it became pretty clear to her that she was in rough shape, her arms felt like they'd been wrenched out of her body and her ribs ached, really ached, and she couldn't seem to catch her breath, only able to take shallow breaths.

The men were near enough but she was having a hard time concentrating on what they were saying. Finally one came over, Lucy wondering why everyone was moving on their hands and knees, were they hiding? In a cave or something?

Lucy managed, "Where am I?"

"You don't remember?"

She didn't answer, the dirt coating the inside her mouth making it difficult to talk.

"They beat you, then threw you in here like this, tied up. We thought you were dead."

She turned her head, spat out some of the dirt from her mouth, the effort hurting her ribs. She found her voice, "So you just left me?"

"What were we supposed to do?"

"Make sure I was alive!"

"We didn't think it possible."

"Where are we?"

"In jail. Locked up like pigs. We have nothing."

"A jail in the camp?" she asked. Then she remembered. The squat building at the far edge of the work camp, the boot on her ribs as she crawled through the door.

Another voice said, 'Yes. We try to leave camp, they came after us, with guns. Guns! Dragged us back here. Locked us up, some sort of cage, bars on the window. It is unbelievable."

Lucy turned on her side, tried to pull herself up. Everything felt like lead. Maybe she wasn't alive after all. She asked, "Do I still have all my limbs?"

Silence, and then a man said, "Yes, of course you do." Then added, "You rest, get your strength back."

Lucy asked, "Where are the windows?"

"The night is too dark to see. You will see them in the morning."

"I just want to see the stars."

A voice scoffed, said, "There are no stars anymore."

CHAPTER
TWENTY-FIVE

Bodine groaned as he slumped into the chair. "Sonofabitch, what a week, slowest fucking train and those damn foreigners, Jesus Christ, glad to be back in civilization," then barked, "Shitty, get me some whiskey."

Shitty jumped up, but Coffin said, "Sit down."

Shitty hesitated, the pull of loyalties making him wince. He looked to Bodine, but he was acting like he hadn't heard anything, leaving Shitty on his own, leaving him hanging him out there like a fool. Coffin nodded to the chair and so Shitty sat down.

Coffin leaned forward, thick arms resting on the table, Shitty wanting to move back but now too worried to move, so he sat, feeling Coffin's whiskey breath on his face.

Coffin said, "So what about Butch?"

Bodine asked, "Is there news? You hear something?"

Shitty couldn't tell from Bodine's tone whether he'd be pleased or not if there was news concerning Butch. Shitty hadn't heard anything. Was pretty sure there was nothing to hear. He figured the man had been eaten. Bear or monster, didn't much matter if a man had been eaten.

"What the fuck would I've had heard?" Coffin said.

Bodine shrugged a big shrug. "Gotten no news Tommy. But I've been up the line, went up like you asked. Got things sorted with JoeBo. Just got back, had no chance to hear anything about anyone."

"There's a steady stream of fellas headed north, some of them must know Butch."

"If I'd heard something, I'd come straight to you. You know that."

"A man doesn't just disappear. Something must be wrong."

"Could've just left town."

"Did you ask down at the train station. I told you to ask around."

Bodine said, "I asked around. The train stations, the stage-coaches, all the teamsters, I've been asking. Talked to any fella that might have known him …"

"Did you say 'known' him," interrupted Coffin, "you think he's dead?"

"No, no, Tommy, just talking. But no one has seen him, like he just up and disappeared off the face of the earth."

"That doesn't happen."

Bodine tried out his shrug again, eyes moving to Coffin's glass of whiskey and said, "Don't know what to say Tommy, maybe he lit out for Montreal, who knows? Now how about that whiskey Shit?"

But Shitty didn't move because Coffin was now staring at Bodine and Shitty thought that maybe there was going to be trouble, real trouble, and it seemed like Bodine thought maybe too because his hands came up, and he said, "Tommy, I've tried, course I've tried, you know we all go way back together. But I can' find the guy if he isn't here! Or if he doesn't want to be found."

"Why would you say that? Why wouldn't he want to be found?"

Bodine shook his head. "I just don't know where else to look. I've asked everyone, went to every mine site, been up and down this street a dozen times, no one has heard or seen him since he headed out to Kerr Lake. Went out there myself, found the makings of his cabin. No sign of him. Don't know what else I can do."

"I'll tell you what you're going to do. You're going to take this piece of shit with you," he said, nodding at Shitty, "round up a few other boys, and you are going to check every building, alleyway, cabin, tent, and fucking shack, and you're going to ask every fucking little rat in this shithole of a town where Butch is. And you're going to come back here with something."

"Yeah, alright."

Coffin leaning back now, tone changing, said, "Bill, I'm telling you, he's here. I know he's here. Me and him were like brothers. He wouldn't light out without letting me know, leaving word. Just send a couple of boys over to the boarding house, the livery, come on Bill, do I have to do all your fucking thinking for you? Now get to it, and meet me down at the livery after lunch, we got something to take care of. And I want some good news from you by then."

Bodine got up, kicked the leg of Shitty's chair, said, "Well get the fuck moving Shitty, sitting there with your gob hanging open, ya dumb fuck."

Shitty scrambled up, grabbing his hat and following Bodine out of the saloon. Out on the sidewalk, Bodine turned and said, "Go north, up to the Foreign Quarter then on out to the LaRose Mine. I'll round up some other fellas and cover the downtown, then we'll spread out from there."

"I'd like to stay downtown. Can't you send a couple of the other guys up the line? Think I'd have a better chance looking around here."

"Don't even try to think Shitty. Just do what you're told."

With that, Bodine headed off, Shitty figuring he was just as likely to head to one of them hole in the wall drinking outfits down Swamp Street as anywhere else. And Shitty decided, and it felt good to be deciding, that he was going to do his own thinking for a change. Had some hunches of his own. Might not need to put up with Bodine kicking him around anymore.

CHAPTER TWENTY-SIX

When he bent over to pick her up, Lucy stirred, said, "I saw you. I knew you'd come."

"Did you now?"

"I did. Saw you plain as day."

"How can you see anything? It's pitch black in here, if it weren't for my match I would never have found you."

"Saw you as clear as if it were noon. In my mind."

He could feel bodies stirring around him. He asked her, "How many men in here?"

"Not sure."

"Can you walk?"

"Maybe. Got no boots though. My sister here?"

"She's waiting, further away."

"Good."

"I'm going to carry you as far as the woods. It's maybe fifty yards. Once we're in the cover of the trees, we'll see if you can walk."

"They might be in the dirt, near the door."

"What?"

"My boots."

He checked, said, "Yes, they're soaked through though."

"Don't care. But what about the others?"

"I'm going to leave the door open behind us," he said. Behind him, still in the dark corners, he could feel the men stirring, waking, one of them asking, "Who's that? What is happening?"

"We're leaving," Modesto answered, "and you should leave too, but don't follow us. Go your own way, back down the trail."

"They'll be caught," Lucy said, a sharp intake of breath as she bent forward to pull on the boots.

"Not if they are careful. But we're leaving, no time left."

"You are just going to walk out of here?"

"Yes."

"They'll shoot us."

"Not sure they are up and about yet. I didn't see anyone when I was coming in. Will just have to take our chances."

He pushed the door open with his foot, then ducked through the low door, said, "Quiet now," then added under his breath, "let's go Biddy, help me out here."

"Ain't no one here but us," Lucy whispered.

"Biddy's always near."

Lucy sighed, rested her head against his green coat and closed her eyes. Then the two of them were in the stillness of the muddied yard. He paused, surveyed their pathway to the forest, the ground churned up into a mess of severed roots, puddles and manure. But overhead the sky was just beginning to show itself, all roses and gold. A good sign he hoped.

The rise and fall of her breathing against his chest stopped, he whispered, "You alright?"

"Holding my breath."

"Will it help?"

"Worked when we was kids, playing hide and seek."

Modesto adjusted his grip on her, held his breath too, and carried her across the yard like they were invisible. And they must have been, because they made it, him turning back to see a few of the men just emerging from the hut, looking around as if they couldn't believe they could just walk out of there. Modesto kept moving.

He hit the edge of the forest and turned onto a small trail, going a short way down before he heard shots behind them. He left the trail, pushing through a tangle of spruce and tag alders, found a small embankment and got down to the bottom of it, setting Lucy down against a big spruce.

She winced. "Guess those shots are meant for us?"

"Either us or the other fellas."

"Might think we're all together."

"Hopefully. We still have some time before they figure it out. Now let's see how those legs of yours feel."

She sat, then with one hand on the tree next to her, she slowly stood. Rocked a bit on her feet. "They feel all wobbly. Sore too. But I can walk. Just don't ask me to carry anything."

"I won't, now let's get moving."

"They didn't see us."

"No, we were lucky."

"Hope those other fellas are lucky."

"When I'm back in town I'll contact the authorities, there is already some concern about this camp. Are you ready?"

"Think I could use a few minutes, my eyes and head are a-buzzing. Stomach don't feel so good either."

She was smaller than her sister, her clothes too big on her. Her hair reached the top of her collar, pushed back behind her ears. Jacket and trousers stiff with mud. Modesto passed her his canteen, said, "Just a few small mouthfuls of the water."

After she drank, she placed her hand on the trunk, said, "The aspens are worried. I can feel their worry. All in their trembling."

"What are they worried about?"

"Can't say for sure."

"No doubt their worry is for themselves, for this forest. Those men will tear it all up to get where they are going."

"Maybe after the railway goes through there will be enough trees left standing to make the forest good again."

"Ireland had forests once, beautiful old forests. Then they were all cut down."

"Trees grow back."

"Not there. My Gran said a people can lose their ability to believe in the forests. Think the land is just pasture, potatoes, and sheep," he sighed, "Too quiet out here. Let's get a move on."

Modesto took hold of her arm to support her, but she said, "I can walk on my own. It'll go faster."

They began to push through the bush, Modesto holding back branches and Lucy ducking slowly under overhangs, and every now and again stopping to lean on a tree to rest. She was quiet, he could feel her watching him, and watching all around her too, skittish. The forest was close upon them, hard to see clear for any distance, the bush a dense mat of tall black spruce and thick undergrowth.

He heard her stopping behind him again, turned and she was leaning with her back against a tree trunk, head tipped back against the rough bark. "The trail widens further up," he said, "I can carry you then."

She nodded, but asked, "How come they got cut down?"

"The trees in Ireland?"

"Yes."

"To build ships, to make farms. But mostly to leave the land bare, expose it, flush everything out."

"Why?"

"I suppose because the English thought it was being wasted, that the land could be better used to make a profit. And that those profits should be theirs for the taking. And my Gran said they were trying to chase out the outlaws too."

Lucy smiled weakly, "Bit of an outlaw myself you know."

"Yes, I know."

"Didn't think to introduce myself properly. Guess that's impolite."

"Introductions are hardly needed, after all, you're quite famous."

"Guess I am," she said. "But I don't know who you are."

"Modesto O'Brien, at your service."

"You hired by my sister?"

"Yes."

"Why'd she pick you?"

"Desperation, I would imagine."

Lucy laughed, but then gasped and gripped her ribs. "That hurt. By jesus that hurt. You know they gave me a beating in there, a real damn good beating. I even thought for a spell that I might already be dead. What you think of that?"

"Dead. Alive. They are complicated ideas. Perhaps you were dead. Maybe we both are. I find things like that difficult."

"Your Biddy person you were talking to back there. She's dead?"

"That is exactly the point, since she's always there, always close, it doesn't matter, and to be honest, I simply can't tell anymore."

Lucy smiled, said, "You are going to be my favourite man ever, I knew it would be you, but I'm just tickled that I was right," but then Modesto felt Lucy fall into him, caught her as she said, "good thing I dreamed of a big strong fella like you, looks like I might need some carrying after all."

CHAPTER
TWENTY-SEVEN

The sky was all knotted up, looked ready to burst. Shitty usually didn't mind it when it rained. When the wagons got stuck, the more horses were likely to go down. Kept Shitty busy—but today he had plans, an idea all his own. So he hoped the rain held off.

He had listened and nodded when Bodine had been telling him to head to the livery, but Shitty was going to follow a hunch he had about that detective. And he might just go straight to Tommy if he turned up anything useful, show Bodine who had the brains around here.

Shitty weaved his way down through the crowded town square then headed north past a series of small stores, catching bits of gossip as he went. The beheaded man and the dead girl had already waned in the town gossip, talk turning back to silver.

"Hey Shiity, have you seen it yet?" was the main question he was asked, first answering 'seen it all boys', dismissive, as if he had other, more important, things on his mind. But the excitement was so intense, coiling through the crowd, that he finally stopped when he saw a prospector he knew from the Bucket of Blood, asked, "So what's this about Mac, place going crazy over this latest find."

"You ain't seen it? Everyone's down at Moore's drugstore, its sitting right there in the window, three hundred pounds! You gotta see it, like the biggest jewel you could ever imagine, it's over a foot wide, damn if it don't look like solid silver," Mac breathless, added, "it's so big the prospector that found it said it looked like it was placed there or something."

"Placed there? By who?"

"I just meant it was sitting right up there all by itself, wasn't saying somebody actually put it there Shitty, but by the size of it, only some monster or giant could'a done it anyhow."

"Ain't no such thing as monsters or giants," Shitty said, stuck on the image now, some big, gnarled hand setting down this glittering chunk of silver.

"I know'd that, it's just a saying. They say it was five feet long!"

"Well, I suppose that's something," said Shitty, feeling his energy leaving him, knowing he had to get going or get caught up in the grip of the place, "Gotta go Mac, see ya 'round."

"That's history you'd be seeing down at Moore's."

"No, got things to do."

He pushed his way across the street, then down a few alleys towards the detective's office. Saw the green door.

He tried the door. Locked.

"I'll be damned," Shitty said.

He stood for a minute staring at it. Maybe he wasn't so smart after all, hadn't even thought about it being locked. And what if the detective was inside—he hadn't thought of that either. Best figure out that part first. Knocked, waited, but there was no answer. Well, that was something. Stood thinking, then tried to picture the room, remembered last time he was there, seeing the light catching in the pretty lady's hair.

He walked around the side. Yup, a window. Up high though. And could he fit?

He glanced up and down the alley, it too was crowded—some fellas at the end, shooting the shit, a few others, map spread out between them, arguing about where to head, and a small group trying to move some lumber through to a building going up at the end of the narrow lane.

And none of them giving him any mind.

He headed towards the group hauling lumber, coming out at the other end of the alley to where they were re-building the Ke Hop laundry. Place did a brisk business and just weren't big enough as it was. Plus part if it had burnt down last month, took two other buildings with it before that fire was finally defeated. Some folks said they should run all the Asians out of town on account of the fire but Shitty didn't care one way or another. And right now he couldn't be bothered to think about that because he was looking for a ladder. And lo and behold, if there weren't one lying against the far edge of the building.

Tapped a fellow standing nearby, said to him, "Give me a hand" and the fella just came along with him, everyone just wanting to be moving, doing something, a least looking like they belonged. Shitty shouted over at a big burly man hauling some tar paper off a wagon, said that he'd be right back with the ladder, but man didn't even nod, didn't even notice in the chaos and noise.

Shitty grabbed one end of the ladder, said, "We'll take it up to the window there," and they hauled the ladder back down into the alley. The man had a thin moustache, clean boots.

Shitty said, "Thanks mister, owe you one, name's Milton, find me down by the livery."

"Al, Al Denman. What are you doing up there? Fixing something?"

Shitty wasn't expecting the guy to stick around and ask questions, could feel his face colouring as Al waited for an answer and Shitty said, "Locked myself out."

"I'll hold the ladder."

Shitty hesitated but thought of Bodine dismissing him, telling him not to think. Well, he was thinking now.

"Alright, obliged for your help," Shitty said, starting to climb, asking, "you new to town?"

"You bet, got in yesterday morning. This is quite the place. Spent last night sleeping in this alleyway."

"Don't you know it, can't get a bed in this town, heard fellas sharing beds, taking turns sleeping."

Denman was grinning, "A fella don't know where to begin around here."

"You a prospector?" Shitty asked, now pulling at the sill, relieved to feel it move, pulling it up and open.

"Hope to be! Got grubstaked by a few fellows I know down Leadville way, hoping to find a big silver sidewalk myself!"

Shitty looked down the ladder. "Well, looks like the window will take me."

"Anything else I can do?"

"If you wouldn't be too put out, you could take the ladder back down the alley. I'll owe you one."

Denman looked disappointed, but nodded, said, "Sure thing, see you around."

Shitty didn't answer but held his breath and wedged himself through the window, shutting his eyes as if that would make the tumble to the floor hurt less. It didn't, hitting the floor awkwardly, his neck bending into his shoulder.

He sat for a moment, letting the pain subside. Wondered about what he was doing, was it a crime? He supposed it was. But he wasn't really trying to steal anything of value from the detective. Just looking to figure out what the man was up to. And even if it was stealing, what was he supposed to do, do nothing? Let Bodine be the big man again, ordering drinks and having Shitty pay for it all? Not this time. Things were going to be looking up for Milton, he could feel it.

CHAPTER TWENTY-EIGHT

The odour hit Modesto just as he heard the strange moaning sounds. Lucy seemed to hear it as well, pulling up short and murmuring "oh no."

It wasn't hard to follow the scent, or to see where the bush had been trampled, and then there they were, in a mess and tangle of alders and spruce. The cow and her calf. The cow was bawling and crying, loud, the calf lying on the ground was bloated, stain of red across its shoulder. Two more cows stood stoically some ten yards away, watching carefully, their pale cream hides twitching to chase off the flies.

"I suppose I have solved Mr. Cooley's case," Modesto said, then explained to Lucy, "a nice old gentleman, missing his cows." He moved slowly towards the cow, but she backed up a few steps, wary, her brown eyes fixed on the body of her calf as if willing it to get up, to stand on its thin wobbly legs, stand so that then they could run away.

"They'd unloaded them off the same train we'd come up on," Lucy said, "but part way to the camp, JoeBo, one of the guards, said they were slowing us down. Just left them in the bush then sent a couple of fellas out later, gave 'em each two bullets, said don't come back with an empty gun unless you have dinner for the men. The fellas looked like they'd never even held a gun in their lives. Came back and said the cows were gone. The guard had a right fit, made them go back out with him, but guess he couldn't really shoot worth a damn either, came back empty-handed himself. The boys telling the other fellas that JoeBo was just shooting wild into the bush. Probably wounded the poor little thing. Been better to eat it then leaving it like this, puffing up and stinking."

The mother was agitated, getting herself tangled further in the mess of grasses and saplings, making sounds between a groan and a mutter now, and Lucy looked at Modesto, said, "She alright?"

"She's keening."

"Keening?"

"Mourning her dead, her calf. Like a lament."

Lucy nodded, tears starting in her eyes, asked, "What we going to do with them?"

"Here," Modesto said, gently touching her arm to move her back from the calf, but she shuddered when he touched her, pulled away from him, eyes glazing, said, "All green. All blackness."

Modesto let go of her, said, "Lucy?"

Lucy was breathing quickly, unfocused, then brought her hands to her face, finally said, "There are days I wish I could shut my mind off. It hurts. Everything hurts."

"Did you see something?"

"I don't know. Just saw those colours all around you. And it was warm and the green was wrapping itself around you, like it was something alive." She sighed, "Never know why, or what it means, just bits and pieces. Didn't mean to scare you."

"It's alright Lucy, here, sit down please, catch your breath. I need to milk this cow out. She's in distress."

"Course she's distressed. Her calf murdered." It seemed then as though the starch had gone out of Lucy, face back in her hands, saying, "Her crying. It's loud. They'll find us."

"Sure we'll be fine, won't take too long," Modesto said, "just keep a watch out while I milk this poor creature and then we'll be off."

Lucy nodded, listened. Sat. Watched as Modesto spoke quietly to the cow, moving her out of the brush, coaxing her to stand, gently stroking the soft light brown hide as he crouched to start milking, sighed at the hardness of the udder, the cow first lifting her leg, stamping, protesting, but then quieting.

"We'll have to bring them along," Modesto said, "Can't leave them out here. Mr. Cooley was right in saying the bush is no place for cows, and he'd be heart broken. It means we'll need to take the main trail. Do you think you can walk?"

"Maybe. I can try. But those men will be faster, 'specially if we're slowed down."

"Perhaps they will be after the other bunch, more of them to track down. We can hope."

"With me and her slowing us down though we might need more than hope. Why don't you pass over one of your guns?"

"Of course, your sister tells me you are quite proficient."

"That I am," she said, "I'm pretty sure about my shooting, it's just the walking that's worrying me."

"Lucy, in my pack, there's a cup, bring it here, you can have yourself some milk, you look half starved," and she rummaged through and brought it out and came over beside him.

"Hold it here, under the teat," and she did, and the milk was coming out as small, hard-won drops, but then the milk came easier and it squirted and sprayed into the cup, and when it was half full she took and drank some and started to cry, placing the cup back under the teat and Modesto too felt tears in his eyes as they crouched beside the cow.

He glanced over his shoulder at Lucy, her face now streaked with tears and mud, and her slate eyes coming up slowly from the cup to meet his own, and he said, "Lucy, sure I'm in love with you."

"I knew you would be. Felt you travelling towards me."

He smiled, rested his head against the flank of the cow as he milked, said, "So it was you drawing me over then was it?"

"Just think it was meant to be."

Then the two of them were quiet, listening to birdsong, the rhythm of the milk hitting the cup, and wondering over the small dead body of the calf.

CHAPTER
TWENTY-NINE

"You think it would be easy to drown a man. For chrissake." Coffin was bent over, breathing hard, wet from the lake water. He'd been in a foul mood when they headed out of town, sullen about Butch, but by the time they were dealing with Alfred Jowsy, Coffin was baying for blood.

After ten minutes of dunking Jowsy's head under the water, and after ten minutes of him refusing to hand over the rights to the land he'd been working, and denying he had any knowledge of where Butch Daly might be, Coffin got fed up and shoved the man's head under the water and right into the sand while the man flailed and writhed and then finally went still.

But it took a while, and in that time, Bodine lost his appetite for being out in the bush, for silver, and just about everything else. Because in that time, he was pretty sure he heard the monster. Or caught scent of it. Or saw it. He wasn't sure what was going on, but he wanted to get back to town.

"We should get going." Bodine was staring down at the body that was lying half in, half out, of the water.

"If you don't mind," Coffin said, "I'd like a minute to catch my breath."

"Looks like rain and we got a ways to go."

Bodine's fear had come over him like a contagion. That was how it was here, one contagion after another. First the silver fever, getting off the train and feeling the energy, even before he'd started up from the station towards the town centre. Then the silver fever faded as talk of the easy money took hold, every other fella running booze or girls or pilfering high-grade silver. But then came the talk of the monster, and the sighting at the train station, and then a couple of prospectors said they'd seen it, plain as anything the other evening out by Kerr Lake. They'd hustled themselves back to town, packed up and headed north, as if the devil himself was chasing them. So now the energy was dark, oppressive, and Bodine could feel it and it unsettled him.

And here he was, standing beside a man's body, listening to the quiet lapping of Kerr Lake. What was a man to think?

Coffin said, "Best to head back in the dark. Don't want anyone seeing where we're coming from."

"No, we oughta get going Tommy."

"Are you afraid of that beastie?"

"Lots to be careful about out here, you know that. Bears, cougar. Come on, let's get going. And what if folks are right about that monster? Them Algonquins say there's big creatures in the woods. Things that disappear into rocks. All kind of things."

"Don't be bringing all your backwards ways along with you. I'm an American, Billyboy, not some backward Mick with his rosary beads and goblins."

Bodine wasn't sure what he was, or where his people were from, but he did know he was afraid. He scanned the edge of the forest on the other side of the lake. "I keep hearing things over there. This is taking longer than I thought and …"

"That right Bill?" Coffin interrupting, "I wasn't aware of the time, it's been such a fucking picnic out here cleaning up your mess."

"Now that's not fair Tommy."

Tommy nodded his head at the body, "You're in the hurry, you drag him out."

"What? Me?"

"Yeah, you want this business finished, find some nice sized rocks, stuff them in the man's trousers, and haul him out into the lake."

"Ain't much of a lake to haul him out into Tommy, I mean it's not much more than a swamp now, can't sees how it'll hide him."

Tommy shrugged. "Alright then, empty his pockets. Then we leave him here."

"Don't feel like touching him."

"Fuck you Billyboy, I didn't feel like holding his head under the fucking brine for half the day, but I did. Because that's what you do for friends, right?"

"No, come on, you know what I mean, I'd just like to get back to town, that's all."

"You need to finish the job, Bill. That's your problem. You never mop up after yourself."

Bill tried not to look at the head of the man as he slipped his hand into his pockets but then Tommy said, "Turn him over, maybe his coat pockets."

Bill nudged the body with his foot. Tommy laughed, "Afraid he's going to jump and bite you?"

Bill ignored the question because he wasn't sure what he was expecting right now. At this moment, as the clouds were turning the color of ash, and a light wind was dragging itself across the surface of the water like something was starting to stir, he wouldn't be surprised if the man did jump up and bite him.

He felt Coffin beside him, pushing him out of the way, cursing, saying, "Jesus Bill, you're a useless shite." Coffin rifled through the man's coat pockets, found nothing. "Good, it'll take a while for anyone who finds him to figure out who he is."

Bodine looked around, asked, "So you're dragging him out?"

"No."

"Thought you said we should?"

"No Bill, if you'd been listening, I said I thought you should."

Bodine hesitated. "Maybe we could just drag him into the bush over there. So nothing gets to him. The idea of something picking or pawing at him gives me the creeps."

"You worried about the desecration of the body?" Coffin asked, "After we drowned the poor bastard? And are you actually talking to me about this monster?"

"Well, yeah, I'm spooked, most fellas are. Hard to know what to think of it all."

"Worried about a monster, Bill?" Coffin said, "Worry about me."

CHAPTER THIRTY

She was tending to the fire when Modesto, Lucy and the three cows straggled into the clearing. She wasn't startled, as if she had heard them coming, just turned to face them, Modesto catching a quick look of relief.

But the rest of the reunion was not quite how Modesto had pictured it. Lucy tentative, Lily wearing the hard look of love that a mother wears. "Lucy, what were you thinking, heading off on your own like that? You've given me such a fright!"

Lucy said, "You sure are a sight for sore eyes Lily."

"And you yourself are simply a sight, now get over here by the fire, what on earth…" Not finishing, but now busying herself with Lucy's cuts, a bit of water and cloth to wipe away the blood, brushing to get the caked blood out of the mousy hair, tidying her up, Lucy's eyes closed, sometimes murmuring.

"What are you saying Lucy?" Modesto asked.

The eyes slipped open, one wandering, she said, "I'm putting a curse on 'em."

"Don't be silly, Lucy," said Lily.

"Can you really do that?" Modesto asked, "Put on a curse?"

"Done it before."

"Did it work?" asked Modesto.

Lucy sighed. "Not sure. Hope so."

"You'll find that Mr. O'Brien is a superstitious man," Lily said. "I find he believes in almost everything."

"Curses are like wishes, Mr. O'Brien," Lucy said, "and I've had some come true."

"Curses and wishes are a foolish preoccupation," Lily said, "when more practical matters are at hand. There is a dampness in the air, we don't want everything getting wet. Should we move under those spruce?"

"Yes, I fear you are correct," Modesto said, "rain on its way. It will make the trip back slower. For now I can move the cows and we can set up our camp where you suggested."

"All it's done is rain," Lucy said, "rained every damn day we were out there. They made us go out and work in it, but you could hardly move, men slipping and sliding in the mud, horses getting stuck. And then at night, the bugs, so many …"

"The bunkhouse looked big enough," said Modesto, "but had a roughshod look about it. I'm sure it couldn't keep out the rain, let alone insects."

"Better than the jail."

"A jail?" Lily sounded surprised.

"Yes, an actual jail," said Modesto, "bars on the window and a door wedged shut from the outside."

"Yup," Lucy said, grinning, "this fella here done found me in the hoosegow."

"Nothing to be proud of, Lucy," Lily said, "and this hair of yours, what a mess!

"I think you woulda been proud of me, standing up for myself. They had ten or so of us in it. Well those bosses they sure were sonsofbitches, and a kid died out there. We had to work right beside the body all day. And then the heat and the flies sticking to us, sticking to the air all around us ...." she paused, "anyway, I tried to speak up but that earned me another beating, a bad one. So I decided to leave, tried asking for my pay and I ended up in that jail, got another beating. Jesus, it was something awful."

Picking bits of dried blood from Lucy's hair, Lily said, "It must have been awful, you're a complete mess."

"Ow," Lucy said, hand to hair, "you're supposed to be taking the mess from my hair not the hair from my head."

"Maybe you should hold still then."

Lucy didn't seem bothered by it, said, "Good thing my hair's not long and pretty like yours. You'd be here a month of Sundays."

"Small mercies I suppose."

"Good thing I was a mess though, probably saved me."

Lily had moved onto to the mud that was caked thick along the bottom of Lucy's trousers, brushing it off with some spruce branches, asked, "Why's that?"

"Otherwise, when I was face to face with Bill Bodine, I might've ended up dead instead of just beaten."

Lucy was looking pleased with herself, for the drama of her delivery, but faltered when she saw the expression on Lily's face, added, "I mean I nearly up and died when I saw him ... why are you both looking like that?"

"Are you sure he didn't recognize you?"

"Don't think I'd be here if he did. But now you two don't seem too surprised about hearing his name come up in conversation all the way out here in the middle of this bush?"

"Your sister had feared you had ended up in his hands."

Lucy, looking between Lily and Modesto, asked, "Why would that be?"

Lily didn't speak, so Modesto said, "I believe your sister had a run in with one of his associates."

"Who? What kind of a run in? What happened?"

"It's alright Lucy. I'm fine. After leaving from Montreal, I got as far as North Bay and ran into some trouble. But I got to Cobalt. When you didn't arrive, after a couple of weeks I was able to employ Mr. O'Brien to help me find you. And in a dreadful coincidence, Mr. O'Brien here also has an interest in Mr. Bodine and his associates."

Curiosity replacing alarm. "That right?"

"Yes, he's up here hunting a few of them. Seeking, in the classic western style, revenge."

"Nothing wrong with that Lily, I've often wondered if we'd been better off to have found some means of slitting those fellas' throats rather than running away," Lucy said, then asked Modesto, "What they done to you?"

"I guess you could say they caused the death of a friend."

"Good enough reason far as I can see." Smiling, causing her lip to split open, fresh drop of blood pooling at the edge of her lip.

"Perhaps." Modesto said, "Some days it seems very important, urgent. Other days I wonder why on earth I've spent all of these years pursuing them."

"You been chasing them down and they've been following us. Well there's something strange about that."

"But am I just the same then?"

Lucy looked to Lily, said, "He's the morose sort, ain't he? Where on earth did you find him?"

"He was the first detective I came across in Cobalt."

Lucy shaking her head, "Oh, I don't believe that Lily, that isn't like you, now come on, tell me, how did you come up with this fella?"

"Must have been the green door."

"Alright, you don't want to talk about it, that's fine. But for now, why don't we hunt them fellas down one by one and be done with it?"

"That is definitely not what we are going to do," Modesto said, "These certainly aren't men to be trifled with. I suggest we head out first thing in the morning, maybe set camp somewhere outside of town to lie low for a few days and then get you two out of here."

"Oh, I ain't going nowhere, been thinking of settling down around about these parts. Got myself a place all picked out, real pretty, right on a lake. We can stay there till I heal up some. Ain't finished yet but it got the makings of a nice little home."

"Lucy, we can't settle down here. This place is worse than Butte."

"No, you'll love it Lily, just like I do. When I came here the first time to meet up with you, I came across it. Once you get outside of town a ways. Tucked away in the woods, makings of a right proper house, most of the timber has been hauled in too, just waiting to be finished. Right near a place called Kerr Lake. Ain't much to the lake now, been harried and dug by those miners, but it'll come back."

"A cabin out there with no one in it?" Modesto asked, "That seems unlikely. Might be risky going there if the rightful owner show up."

"Well, that ain't likely, it'd already been stolen by a fella who kilt another fella to get it."

"Are you sure?" asked Lily.

"Course I'm sure."

Lily shook her head. "That's even more reason to avoid it. I wonder about your common sense sometimes Lucy."

"Don't have to worry about the killer coming back."

"How can you be so sure?" Modesto asked.

"I'm sure because we know the fella Lily, and he's nothing but a lowdown thief and murderer." Lucy looking smug.

"Who?"

"That coward Butch Daly."

Both Lily and Modesto simply stared at Lucy, so she said, "You two are acting awful peculiar here today, keep gawping at everything I say. What now?"

Modesto said, "Daly, he's one of the men I'm hunting."

"Oh, well you can stop hunting." Lucy said.

"You know where he is?"

"I shot him."

"You what?"

"Yeah, right on the shore of that nice lake I was just telling you about."

Modesto stared at her. "You killed Butch Daly? Are you sure?"

Lucy nodded, "'Course I'm sure, know who I'm shooting don't I?"

"Did you shoot him to get his cabin?" Lily asked.

"Don't need no reason, reason enough he was Butch Daly."

"Did he recognize you?"

"Not at first. But I set him straight just on who I was and what I wanted. Told him I was looking for my sister, and given the fellas he ran with, I was sure he knew something about you going missing. Said it weren't no coincidence, him turning up here after dogging us all these years."

Modesto said, "So the man is dead."

"Surely is."

"It's surprisingly unsatisfying, to find that out."

"Not getting to do it yourself?"

"Perhaps. I'm not sure."

"Well, you got a couple more on your list there don't 'cha?" Lucy said, grinning, the spot of blood now pushing from the corner of her mouth to drip down onto her chin, her dragging her hand across her mouth, saying, "No need to be moping about over it. Plenty of time to find satisfaction."

Modesto said, "Yes, I suppose so. What did you do with him, there has been quite a search out for him, I've been asked several times if I've seen him."

"Not looking very hard for the bastard I don't think," Lucy said, "left him lying out on the shore of the lake. Plain as day."

"That is odd. Perhaps some animal dragged him away? I'm sure if you just left him …"

"I think we've talked about this enough," Lily said, getting up, "might be time to get ourselves something to eat and then some sleep. Lucy might not be feeling the ill effects of her captivity now, but she will sooner or later."

Modesto smiled, "Of course, I'll gather some kindling."

When he returned, Lucy was holding onto the cow's lead.

"You needn't hold her, I don't think she'll wander off."

"I'm not worried about her, it's helping me stay still."

"Are you wanting to run away Lucy?" he asked.

"Lucy is just talking nonsense," Lily said, "like she often does. It would be easier for her to settle down if you don't pick up every scrap of conversation she throws out and examine it like some profound philosophical tract. Now perhaps we can get through this supper of ours and get this dreadful day over with."

So the fire was started and Modesto busied himself with dinner. Lucy said she was starving and after he'd dished out the food, and he refilled her plate, she said, "You make a nice stew, Mr. O'Brien."

"Why don't you call me Modesto, both of you, please."

"I don't really like that name," Lucy said, "Why do you have such a funny name?"

"Lucy!"

"No that's fine, Lily," Modesto said, "I don't mind. It is an unusual name."

But then quiet settled over the three of them, and they finished eating, cleaning up and clearing a place for bedrolls.

"Should we take turns, staying up?" Lily asked.

"Might be a good idea."

"Why don't you get some sleep then, I can stay up."

"No that's fine, I'll start off, need to milk the cow anyways."

"You know she will slow us down tomorrow."

"True enough," he said.

"We're not leaving her." It was Lucy, stretched out now on her blanket, not bothering to open her eyes.

"Not to worry. We won't leave her," said Modesto.

He brought the cows up, tied them just out of the ring of light cast by the fire, sat and began to milk, humming as he did so.

"Some charming little tune from the old country?" Lily asked.

"Not exactly charming. But yes, from my Gran."

"She sing to you? Lullabies?" Lucy asked, twisting her head in the fire light to see him.

"Yes, she did. My Gran and my mother were always singing."

"Our mother only sang on stage, never at home. Didn't like to."

"Lucy, I'm sure Mr. O'Brien is not interested in our childhood."

Lucy looked back into the fire. "I think he is, aren't you?"

"Very much so."

"Well, not much to tell I suppose," Lucy said, "my mother was never home. And she was very beautiful. Everybody said so. Had lots of suitors. Like our Lily here. You find my sister beautiful?"

Lily stood up, "Really Lucy, would you please stop asking your childish questions. You frustrate me to no end. Now get your rest, we have a long day ahead of us."

"Sing me your lullaby, it'll help me get to sleep," Lucy said to Modesto.

"It makes me too homesick."

"Homesick for where?" asked Lucy.

"A small place called Ardroe."

"Where's that?"

"Ireland."

"You lived in Ireland?"

"No, never."

"You are a strange one," she said, then asked, "would you sing for me?"

So he sang, a few lines. *"Last night as I laid dreaming, of the pleasant days gone by,*

My mind being bent on rambling and to Erin's Isle I did fly. I stepped on board a vision, I sailed out with a will, And I quickly came to anchor, at my home in Spancilhill".

"Sounds sad. Think if I were a baby it'd make me cry."

"Yes, more of a lament than a lullaby I suppose, but it meant a lot to Biddy, that's my Gran. And my mum."

"They both dead?"

"Yes. Otherwise I'd still be there with them, in Butte."

"Hell of a place to be."

"Yes. Dreadful."

"But you would have stayed for them?"

"Of course."

Lucy didn't say anything, rolled on her back, staring up at the stars. Lily was watching Modesto, said, "My sister wants to settle down. She doesn't like moving around."

"I don't suggest Butte."

Lucy said, "I mean it about staying in that cabin, you know, the one I found. Getting us a cow and a garden. Fishing is good around there."

"I'm afraid Kerr Lake won't be much different than Butte," Lily said, "not with the silver they say they're finding out there."

Lucy didn't answer, watching the fire, flames casting a glow to her face, then finally saying, "I suppose I should be thanking the both of you for coming to get me. That was some terrible place to be in. Thinking though I might be having to go back there and get the rest of them out."

"I think we best get you both tucked away somewhere safe, and then I'll see what I can do about these other labourers."

"Glad you hired this fella to come and get me, Lily," Lucy said, added, "you know I dreamt him."

"You saw him?"

"Clear as anything. Even his coat. I like that coat."

Lucy turned her head towards Modesto. He had settled into the milking, the rhythm of the milk into the bucket and the humming still.

"What's my sister paying you?"

"Perhaps you should ask her."

"She won't tell me. Lily don't tell me things."

"My arrangement with Mr. O'Brien is between he and I. You needn't concern yourself with it."

"He expensive?"

"I work for whiskey."

Lucy turned to him, "What? What kind of a policeman gets paid with whiskey?"

"Probably all of them in Cobalt," Lily said. "And he's not a policeman, he's a ..."

"Fortune-teller..."

"I was going to say a detective and gunman."

Lucy looked from one to the other. "Best you two get your stories straight."

Lily sighed. "I'm tired. Tired of this bush, these bugs, and tired of all your questions. I'm going to sleep."

She unrolled her bedroll, smoothing it out, rolling her coat for a pillow, "Good night."

Lucy sat up, "Goodnight Lily, didn't mean to upset you none. You know me."

Lily was quiet, only the sound the Modesto tying up the cow, humming to it, off in his own world.

Lucy sulked for a few minutes, then was grinning as she propped herself up on her elbow and looked across the fire at Modesto and said, "Why Lily, I swear this here fella is almost as pretty as you are," and then she crawled around the fire towards him, eyes now shining like pewter, asked, "Why d'you got such long hair. You look like one of them outlaw types, you know, like what's his name...?"

"Leave Mr. O'Brien alone, Lucy."

"Sure, I don't mind explaining," Modesto said, "my Gran always had me in long hair. She was such a fan of the likes of Billy the Kid. She always said that what got Billy into trouble was his loyalty."

"Think his gun got him into fair a bit of trouble," Lucy said.

"Not according to Biddy," Modesto said, "she said he was a hero, a young man like that seeing the man he idolized gunned down, what else was he to do?"

"It was a fight over cattle, wasn't it?"

"Yes, Biddy would also say that all fights were over cattle. Cattle or land."

Lucy said, "This mama cow, can she stay with us?"

"I'm afraid she belongs to Mr. Cooley, who is missing her dearly."

Lucy looked wistful. "Always wanted a cow."

"Well look up there," he said, pointing to the thick trail of stars crowded across the night sky, "Biddy called it the river of cows, said she heard it in one of the old stories about a famous cattle raid, she'd say *see, up above us, what they call the Milky Way? it's the white cow and her herd, making trail.*"

Lucy was staring up at the sky. "Starcows."

"Yes, that's right," Modesto said, "starcows."

CHAPTER THIRTY-ONE

Bodine didn't know what to think. After getting back from the lake, he'd headed back out to keep looking for Butch but he'd learnt nothing new. Tired, hungry and fucking thirsty, he stumbled into the Bucket just after supper time and for chrissake if he didn't see Tommy and Shitty, laughing together, coffee cups on the table and an empty bottle of whiskey and two dirty plates pushed to the side. They both looked tired, red-eyed, but pleased with themselves. What the hell was this?

Pulling up a chair, pushing the dirty plates towards Shitty and, thinking the less said the better until he knew what the fuck was going on, opened with, "Evening."

Shitty said, "Good evening, Bill," a little too loudly, but Coffin didn't say anything, just smiled slightly at Shitty's exuberance and took a slow sip of his coffee.

"What the fuck happened to you," Bodine asked, turning on Shitty. Annoyed, confused too by the tone at the table, he added, "I turned around and you were gone, lazy bastard, you never even showed up at the livery."

"Now, now, Billyboy," Coffin said quietly, "before you think to take a round out of your man here, best find out what he was up to."

Bodine glanced at Shitty. The man seemed drunk, his watery eyes shining, so Bodine asked, "What trouble did you get yourself into Shitty?"

Shitty hesitated, frowning now that he was put on the spot and Bodine, impatient, said, "For chrissake, spit it out man."

Coffin held up his hand, "Let me explain, you mind Shitty?" Not waiting, he continued, "So your man here showed a fair bit of initiative, you didn't tell me he was such a resourceful fellow."

"Is he now?" Bodine getting worried, glancing sideways at Shitty, him now grinning his fool head off.

"Well, he had the same feeling as I had about that detective fella, the fortune-telling one. I knew something was up with him. Knew as sure as we're sitting here that something was wrong."

"What's this all about Tommy?"

"Do you know who he is?"

"Who? The detective?"

"That's right."

"O'Brien, that's his name."

"Yeah, Modesto O'Brien. From Butte. Remember, we talked about him the other day. Do you recall exactly who he is Bill?"

Bodine said, "Fuck's sake, what's this all about?"

"Coincidences worry me," Coffin said, "That he's here, and we're here."

"Everyone's fucking here Tommy, half the fucking world is in Cobalt. Why shouldn't he show up too?"

"That's not the coincidence."

"Then what is?"

Coffin drew out a folded newspaper from his inside coat pocket, opened it and stared at it for a few seconds, then cleared a space on the table and set it down in front of Bodine, smoothing it out, said, "This is what Shitty found for me. In the drawer of that detective who you seem to think is nothing to worry about."

Bodine was staring down at the drawing of the Nail sisters. He could feel Tommy's eyes on him, waiting, but he had nothing to say. He was thinking now of being back in Butte, remembering how good they'd felt creeping through the dark towards the house that night, him and Butch drunk and laughing, eager to teach the two sisters a lesson, scaring the bloody hell out of them. But Tommy hadn't been laughing. He was raging. He'd jammed the back door shut, Butch telling Tommy he was making too much noise, but Bodine just remembered laughing, not paying attention until Tommy started the small fire under the porch saying it served those evil little bitches right.

Then the face of the weird one was suddenly there at the porch window, seeing them, and then the three of them having to scramble as the flames took hold too fast, the loud crackling sound following them as they reached the laneway and ducked into the darkness, trying to lose themselves in the crowd that came running, people shouting "Fire!" as it spread from the house to the laundromat then right through to the boarding house on the corner until it finally got put out. He thought for sure they were going to get rounded up and hung that night.

"Nothing to say Billyboy?"

Still staring at the newspaper, unable to focus on the words, to read what it was about, he said, "Guess this complicates things."

"Would seem so."

Bodine was silent, still staring down at the page. Trying to calm himself down, surprised at how jangled up his nerves felt right now, finally managed, "This fella, O'Brien, maybe he's hunting them. There's a reward."

"Shitty here doesn't think so."

Bodine couldn't decide whether he was angrier at Tommy for embarrassing him or Shitty for going behind his back, making him look stupid. "Didn't know Shitty did much thinking."

"That's where you'd be wrong," Coffin said, looked to Shitty and said, "Go on, explain it to him."

It took all of Bodine's restraint, and he'd be the first to admit he didn't have much of it, to not just up and hit Shitty's smug face. But he sat, listened, as Shitty said, "I seen him with a woman, could swear she looks just like …" pointing with his greasy fingertip, "this one."

Lily. The one that had started all this trouble.

Jesus. He'd followed Tommy from town to town, Tommy always saying it was for one scheme or another, but he was pretty sure all along the way they were following after rumours and whispers of Lily Nail. Tommy didn't talk about her much, but one night, they were down in Mammoth, Arizona, Bodine said he was ready to head back to Butte. Butch, heavy into the drinking, said that Tommy hadn't been himself since they'd left Butte, wasn't likely to want to go back. Bodine was drunk too, had long forgotten about the face at the window, so he'd asked why, what was wrong with heading home, and Butch told him he was a dumb sonofabitch, "Don't you recall Bill, we burnt those crazy girls out. Tommy says when he was talking to her he saw that her eyes were like amethyst, that she had an evil eye. And Tommy thinks the mad one put a hex on him."

Bill dragged his eyes away from the spot of grease from Shitty's hand that was turning the newspaper translucent around Lily's picture, said, "Looks like you caught up with her."

"What the hell does that mean?"

Bodine trying to pull himself together, said, "Nothing Tommy, nothing, just thinking maybe they're working together?"

"I think this here lady hired the detective," Shitty said, "That was my impression."

"Your impression?" repeated Bodine, "Seems to me like maybe you are just telling tall tales."

Shitty sat up straight. "You hang on a second there, Bill, now there's no need to be talking like that. I seen that woman sitting in O'Brien's office, like she was a customer."

Bodine didn't say anything. Trying to get his wits about him, this shifting of allegiances happening right in front of him. There was just too much going on and his head hurt, and he wanted to sleep.

"I think it's time you rounded up a few of the fellas, we got our work cut out for us."

"Not sure I follow Tommy, what kind of work?"

"Find that hellcat, we find Butch."

"What? How do you figure that?"

"It's what I was saying Bill, about coincidences. I don't believe in them."

"Alright I guess," Bodine said, scratching his head, not sure what to think of Tommy's logic, "but there aren't too many fellas around that I can trust, most are up past end of steel, working that railway job."

Coffin, dismissive, said, "Call some of 'em back."

"I don't know Tommy, I was thinking of heading back up there myself, it's pretty haywire up there, got their hands full with that crew of foreigners."

"Can't handle a few Italians?"

"Don't think they're Italians, don't know what they are and don't really give a damn, just know they're a pack of trouble. Lazy devils too. And we've had a few runners. We ain't going to be making no money if they don't get a move on ..."

He stopped, remembering now that kid being dragged into the room up at Driftwood City, the skinny arms jutting out of the loose, too big coat, and then JoeBo knocking the kid's hat off, and that kid looking back at him ... the fucking eye, Billy now tapping the newspaper, said, "Goddammit, been under my nose all this time. Should have known, the kid not right in the head with all that gibberish. Jesus."

"Who?"

"The mad one, Tommy, your spitter."

"Lucy Nail?"

"The one and only."

CHAPTER THIRTY-TWO

Modesto thought it would be a good day to be a raven. A few of the shaggy black birds were perched high up in the topmost branches of a big spruce. Wasn't much for them to see, the trio below moving slowly, cows walking ahead of the riders, the ground mucky, the damp morning heavy with fog, feeling oppressive.

It had been slow going getting this far, taking the bush trails until they had gotten to the railway station in Englehart, loading up their cattle and stashing Lucy in with them. She said she crawled under a canoe and went to sleep near the cows, rocked back and forth like a baby until Modesto woke her once they reached Mill Creek. The small settlement was hectic, so they stopped just long enough to pick up a few supplies, then fetch Molly. When they got to the livery, Lucy said her and Lily needed a horse, the trail they would be taking was rough, and anyways she wasn't going to ride in no buggy. Took her no time at all to pick one out, Modesto spending the last of his money on the tidy palomino with a bleached-out blaze on her forehead and a splash of light pink on her muzzle.

They had decided not to go back to Cobalt, chances were Bodine would be back soon if he wasn't there already, so instead they were heading towards the cabin Lucy had found out near Kerr Lake. It seemed a good enough place to lie low, giving Lucy time to heal up. If they'd landed in any of the boarding houses or hotels in Cobalt they were sure to attract attention. Word would get around.

They swung south, the pair of horses struggling, hooves sinking into the mud, slipping on the ruts and gouges left by the riders and wagons that were traveling up and down the ever-widening trail. But they took their time, Modesto letting the cows and Molly set the pace. He didn't mind the slowness, he needed time to think.

He glanced back, saw the stony expression on Lily's face, saw Lucy behind her, head resting on Lily's back, her eyes closed, no doubt dozing on and off. She wasn't in the best of shape but she put on a brave face. It would be good to get them off the beaten track and settled, give him a few days to try and figure things out. Modesto could feel something stirring, but he couldn't pin it down, though he was absolutely certain it had to do with these two sisters, with the men he had been hunting, and with the strange spirits set loose in this landscape.

The ravens had followed with them up the trail, now sat in the bare top branches of an old birch, Modesto looking up at them as they started in with their *caw cawing*, raising a ruckus.

He slowed to let Lily ride up beside him, said, "They seem agitated."

"They are waiting for fair payment," Lily said, but then seemed to regret it, added, "Yes, just agitated. Ravens always seem agitated."

Modesto said, "I have nothing to give them."

"Never mind, Mr. O'Brien, I was talking nonsense."

"I doubt that very much," he said, "but it still remains that I have nothing to offer them. Perhaps when I come back I will have a chance to make amends."

Lily smiled, "Making amends is an elusive endeavor."

"Yes, but it might help if I was more knowledgeable as to what I was making amends for?"

Lily stared at him for a brief moment, hard eyes softened to mauve by the grey skies overhead, then said, "Lucy, for godssake, how much longer to this paradise of yours?"

Lucy opened her eyes, trying to get her bearings. They were well past the few mines along the road. They had stopped near the first mine, Modesto taking his little herd of cows to the blacksmith's yard and asking if he could leave them there, pick them up on his return trip. The smith just nodded, not bothering to stop working to converse. It was part of the mining frenzy, Modesto supposed, stop working and the silver might stop too. So Modesto left the cows, the man ignoring him too when he reassured the cows he'd be back for them. Then he rejoined Lily and Lucy further up the road. Now the trail was lined with looming white pine and birch, thick and towering, making the trail feel as if it were closing in over them.

"Not far now, just a mile or so more," Lucy said.

They plodded along in the mud a bit longer, and then Lucy was directing them to a narrow bush trail, then up a slow sloping hill covered in thick tangles of dogwood and alder, until they pushed through to a small clearing, Lucy pointing, said, "There she is!"

It was small, rough, the front window uncovered and opened to the elements, but Lucy was excited, slid off her horse saying, "We'll get those closed in 'fore winter. But it's coming along. Keeps the wind out, already's got a stove inside, even the chimney pipe. Floors in and that's the main thing," glancing over at Lily, seeing her expression, said, "It's got a ways to go I guess."

"It certainly does," Lily said. She dismounted, peering in through the doorway, said "Oh to be clean again."

"It's all right Lily, we got a lake not too far from here."

"Is that Kerr Lake?" asked Modesto.

Lucy nodded, said, "Yup, not too pretty right now but it will be one day."

"Well monster or not, I need to get water for the horses," Modesto said, "you ever hear or see it when you were out here Lucy?"

"Can't say I did, but it was scary enough down by that lake. Them mining fellas did a damn poor job of sucking all the water outta there. Left all those poor fish stranded. First night I slept out here, I was close to the lake, swore I could hear them all gasping for breath. Gave me bad dreams. Moved away from the lake after that. Found this cabin on account of that. But just 'cause I didn't hear it doesn't mean it ain't out there."

"Lucy!" Lily said, "don't be silly."

"Well I was just saying it ain't impossible. Not like you don't believe in things other people can't see or understand."

"Lucy, please, let's get settled and stop talking nonsense. You need your rest."

Modesto watched the two sisters, Lucy glancing sideways at Lily, worry in her crooked eyes, but Lily now looking directly back at him, still, skin almost translucent. Were her veins silver? He could see it then, the slither of the metal through her lean body, hitting the heart like rapids, spilling back through, and she said, "Mr. O'Brien, you're staring."

"I am sorry," he said, "but sometimes I am quite certain you are some sort of enchantress."

Lily shook her head, simply said, "Hardly that."

"You think my Lily is a witch?" Lucy asked, sliding the saddle off the palomino, wincing as she bent to set it on the ground. "You wouldn't be the first man to call her that."

"I believe there is a difference between an enchantress and witch, Lucy, though I have no trouble with witches. Some of our neighbours in Butte thought both my Gran and Ma were witches. People can get suspicious of things they don't understand."

Lucy said, "Can't do much about that."

"No, true enough," Modesto said, then added, watching Lily carefully, "Have you seen the monster, Lily?"

Lily stared at him but said nothing, long enough to make Lucy turn and see why Lily was not answering. But Modesto was good at silence. And good at waiting too. Giving her time to arrange her thoughts and finally she said, "You really are quite absurd. You can't see something that doesn't exist."

"I had dismissed the idea of the monster at first, but now I have a sort of personal interest in the whole matter."

"And why would that be?" Lucy asked.

"Because I saw it. And it is something that is hard to unsee. Now I feel that it is with me all of the time, I can't turn any which way without feeling such a strange presence inside my mind. It is getting troubling."

"You scared of it?" Lucy asked.

"No, not really, I feel afraid, but not of it. If that makes any sense."

"Maybe it's looking out for you then," Lucy said, "maybe it's making sure no harm comes to you."

"A protector? I hadn't really considered that possibility."

"From what I've heard, I'm not sure it's even hurt anyone," said Lucy. "Seems to me it's the men out here that are killing each other over this silver. And for all we know, this monster could be some sort of big 'ole bear folks thought was extinct or something. Don't need to be no cold-hearted monster."

"I don't know Lucy, I saw it holding the head of John Moberly, a bullet hole in his head. It was unnerving. At least I think that is what I saw."

Lucy frowned, said, "John Moberly? Ain't he the fella that was teamed up with Butch Daly?"

"The one and same."

"That is right peculiar, but not regrettable."

"Yes, I suppose you're right. Though I now believe that this creature or apparition or whatever it is has become part of our story. Yet it is a complication that doesn't have a clear explanation."

Lucy shrugged. "Somethings just don't get explained, that's all there is to it."

Modesto could feel Lily's eyes moving slowly back between Lucy and himself, maybe she was calibrating the risk of some strange truth slipping to the surface. All manner of weird was moving up through the fissures and fractures, maybe carried by the veins of silver, maybe slithering up on its own. But the ground felt unstable beneath him.

"I'm quite certain," Lily said, "that nothing is to be gained by fixating on this creature. We have enough troubles right in front of us to deal with, like getting Lucy safe and settled in this charming hovel of hers."

"It is troubling to me, though," he said, "that I cannot fully explain all the events that have occurred, even those occurring right in front of me. Some things are clear. Lucy killed Butch Daly, thinking he was somehow responsible for you having gone missing. Daly was partners with Moberly, who also turns up dead, shot in the head after a very public brawl with Bodine. You assumed Coffin, and his associates Daly and Bodine, were responsible for Lucy missing and hired me to kill them and find Lucy ..."

"As entertaining your summary is, Mr. O'Brien," Lily interrupted, "I did indeed hire you and perhaps this is a good time as any to conclude our relationship."

"Don't fire him, Lily." Lucy said, "not yet. Not now. We'll need supplies brought out, least for a while, until we deal with Coffin."

"We will be on the first train out of here once I take care of a few things," Lily said.

"But I ain't leaving, I'm staying put. This is my home now. Look at those aspens, they're so tall and beautiful. And the rock cliff over there, it'll protect our backs, slow down those winter winds. I think it's a perfect place. We could clear out enough room for a good garden, maybe even a few chickens. Plants some flowers there, near the house."

Lily was shaking her head, "They're going to come here."

"They won't find us. Or we'll get O'Brien here to kill them for us. Or I'll do it."

"But everyone will come, don't you see," Lily said, "it's not just them. How could we stop it? Stop the fever for silver? They'll come here and tear this place up like everywhere else."

Lucy digging in. "Maybe the silver will run out. I sure hope it does. Just don't fire him yet."

"I think we can solve our own problems now."

"Of course you can," Modesto said, "but don't you both find it strange, that for these past few years Coffin has pursued you, and I've pursued him? The three of us have followed the same path, unwittingly, missing each other, only to finally be brought together here. The very place the Coffin and Bodine have ended up. I wonder if it isn't some sort of destiny that has brought us all here, to finish this strange entanglement."

Lily said, "Best be on your way, Mr. O'Brien, don't want to be dragging these poor cows through the bush after dark."

"No, of course not," he said.

• • •

They watched him leave.

Lucy said, "It'll be what we always dreamed of, a place of our own. We'll have a garden, and a little cow, we'll have everything we need out here. Long as folks leave us alone, we'll be alright. I'm going to plant irises and violets, they'll make me think of you Lily, just in case you decide not to stay with me."

"Don't be silly, I'd never leave you."

"No matter what?"

"No matter what."

Lucy was quiet for a minute, then she turned to Lily, asked, "We're going to be alright, aren't we?"

"I hope so Lucy. I really hope so. At times I wonder if we're not in over our heads."

"You'll think of something Lily, you always do."

Lily nodded but said nothing, both of them just staring at the small clearing with the half-made cabin. The palomino snorted, restless, so Lucy took the reins, said. "I'll get this one settled. You sent O'Brien away before he got the water, I'll go fetch it."

Lily didn't answer, still just staring, distracted.

"Sure in your own world Lily, what are you thinking on?"

"Silver."

"Silver! Everyone's thinking on silver. How we going to get ourselves some, we know next to nothing about prospecting? Maybe O'Brien knows something, we could ask him?"

"Perhaps it is simply the illusion of silver we need. But I think the real thing would be better. Regardless though, there is no need to discuss anything with your Mr. O'Brien."

Lucy didn't ask anything else but was thinking that she liked the sound of *your* Mr. O'Brien. Liked the idea he might be hers, with his eyes the colour of lichen and skin the colour of birch trees.

CHAPTER THIRTY-THREE

Modesto thought they must make a peculiar little parade, the three cows, his big grey horse, all moving along the rocky mud trail in single file. Molly, he felt, was making a show of it, moving slow and almost prancing. She had done a good job in getting them this far, the mud slick underfoot, the cows balking at times, but the mare kept everyone moving.

They turned down towards the livery, the light dimming behind the horizon but bright enough to see the man leaning against the barn, watching him come in.

"Good evening. I'm back with Molly."

"I'll be damned if that horse don't look better every day. She's really coming along."

Modesto dismounted, patted Molly's shoulder, said, "She is a fine fellow traveller."

The livery man cast a glance over at the three cows. "What's this?"

"I was wondering if it were possible to leave these cows here for safe keeping. Until Mr. Cooley can come fetch them? I'll send word for him to come."

"These are Cooley's cows? Thought they'd been up and stolen, the whole lot of them."

"They were," Modesto said, "but what was lost has been found."

The man didn't say anything, so Modesto said, "It's a saying, from the Bible. You may have heard of it?" but the man just grunted, said, "You got till noon tomorrow."

"Good enough I think, if not I'll be back to make other arrangements."

Modesto made his way down the hill towards his office. The town seemed subdued, none of the exuberant silver mania he was expecting, only a dark thick energy pooling in the open cuts, its grease curling through the rocks and crevices that cut through the town. It showed in the surliness on the men's faces, huddled in smaller groups, talking among themselves. Everyone seemed in a grim thrall. He picked up his pace, worried it might latch onto him. He was just rounding the corner to the alley and he heard his name. He ignored it, kept moving, heading to safe harbour.

Shitty caught up to him, yelling as he clamped his hand onto Modesto's shoulder, "Hey, didn't you hear me?"

Modesto would have kept walking but for the clasp of the hand. Such sureness in the hand. Not like Milton at all. He paused, turned, said, "Sorry Milton, my mind was elsewhere."

And then yes, the look on Shitty's face, smug. That was different. Modesto wasn't sure he wanted to know. He was tired, wanted a bit of whiskey, and then to stretch out on his bed and sleep.

"Yeah, what was you thinking on?" Shitty asked, almost bouncing along beside him.

"Just a case I'm working on. Has me preoccupied. I'm afraid I'm not good company."

"What's the case?"

"I'm not at liberty to say."

"It got to do with Cooley's cows? I heard you done brought them back."

"You certainly keep up with what is going on in this town, I only just delivered them. Always have your ear to the ground."

Shitty pleased, said, "You bet I do."

"I'll tell you a secret then. Can you keep this to yourself until I speak with the Constable?"

"Oh, I sure can."

"The little calf had been killed. Shot."

Shitty was surprised by that, said, "Shot? Was it sickly?"

Modesto paused, took in the rise and fall of Shitty's sureness, said, "Not at all. It was at that rail camp up there, a sad combination of greed and incompetence. They only wounded the poor thing, then left it for dead in the bush."

"You don't say," Shitty said, his eyes moving back and forth, Modesto could almost see him turning the news over in his mind. Trying to make sense of it, the waste and wrongness of it all, and Modesto said, "You know anything about the rail camp, the men who run it?"

The expression on Shitty's face shifted again, moving to where he was more comfortable, suspicious, wary. He asked Modesto, "What were you doing up around those parts anyhow?"

"Well one of those very men came into my office to hire me. I didn't like him, but he insisted. I headed up on my own to see what I was getting into. Came across the cows so simply returned immediately to restore the cows to your friend Mr. Cooley."

Shitty was slow to respond, finally just said, "He ain't really my friend, I knows him is all."

"Regardless, I believe it will be a police matter now, about the calf."

"That right?" but he wasn't paying attention.

"It certainly is. And do you know these fellows? You seem to know everyone in this town."

"Can't say for sure."

"A man called Tommy Coffin? He's the man that hired me. You know him?"

Shitty just stared at Modesto, then his face hardened, said, "Maybe I do, maybe I don't."

Modesto watched as Shitty ambled away down the street. He felt Biddy beside him but then she left to trail after Shitty Mitty, whispering as she left, *Tommy Coffin, Tommy Coffin, the name is like a bad spell, turns men mean. You've seen it before, the curse. Now it's on this one*

He knew she was right. Coffin exerted a strange power over men, but how to fight it, something that can so easily take hold and turn men mean? Then Biddy turned, said over her shoulder, *find a worst curse.*

• • •

Mr. Cooley was beside himself when he laid eyes on the cows. "God rain down a thousand blessings on you, Mr. O'Brien, you have saved me from ruin."

He stared wistfully at the light brown cow, her head coming up as he spoke, ears forward. He touched each of the three cows on the head, as if counting them, or perhaps testing their corporeality.

He said, "Breaks my heart about her calf though, breaks my heart. What kind of men could do that. Leave the poor thing for dead. Sure it's a shame that they are going to get away with this, the stealing, the abuse."

"We'll see Mr. Cooley, I'll keep my ear to the ground, maybe we'll turn something up."

Mr. Cooley was suddenly serious, the watery eyes turning sharply to Modesto, "Now, Mr. O'Brien, there'll be no pursuing those men. I'll not have that on my account. As far as I'm concerned, it's over, I have most of my cows back, and for that I am grateful. But this bunch must be some bad characters, and there is nothing to be gained by antagonizing them. I don't want any more trouble coming your way," then leaning in, he said in a hushed voice, "This is a rough town, O'Brien. Sometimes I think that just a little bit of hell pushed up from below when they started that trenching and blasting."

"I appreciate your concern Mr. Cooley, and I will consider the matter closed. But I think you might be mistaken about the hell here. I don't think it slipped up from the trenches and shafts. I think it came in on the train."

CHAPTER
THIRTY-FOUR

There was a commotion along the bar. Shitty had just arrived, looking for Coffin but just finding Bodine, the man ignoring him. After the three men had talked earlier, Coffin sent Shitty to check the hotels, see if Lily Nail was staying at any of them, told Bodine to head back up north to the camp and get Lucy. Use her as bait. Bodine had belly-ached about that but Coffin told him to shut the fuck up, said it was time he started pulling his weight. Bodine said he'd go but Shitty figured he had no intention of heading anywhere but the Bucket, so wasn't surprised to see Bodine sitting alone in the corner with a bottle. Shitty wanted one himself but didn't even have time to order a drink when all the men started to file out.

Bill pushed past Shitty, grabbing a fella's arm as he passed, asked, "Hey, what's going on?"

"It's Jowsy, they found him."

"Jowsy?"

"Yeah, dragged his body out of Kerr Lake."

"Well, I'll be damned." Bodine said, "imagine that."

"And that's not all," the man said.

"Oh?"

"Another fella too," then he seemed to realize who he was talking to and lowered his voice, said, "and sorry about this, but someone said it might be Butch Daly."

"Butch?"

The man shrugged, said, "That's what fellas are saying."

Bodine turned, saw Shitty hovering in the doorway, said to him, "Find Tommy. Now."

• • •

Bodine followed the man outside, then pushed his way to the front of the crowd just in time to see Modesto stepping off the wooden sidewalk and joining Constable Calder next to the wagon.

Calder surveyed the jostling crowd, looked worried as he turned to Modesto, said loudly, "Thanks for coming, Mr. O'Brien," like it was an announcement for the crowd of onlookers, "seems we have ourselves some unfortunate circumstances to deal with here, thought you might be of some help given your background."

Modesto moved around to the back end of the wagon. On the back were two bodies, each covered in a grey blanket. The blankets were moth-eaten. Directly above the wagon, along with the crowd of shopkeepers and prospectors, was Bill Bodine. Good.

"Of course, glad to assist anyway I can," Modesto said, mind now drawn to the small holes in the blanket made by the moths, thinking about the taste of wool. Did all wool taste the same to a moth?

"I know from our earlier conversation that you know a thing or two about the science of all of this ...." Floundering for words, so Modesto offered, "Death?"

"That wasn't the word I was looking for, but let's just get on with this," said Calder, pulling back the first blanket, asking Modesto, "Do you know the man?"

Before he could answer, one of the prospectors on the sidewalk shouted said, "Yup, that there's old Al Jowsy. He's a mining man."

"A prospector?" asked Calder.

"Prospector, miner," the man answered, "and one of them there speculating types."

Calder nodded, glanced over at Modesto, said quietly, "I want you to see something else." He moved around to the side of the wagon, said, "Prepare yourself..."

He gingerly pulled opened the top of a burlap sack, holding it open for Modesto to see. Modesto could feel the crowd, perhaps the entire town, even the birds overhead, lean forward, craning to see what was inside the burlap sack. The mottled head of Moberly, what else could it have been?

Modesto sighed, "Yes, I see. The missing part."

"Keep your voice down now, don't want to cause hysteria. Word gets out about this I'm not sure what will happen. Folks are quite stirred up by all the goings on of late."

Modesto peered into the sack. The creature he'd seen, or imagined, must have taken the head out to Kerr Lake? To leave it with the bodies of Daly and Jowsy. How strange. Was the thing bringing the remains there, perhaps some sort of site that was of importance to the creature? Could an imagined creature carry physical objects – that was something to wonder about. He would have thought not. And if not, then could the thing he saw have been real? A true thing? He wasn't sure which possibility worried him more, an unfettered imagination taking over his mind and his logic, or the actual existence of the creature. But then a real creature, that was something, seeing it there, the head swinging at the end of the arm of mist and ice.

The head was so damaged with the pecking and weathering that it seemed unlikely anyone, including Calder, would have noticed the bullet hole. Modesto asked, "Did you inspect it?"

Calder coloured, "Not sure what for. Can see plainly what it is."

"What's in the sack?" someone shouted, and with that Calder reached past Modesto and tightened the closure of the sack, said,

"Evidence. And we're not sharing it with the public. Now could you all stay back and quiet down, give us some room here."

"It's Moberly's head," someone shouted.

"Now I want everyone to calm down and back away from the edge of that sidewalk, someone's going to get hurt here," Calder yelled, angry about the lost secret, the mob and the bloody mess on the back of the wagon. "I don't want to have to start hauling in any of you troublemakers!"

Modesto moved away from the head, skirting around the back end of the wagon and asking, "And the second body?"

Calder grimaced, "Pretty chewed up, can't say much of it left intact. Been out there for some time it seems."

"So unlikely any of them met their end at the same time."

"Would seem so."

Modesto carefully lifted the edge of the blanket and peered under, the torso covered in the crust of a shirt now discoloured by dried blood, the face pecked at and gnawed upon. No doubt about it though, it was Butch Daly.

"And who found them?" Modesto asked.

"This man here, Beaton," said the Calder, pointing to a thick-set man waiting with the team of horses, "he and his partner found them."

"I can't tell you much sir," Beaton said.

But Modesto was staring at the drooping moustache sagging over Beaton's mouth, the thing moved slowly when the man spoke, when he said, *'I can't tell you much'*, the sad, furry thing went up and down. Would it stay put, was it moving, crawling off the man's face?

"Mr. O'Brien, do you have questions for Beaton here? We should be moving this thing along, making quite a spectacle of ourselves."

"Yes, sorry. Was just concentrating. Now Mr. Beaton, tell me, this one here," he asked, pointing to Jowsy, bending to peer closer at the body, "was he in the water, or on the shore?"

"Half in, half out I would say, can't recollect for certain."

"Which half was in the water?"

"I guess his head."

"Face down or up?"

"Down."

"And his legs, straight out? Twisted? Bent?"

Beaton hesitated, squinted, like he was picturing the scene, turned to glance at Calder, the moustache moving with his face. Modesto was relieved. Calder said, "Answer the man!"

"Uh, well, I don't rightly recall. Wasn't expecting to come across something like this."

"No, I don't imagine," Modesto said, "but just do your best to remember, it might be helpful in determining how this man died."

"Seems to me," said Calder, "that this man might have collapsed from some kind of medical reason. Fell face down onto the shore."

"Possibly," said Modesto, "though there are some signs of violence on Mr. Jowsy."

Calder frowned, "I don't see that myself."

"Yes, you are quite right," Modesto said, "it is very difficult, both due to the natural exposure and degree of decomposition, but his hands are reddened, torn up, there is sand packed under the nails, and on the back of his neck it appears there might be bruising but we would need a closer look. I believe the possibility exists that this man was forcibly drowned."

Modesto looked up to the crowd, found Bodine's face, asked, "Anyone have any information that might be helpful in determining what happened to Mr. Jowsy?"

Bodine didn't flinch, stared back at Modesto.

Calder, sounding frustrated, said, "Nothing but gossip twenty-four hours of the day in this town and now no one knows anything? No one?"

Beaton said, "I never seen anything so awful as finding these, these ... bodies. Ain't natural. Has to be that monster out there."

"That's right, that was where it was seen," a man from the crowd said, "right around Kerr Lake. I'm telling you, it's out there!"

"Now, now, fellas," Calder said, "best just settle down. We ain't little children, got no reason to believe in ghosts and monsters."

"I'm telling you, it's out there, seen tracks and everything. Not going back either, can tell you that much, not after finding this," Beaton said, nodding towards the wagon.

"Finding what?" Tommy Coffin asked, pushing his way to the front of the crowd, the energy shifting, men moving out of his way until he was right beside Bodine. Shitty left stranded at the far edge of the crowd.

Beaton said, "Found a couple of bodies out by Kerr Lake."

Tommy Coffin glanced down at the wagon, asked, "Who are they?"

"Fellow by the name of Jowsy."

Tommy shook his head, dismissive, said, "Quite the crowd for just another drowned prospector."

"That's a hard-hearted assessment," Modesto said, "but your partner there beside you is looking rather distressed. Mr. Bodine, do you know this man?"

Coffin gestured at Modesto, asked Calder, "What's he got to do with any of this?"

Calder, sounding even more frustrated, asked, "Who the heck are you?"

Coffin, smiling, said, "Just a concerned citizen."

Modesto said, "I think the Constable here thought, given my background as a detective, I might be of some use in this situation."

"You aren't a detective, you're nothing but a damn charlatan."

Men leaning in, they hadn't been expecting this. There was some murmuring, and one guy said from near the back, "That's right, this man is one of them fortune-tellers."

Modesto was surprised he had lasted this long, had felt suspicions sliding down along his spine since the day he had walked out of town with the bear, the good-natured crowd turning surly. Modesto said, "Just trying to be of assistance, but perhaps I've assisted in this matter as much as possible."

"Now, now, boyo, don't go running off," Coffin said, "tell us what you think happened to this poor fellow, this Jowsy."

Calder said, "Now Mister, not sure who you are, but best leave this matter to me, move along now."

"Surely Constable," said Modesto, "you've come across Mr. Coffin before."

"Can't rightly say I have," Calder said, "and can't rightly say I appreciate all of this back and forth between you two, seems to me like it has nothing to do with the matter at hand. Now I asked Mr. O'Brien here to give his opinion as he seems a man of science and observation and that's that. Now I don't care who you are Mr. Coffin…"

"Perhaps," Modesto offered, "Mr. Coffin's name came up in the matter raised by the authorities from the Austrian Embassy?"

"Austrian Embassy?"

"Maybe it was the French? I do believe his name was mentioned in connection with those abused foreign workers? I read something about it, perhaps in the *Montreal Daily.*"

Calder shot Modesto a look, "What? Oh yes, that matter. How is this man involved with that?"

"It's his gang laying the railbed up there at Driftwood City."

"That a fact?" Calder now turning to size up Coffin more closely, "You running that railway outfit up there?"

"You've got a pair of dead men stretched out right in front of you," Coffin said, "and you're asking me about my business interests."

"Mr. Coffin," Calder said, indignant now, "I am well aware there are two bodies stretched out here."

"Perhaps Mr. Coffin would like to assist in the identification of the second body," Modesto said, moving around to the top of the wagon to be closer to the head, pulling down the blanket, it was rough in his hand, damp along the frayed edges, "Do you know this gentleman Mr. Coffin?"

Bodine groaned loudly, looked away, and then there was only silence, and every pair of eyes fell away from Tommy Coffin to the waxy, discoloured face of the body stretched out on the wagon.

Modesto said, "Does anyone recognize this poor soul?"

Many of them would have known Daly, but the dread expression on Coffin's face was so possessive, it was like he owned the very death of the corpse, so no one spoke. They all stood staring down at Butch Daly's mottled face until Calder said, "What the hell is going on here, who is this man?"

Coffin said, "That's my business partner, Butch Daly."

Beaton said, "Looks like this Daly's been mauled, dragged or something. Maybe he's what Moberly saw out there by Kerr Lake, that the monster had."

That set the crowded humming, but Calder barked, "Enough of this monster business. Stay out there long enough, animals are bound to get you. Now let's finish up here."

Modesto pulled up the blanket, but his attention was drawn away from the corpse by the uncanny calling of the gulls overhead. The fog hung low over the small lake at the centre of the town, turning the gulls to ghosts, pale outlines of the birds as they flew over. Modesto remembered Biddy saying, *Oh how we pity those poor Children of Lir, turned to swans by the terrible stepmother, left so lonely by the lake, but oh how they loved each other, could fly so high above us, fly away from us, their minds full of clouds, I envy them that, but not being able to go home, well, that was something else.*

To Modesto's ears the sound of the gulls as they conversed was bird and human and otherworldly all at the same time. Perhaps the story of the Children of Lir was true after all. And if true, could he be turned to a gull, fly away? But he was drawn back down from the mists by the weight of the crowd's eyes upon him. He felt they were waiting for him to offer an opinion on the question of the monster, so he said, "The Constable is quite right, I'm sure if we search there'll be animal tracks all around where these men were found."

"I seen tracks alright," Beaton said, "and just like Moberly said, they were big, not like any animal I ever saw."

And Modesto thought yes, why not an animal, or the monster? Lucy had said she shot Daly, but time and exposure would have taken their toll, obscured the gunshot. So why set the Constable searching for a killer, it would only be a matter of time before someone made the connection to the Nail sisters.

"It would be hard to be sure," Modesto said, now doing his part to reinforce the story of the beast, "what sort of creature might have gotten to the bodies."

"I've heard it," Beaton interrupted. "Heard that thing out there howling at night, we've all heard it, don't say you haven't."

"Wolves, nothing but wolves," Calder said.

"Don't sound like any wolves I've ever heard," answered Beaton, "and I've heard stories, was told that there were legends, says there's a creature out there. Local people say it's madness that we're disturbing the lake out there. Digging in the earth. That it lives under there."

Calder said, "I've heard just about enough nonsense from the lot of you. Now I'm sure you've all got somewhere to be. Now time to move along!"

The men reluctantly began to pry themselves loose from the spectacle, and Beaton slowly mounted his rig and turned it towards the livery. Calder called after Coffin, said, "You! Coffin! Best come with me, got some questions for you about your business partner."

"Want me to come along Tommy?" Bodine asked, hoping the man said no.

"You're nothing but a fuck up," Tommy said, spitting onto the sidewalk before hopping down and following Calder, "think I can manage without you."

It wasn't the kind of 'no' Bodine had been hoping for.

CHAPTER
THIRTY-SIX

The scarlet hat and jacket were shocking against the dull browns and greys of the mud and rock. From the top of the street the men watched as she slowly made her way down the street, watching still as she lifted her skirt to show the red boots tipped in dark mud, the steps landing gingerly between the rocks, stepping over the rivulets of sludge and sewage that criss-crossed the road, past the piles of boards and debris, waiting as a cart passed by, the turn of her face away in case there was splashing.

Approaching a row of men lining the sidewalk, Lily called out, "Could one of you gentlemen point me in the direction of the Mining Recorder's office?"

That was too much for them, this dreaded combination of womanliness and mining. No one spoke. Just stared.

She smiled politely as she passed their gawking. Several yards on, she paused, stopped and glanced around, tilted her head back a bit as if sniffing the air, then turned and walked right through the doors of the Bucket of Blood Saloon.

There was a suspension of time for just a moment, then a ripple, a current passed through the crowd of men who went from slouching along the bar and in their chairs to sitting upright, some leaning to get a better look at this strange spectacle of a scarlet woman. They glanced at each other but said nothing, and an awkwardness, paralytic and quiet, settled over the raucous room.

She said, "Anyone able to assist a lady find her way to the Mining Recorder's office?" Lily cast a look about the room, eyes settling on an older fellow close to her, and she said, "Sir, could you be so kind as to escort me?"

He smiled awkwardly, said, "It isn't too far up the road, Miss, but I'd be happy to escort you, you know, the traffic can be a devil at times, those teamsters never looking where they're going, just in a hurry to get there."

"That would be very kind of you."

"George Johnstone, at your service," he said, and he offered her his arm, which she took gingerly with an ever so slight nod of her head. She moved slowly, delaying her exit, and then yes, she heard the voice she was waiting for, "Well, well, well, if it isn't Lily Nail."

She ignored it, Coffin then calling across the room, "Lily Nail, Queen of the Thieves from the Dublin Gulch."

Lily was brought up short by Johnstone stopping, saying to her quietly, "I think that gentlemen was calling to you?"

She turned her eyes on Johnstone, "Pardon me? What gentleman?"

Johnstone gestured with a slight nod of his head towards the back of the bar where Coffin was at a table, had been playing cards with Shitty Mitty and two other men.

Coffin said, "Come on Lily, I'm sure you haven't forgotten me, have you?"

Lily glanced back as if annoyed and said to Johnstone, "I think he has me confused with someone else, should I answer him?"

Johnstone looked flustered, said, "Well Miss, I'm not sure I am a suitable judge of appropriate behavior."

Coffin, even louder, said, "Not surprising that I would run into Lily Nail in a town like this."

Lily released the arm of Mr. Johnstone and turned to look at Coffin. "I think you have me confused with someone else. I'm Theodora Bow, here with the travelling show, Colleen Bawn? Perhaps you've seen it?"

Coffin, grinning now, said, "You can certainly act. But you can't lie about those violet eyes of yours, can you?"

Lily rested her hand on Johnstone's arm to bring him along with her as she took a few steps towards Coffin. She sighed and said, "Sir, you really are confused," and then smiling patiently turned to Mr. Johnstone and said, "Mr. Johnstone, what colour are my eyes?"

He flushed deeply, said, "Miss Bow, by all accounts they appear to be a dark brown to me."

She turned to Coffin and said, "You see, as Mr. Johnstone can attest, I am not your lady friend, now please, if you don't mind, I have business to attend to."

"I know damn well you're Lily Nail. You and that crazy sister of yours are up here running some sort of swindle." He then said to the men mesmerized by the scene unfolding before them, "She robbed some fellas back in Butte of their hard-earned money. Not sure what kind of women's trickery she's using here, but that there is Lily Nail and there's a reward on her head. I know that as sure as my name's Tom Coffin."

"What an unfortunate name sir, and though I cannot attest to the veracity of your name, I do know the colour of my own eyes. And as everyone here can plainly see with *their* own eyes, they are brown, not violet. Now I really must be off. I am in quite a hurry," she said, even as she was still moving slowly towards him.

"Hurrying off to church?"

"The Mining Recording office. I have a claim to register."

"A prospector as well as an actress Lily?"

"As I said, my name is Miss Bow. And actually, I have an agent working on my behalf," she was saying as she continued towards him, "A Mr. Campbell, and I believe he has done well by me."

Coffin frowned. "Campbell?"

"Yes, a Mr. Campbell. I suppose you know his eye colour as well." A few men snickered and by now Lily was right at his table, able to view the cards laid out there, most face up, the men at the table having just finishing a round.

"What claim?" asked Coffin.

"Oh, I'm really not too sure. Not that it is any of your concern, but Mr. Campbell just said a piece of ground had become available owing to some tragedy. He said other prospectors working in the same area were reluctant to work the property. He further explained that the area had great promise even though there had been accidents, then of course stories began to circulate. Mr. Campbell explained that miners were a superstitious lot. But of course, a woman does not have the same opportunities as a man, we can't afford such superstitions, so I took it."

There was a murmur through the crowd, and a man leaning on the bar called, "Out at Kerr Lake?"

"Oh maybe, that sounds familiar." Smiling, asked him, "Am I going to be rich?"

The man glanced uneasily at the others around him but didn't answer.

"You're staking out at Kerr Lake?" Coffin asked.

"As I said, I really can't say for sure as I was relying on the good nature of Mr. Campbell to assist me. Just before he left town, he contacted me to say he had finalized everything, and I was to stop by the Mining Recorder's office and pick up my documents. So that is where I'm off to."

"I was working with Campbell."

Men in the bar were rivetted now, sensing now the growing trouble in the air between this man and the woman. No one seemed to know too much about him, knew he was a relative new-comer in a town of newcomers, that he'd come up from Montana and now they knew he had been partners with Butch Daly. But his energy said he was a force to be reckoned with, and the crowd was jealous of the three others sitting mutely at the table with him, of their front row seats to such drama, jealous too of Johnstone.

Lily said, "Is that right? Well good luck to you sir", and then glancing back down at his cards said, "Oh goodness yes, you certainly will be needing it," her pale hand now reaching and spreading out the cards, murmured, "my, my that is quite the hand you have there."

"This is poker darling, not one of your parlour games," Coffin said.

"The cards never lie."

"What's he got, Miss," a man along the bar called out, "a dead man's hand?" A few men laughing.

"No, he has a pair of fours, and an eight and seven of clubs, and the ace of spades."

"Not taking home the pot with that one," someone yelled, and again laughter.

"Oh, but it's quite the hand."

"Shut your mouth," Coffin said, now reddening, mad, not used to being laughed at.

Lily said, "But there is so much to see here, and it's a bit more complicated than the dead man's hand. See, look here, this one, the diamond," then glancing up at Coffin asked, "Sorry, sir? What was your name again?"

A man at the bar shouted, "Coffin."

"Yes, of course, pardon me, Mr. Coffin," she said, then focused her attention on the cards, touched the four of diamonds, said, "Seems like you must have a friend you shouldn't be trusting."

"That'd be Shitty!" the man at the bar shouted, getting another few laughs.

"And this one, your eight of clubs, a card of caution, for coveting. Do you covet something Mr. Coffin? And here again, dear me, yet another caution with your four of clubs. Imperiled by your short temper perhaps?"

Coffin could not but help glance down at the cards as she said, "But these last two, they really help tell your story. The seven of clubs, danger from a member of the opposite sex, goodness, that could spell rack and ruin for you Mr. Coffin."

"What about the ace?" the man at the bar calling out.

"Oh that's simple. Death. Perhaps in a duel. How old fashioned."

Coffin grabbed her hand, his grip strong, said, "Get out of here."

"If you want me to leave, sir, you will need to release my hand."

He stared at her for a few long seconds as she stared back, the men watching rapt, and she said, "Let go of me."

Then Coffin jerked his hand away as if burned, "You little bitch, I'll be seeing you later, you can bet on that Lily Nail."

Mr. Johnstone cleared his throat, seemed to try and avoid looking at Coffin when he ventured, "Come along Miss, I think we best be going."

"Yes, indeed, the tone is really quite unpleasant in here," she said, and she took Johnstone's arm and made her way to the door.

The energy drained from the room in her wake. As the red jacket passed by, each man seemed to turn away from the spectacle and back to their beer and whiskey, their dreams of silver already wasting away, a sour taste in their mouths.

CHAPTER
THIRTY-SEVEN

As she passed through the doors with Mr. Johnstone and onto the boardwalk, she almost collided with Modesto O'Brien.

"Excuse me," she said.

He stared at her. At Mr. Johnstone too.

"No, not at all," Modesto said quickly, "entirely my fault, Miss, I assure you."

Since he didn't move, she said, "We were just on our way."

He glanced at Mr. Johnstone and said, "Would you please excuse us for one moment, that I might have a quick word with the lady?"

Mr. Johnstone looked to Lily for guidance. She smiled, "Yes, if you wouldn't mind, could you be so kind?"

Confused, he stepped back a couple of feet, but both kept watching him, so he retreated several more feet, and Modesto leaned into her and whispered, "You left Lucy?"

"She's fine."

"Why draw attention to yourself now? You both need to be on the train and far away from here as soon as possible. You can't forget about the reward, you are both still at great risk."

"Lucy is right though, he'd follow us, like he has always followed us. The man is possessed. It's time to deal with this once and for all."

"But why leave Lucy? And put yourself at risk. Better to put some distance between yourselves and Coffin, come up with some sort of plan later."

"Mr. O'Brien, perhaps if you are so concerned with my sister you should attend to her. I am off to the Mine Recorder's Office with the very kind Mr. Johnstone. I have kept him waiting long enough."

She walked a few feet towards Johnstone then turned and walked quickly back to Modesto, brought her hand up to his cheek, fingertips on his face felt like ice, and she said, "Take care of her."

Modesto watched as the pair made their way slowly down the street. Near a large pile of timbers, they turned, and then were out of sight.

CHAPTER THIRTY-EIGHT

Inside the Bucket of Blood, the men were quiet, thinking of the lady in the red jacket and of the man left sitting with Shitty Mitty and a bad hand of cards. Nobody was envying Tommy Coffin right now.

But outside, Bodine had watched as the man in the green coat leant into the woman in red. It was that detective. Whispering. Knowing each other. And then her, touching him like that, now that was something, Bodine feeling himself drawn to her, like the first time he had seen her. Maybe she had that animal magnetism too.

But all in all, it was making him angry, thinking about trailing along behind Tommy all these years, this woman somehow taking over his life. They'd been the Kings of the Dublin Gulch, but nothing had been the same since they'd burnt that house down. Maybe Tommy was right, maybe here was a curse. They'd had some good times over the years, but just when Bodine thought they were getting the old charm back, there'd be another sighting. Tommy would always find some excuse about why they should move on, but it was always the Nail sisters.

Goddammit, he wished he could do that night over. Or have waited until later, another time. Or until they were sober enough to do it right. But he'd been excited, so had Butch, both drawn to Tommy's energy that was dark and raging and magnetic. And he had been exhilarated by it, by the flames, the crowds running, the commotion.

But things were never the same again after that night. Folks remembered, remembered seeing Tommy trying to haul Lily Nail across the backyard, so even if they weren't sure about why the fire started, the doubts were always out there. And they remembered too the other sister rushing out, wild-eyed, laying down the curse. People had always been afraid of Tommy, but they had also admired him. He was tough, connected, good at getting his way. But the possibility of a curse weakened him in the eyes of folks, and made Tommy edgy, meaner. And then after the Nail sisters' first robbery, the glamour and notoriety of it all, it was just too much for Tommy, he became obsessed.

And now, Shitty was sitting inside with Tommy while he, Tommy's oldest friend, was on the outside. Well, maybe he'd just have to finish this business with the Nail sisters, once and for all.

He had watched as the woman headed down the street with the man she'd come out of the bar with, leaving the detective standing and watching her go. After several long seconds the detective left, heading in the opposite direction. So the question was, which one to follow.

The red coat beckoned, and he followed. That is what he would tell Tommy. Sounded pretty good in his head, he could see himself, maybe holding some belonging of the woman, the hat maybe, that would get Tommy's attention, and then he would say something like, *'You wanted her, well I got her out in that cabin, ready and waiting for you.'* Or he could bring in the hat, say, *'This is for you, all that's left of that witch.'* He wasn't quite sure what he was going to do, but he was going to do something.

He saw the pair enter a building at the end of the street. Sauntering up towards it, he saw the man who'd escorted Lily emerge from the doorway looking a little lost, and then awkwardly amble back towards the Bucket of Blood. Bodine stepped up onto the sidewalk to get a closer look at the small sign beside the door: Mr. J. G. Murdoch, Mine Recorder.

He could hear voices inside, probably Lily and the Murdoch fella. He leaned against the wall beside the door, heard Lily ask Mr. Murdoch to call her a buggy from the livery, she was going to head out to the claim, Murdoch saying, "I do not advise you to head out there alone. There have been too many accidents out there. Wait, and in the morning we will send a man with you," but her saying she could look after herself. And so Mr. Murdoch leaned out the door, called to a boy on the corner to go tell Mr. Carr to send a buggy over.

Perfect.

Bodine was right behind the boy when the livery came into sight. Grabbed the boy by the shoulder, said, "Never mind about the buggy, I'll handle it."

The boy started to protest but Bodine said, "Go on, git," and the boy did. Bill pushed his way into the stables, called, "Hey, Carr, got a buggy ready to go?"

Carr came around the corner, asked, "What would you be wanting with a buggy? Never mind, don't got none left anyhow. Busy as hell today, everybody's either coming or going. Got a wagon though."

"No buggy?"

"Nope."

Bill scratched at his head, thinking, then said, "Wagon'll do. Maybe best anyways."

"Where're you taking it?"

"None of your business."

"Of course it's my business."

"Just heading out Kerr Lake way."

"That right? No one's heading out there."

"Well, I am."

"And when'd you get interested in mining?"

"I'm going out to Butch Daly's cabin. Do right by his family back in Butte, send on his belongings."

"Butch had a place out there? Never said nothing about it."

"Smart enough fella to keep his mouth shut, mind his own business. Maybe you should try it, 'stead of wasting my time, now get me that wagon."

"I'll get it, but you bring it back in good shape or you'll be buying the team and wagon."

"Don't worry, just get a move on."

But Carr moved as he moved, which was slow and steady, giving Bodine time to get his guns from the saddle bags he kept with his horse, and still be waiting on the man to come around with the wagon. By the time Bodine was pulling up outside the Mining Recording Office, both Mr. Murdoch and Lily Nail were peering down the street, impatient.

Bodine pulled up, said, "Carr was slow. Busy down there today."

Mr. Murdoch frowned, "What's going on here Bodine, you don't drive for Carr."

"Do today," Bodine said, now grinning, having fun, this was something different, adding, "helping him out, he's short-handed."

"Haven't known you to help anyone out," said Murdoch, then turning to Lily said, "I think I will send for another driver."

"Now hold up there," Bodine said, protesting, trying to look injured and wronged but thinking about coming back after he was all finished up with the woman and giving this pompous ass a good beating, "I think you're a little out of line."

"Miss Bow, I must insist... we can view your property tomorrow. It is very late in the day."

"It is alright Mr. Murdoch," Lily said, "I have no reservations about this driver. His arrival is in fact very opportune."

Speaking quietly and turning his head away from Bodine, Murdoch said, "You don't know what kind of a man he is ..."

Lily, laying a hand on Mr. Murdoch's arm, smiled and said, "Oh, I know exactly what kind of man he is."

Murdoch helped Lily into the wagon, said, "Are you sure I can't persuade you to wait, I would be happy to escort you out there myself first thing," but Bodine gave the team of horses a sharp snap of the whip and the wagon lurched forward. Lily called over her shoulder to Murdoch, "Not to worry, I'm sure everything will be just fine."

• • •

Bodine felt in his element, chatting all friendly like to the woman as she told him everything he needed to know. Women, he thought, couldn't help themselves but talk, talk, talk. She told him how she had come by her claim, why she thought it was valuable, and what her plans were for developing it. What was nagging at Bodine though was the detective. What was her relationship with him, and did she tell him?

He was trying now to figure out his best course of action. Go straight to the cabin and have Lily Nail and the claim? What about the sister though? Maybe she'd come, he could use Lily as bait, draw the other one out. But how would she know he had Lily? So maybe he should just turn the wagon around and drive her straight over to the Bucket of Blood, haul her in there and say to Tommy, look what I found, you been looking for this right? Or something like that.

Except when he'd seen her she'd just left the saloon, and he knew Tommy was inside. So obviously he'd seen the woman. So maybe first he needed to make sure he had everything under control. Show Tommy that he'd made a big mistake in underestimating ol' Billyboy. Have the woman and the claim.

He said to Lily, "So I'm not sure that you are aware, Miss, but some fellas think Mr. Murdoch isn't always a straight shooter, if you get my meaning."

Lily said, "No, what do you mean? Mr. Murdoch has been very helpful to me."

"Sometimes, now I cannot verify this from personal experience or anything like that, but sometimes he's been known to hand out a bad claim, just little things a fella is likely to miss, but something like a wrong date, name misspelled or some business like that. Then that buys another fella time to get in there and lay the claim properly, and according to the law. Now did you have a good hard look at that document he provided you with?"

Lily said, "I tried to look it over, but I really don't understand mining all that well."

Bodine reined in the horses, then took the reins in one hand, and held out the other hand towards her, said, "Let's have a closer look then, shall we?"

Lily, hesitating, saying, "I really have no reason to question Mr. Murdoch."

But Bodine gestured with his hand for her to give it to him, shaking his head and smiling, saying, "You just can't trust anyone in this town, best be sure, now let's have a look."

CHAPTER THIRTY-NINE

When Tommy Coffin came into the room, Modesto was sure even the walls wanted to retreat, move away from the man's energy. Modesto should have had his guard up, been more careful, but he was rushing, focused on getting his guns from the case when Biddy said *he's afoot, he's stirred and is coming, the foul thing that he is*, but then there was no time, Coffin through the door saying, "You fucking little Irish bastard."

Coffin hauled a chair over to the small table where Modesto was sitting, spun the chair around and straddled it, resting his arms on the chairback, "I was sure I knew you from somewhere. Little Moddie O'Brien."

"Only my Gran was allowed to call me that," Modesto said.

"You were always a strange one. You and that mad old woman."

Modesto said nothing. Felt calm now, felt too the gun on the inside of his coat. How had it gotten there, the case now empty and sitting between he and Coffin on the table, Biddy saying, *Such pretty pistols* and he smiled, and Coffin said, "What the fuck you smiling at? You wouldn't be smiling if you knew what I'm going to do to you. But first, we have ourselves some unfinished business."

Modesto had known it was only a matter of time before Coffin came after him, but right now was very bad timing. He was worried about Lucy, wanted to get out to the cabin and see her, make sure she was alright. And then get Lily, get them both out of Cobalt. The only good thing about the present situation was that Coffin was here in town, and not headed out to Kerr Lake.

"We do indeed have unfinished matters," Modesto said, "but now is not the time. I have somewhere I need to be so if you'll excuse me…"

Coffin called over his shoulder, "Come on in here boys," and two men slouched around the edges of the door, arms crossed. "Your business will have to wait, and these gentlemen are going to help ensure that I have your close attention. I need to have little chat with you, find out what the great detective here is thinking about those two bitches. Or are you a fortune teller today? Gunman?"

Modesto didn't respond so Coffin said, "That's right Moddie, no point talking back. Now you answer my questions and I might be inclined to leave you in one piece today."

"Ask."

"Simple question. Why are you in Cobalt?"

"Why do you think?"

"That's not a fucking answer. Now answer me, and don't bother telling any tall tales."

"I'm here for the same reason everyone else is."

Coffin smiling said, "The sorry bastards in this town are here for the silver. You don't strike me as the prospecting or mining type. But I can wager a fine guess as to why you'd show up here."

"The Nail sisters have nothing to do with me being here."

"Careful, O'Brien. Shitty, you know Shitty, well he found your little newspaper collection, so don't be wasting my time. Now the way I see it, maybe you trailed them here thinking about the reward, but then that cold bitch got her claws into you. Am I close?"

"No, not at all."

"Alright then, you tell me."

"I was looking for you."

Coffin was surprised. "And why would you be interested in looking up Tommy Coffin?"

"To kill you."

Coffin burst out laughing, "You're having me on!"

"Bodine and Daly too."

Coffin looked baffled. "Why?"

"Because of the boy."

"What boy?"

"Kit Murphy."

Just the name was enough to shift Modesto's thoughts, send them scurrying, the small shed, too hot, claustrophobic, and the blonde hair tangled, and Biddy said *Go easy Moddie, the foul thing can smell your fear*

Coffin was frowning, "Murphy?" Then shaking his head said, "Who the fuck is that?"

"You cut his hair."

"What?"

"You dragged him out of school …"

"School! You're talking about something that happened when we were boys?"

"Yes."

"Jesus to god man, what's the matter with you? How do you expect me to remember some school yard prank?"

"You don't remember?"

"No, why should I?"

"He took his own life because of your schoolyard prank."

"What's that got to do with me?" Then the memory slid into place and Coffin said, "Right! That little puss! The one always playing cowboy, for godsake man, all we did was try to clean him up, couldn't have him looking like a fucking girl could we, needed his long blonde locks trimmed up? Is that the boy?"

"Yes."

"What's he got to do with you?" Coffin asked, "Not your people?".

"He was a friend I suppose."

"You're aiming to kill me over someone you suppose was your friend?"

"Yes."

Coffin was shaking his head, laughing, said, "Well, you are one exceptional bastard, O'Brien. But I'm not interested in this Murphy kid, or you for that matter, I'm interested in Lily Nail. Now you just tell me where she is, and I'll be on my way."

O'Brien found he was gripping the table. "I don't know where she is. But you would be best to leave her and her sister be. I wouldn't want to have to involve the authorities. They already have an eye on you."

"Did you think that was a clever move then, O'Brien? Sending the Constable my way? I'll tell you right now, nothing's going to keep me off the trail of the Nail sisters? So you do right by me here and I'll spare you the worst of it."

Modesto didn't answer. Was wondering what the worst of it was, was it to take someone from themselves, take away who they thought they could be in the world? Was that Tommy Coffin's specialty? Or was this thuggish man too dull for that, too stuck in his muscle and blood, would rather just get to the killing of Modesto, right here and now?

"Quiet now, O'Brien? Nothing to say? Maybe now you're not so sure now about taking on Tommy Coffin, are you?"

"Nothing to be afraid of from you," Modesto said, seeing the heavy thickness that hung in the air all around Coffin, surrounding him with mud-coloured pulsing, the drippings and the seepings. The man was terrifying.

"That right? We'll see about that," Coffin said, half turning to share a smile with the two men behind him, "We'll see about getting some justice for Butch."

"I doubt you understand much about justice, Coffin, and to be clear, I haven't seen your esteemed colleague since I was a schoolboy."

"You might be right about that, but the Nail sisters sure as hell are responsible for what happened to him. So to me, there's no difference. And when I'm finished with you, I'm going to go and see your girlfriends, have some fun with them, make them sorry they ever crossed my path."

"I'm quite sure they already regret ever laying eyes on you. I certainly do. But you might be disappointed. They've likely long gone, headed back down south I believe."

"Now I know you're lying. So why don't you tell me how she did it?"

"Do what?"

"Disappear again. She is a fucking witch, must be. How? She came into the bar. Went up the street. By the time I got there, the Mining Recording office was already locked up, not a soul insight, and no one had seen her, seen where she went. Fucking broad was wearing red and parading in the streets. But she vanished, just like that. So what's the game? You tell me, you're working some angle, got some fucking scheme up your sleeves, what the fuck is it?"

Coffin was yelling, the two men with him hovering in the doorway, not sure when to step in, wondering maybe what they'd gotten themselves into. Modesto said, "There's no game. They've left by now."

"Both you and me know that's a lie. And you know how I know? Because Lily Nail is like a bitch with a bone, she isn't going to leave me alone any more than I'm going to leave her alone. She's gone for our claim, for Butch's cabin. I know it."

"I think you overestimate her interest in you."

The fist coming down on the table sent the case flying, Coffin yelling, "What would you fucking know?"

His yelling made the two men move further into the room, alert now, smelling the hope of blood and bruises in the air, and Modesto stood, backing away from the table and said, "I thought Mr. Bodine did your dirty work for you?"

Coffin stood as well, tossed his chair aside, then the table. "Now why would I leave all the fun for him now? Where's the sport in that?"

"I think it likely we have different notions of sport."

Coffin took a few steps closer to Modesto, "I don't give a fuck what you think." And with that, the hard hand slammed up and across Modesto's face, knocking him backwards and down to the ground, Coffin spitting, then saying, "I'm going to give you a beating like no other O'Brien. You're going to wish yourself dead."

As the first kick landed into his ribs, then another, and he watched the other two men moving over to join in, he thought yes, it was going to be a beating like no other. But he wasn't ready for dead. Not yet. Not yet ready to wish himself dead.

CHAPTER FORTY

"**G**et the horses."

That was all Coffin had said to him, but Shitty was happy to oblige, to get out of the bar, away from the sourness in the air. He'd been sitting across from Coffin when the woman had come into the Bucket of Blood, his back to her, unable to see her but feeling the presence, almost paralysed by it. It was suffocating. Strangest damn thing.

When the woman left, Coffin had sat there staring at nothing and then after a few minutes he just up and bolted out of the place, leaving Shitty sitting there alone like an idiot, none of the other fellas wanting to be near him. Thinking Shitty was bad luck due to the company he kept. He was relieved when Coffin had barged back in sometime later, demanding a bottle and sitting heavily down in the chair across from Shitty. His knuckles were roughed up and his colour high, but he just sat drinking in silence. After a couple of shots of the whiskey he took a deep breath and told Shitty to go get the horses.

Shitty hadn't bothered to ask Coffin what horses he was supposed to get or why, just glad to get the hell out of the bar. But now he wasn't sure what to do. He supposed he could take Bodine's horse, unless Coffin was figuring that all three of them were going somewhere, he didn't really say, but Bodine wasn't around and that was making Coffin even more agitated. The man was darn right snarly now.

Carr was out front when Shitty got there, shouted out at him, "Wasting your time, he isn't here. Already left."

"Who?"

"Your man Bodine."

Shitty, not wanting to look like he didn't know what was up, said, "Right, yeah, said he was going," paused, then asked, "When'd he head out?"

Carr shrugged, said, "Don't keep track of every jackass who rolls through here."

"Huh," Shitty said, wondering now about getting the horses if Bodine's was gone. Didn't have much money on him, but if he just came back with Coffin's horse the man would be some sore.

"Quit standing around gawping, state your business or beat it."

"Well, I came to fetch a couple of horses for Mr. Coffin, Bodine's was one of them, but guess I'm out of luck."

"Nope, his nag's here, he took on outta here in a wagon, but was wanting a buggy."

"A buggy?"

"Yup, guess your friend is doing some courting behind your back Shit."

Shitty was thinking that was unlikely, Bodine didn't waste no time courting women, just got down to the business with them, but said, "Say which way he was headed?"

"Didn't even know himself where he was going, the damn jackass! Said he was heading to Kerr Lake but then drove that wagon straight into town."

"Kerr Lake?"

"Said he wanted to go collect Butch Daly's personal effects, to mail home to his family. I doubt that," scoffed Carr. "Pity the poor woman he might have been picking up if he's planning on a picnic down at Kerr Lake."

Hesitating, not sure what to do, Shitty knew he was doing just what Carr had told him not to, standing around and gawping. Took a chance, said, "Did he actually say he was collecting a woman?"

Carr, impatient, said, "Not in so many words, but most fellas don't take a buggy to go prospecting. And Bodine never seemed inclined to work anyways. Now get the horses and get out of here. You're bad for business."

Inside the stable Shitty felt more comfortable. Horses were something he knew. Most times he could handle himself around them just fine, even around a big team of workhorses. When Bodine had first got into town he'd said, 'go get me a horse,' the man thinking they were a dime a dozen round here, but it was hard to find a good one, loads of horses coming in but not fast enough. He'd found a nice bay with a wide blaze of white down his face, white stockings, knew Bodine would like that, horse had a touch of style to it. By the time Mr. Coffin had gotten into the town, things were even busier, but Shitty still managed to find the man a heavy-set chestnut.

Wasn't hard to locate either of their horses in the stable, they seemed to be almost the only ones left. Carr must be doing alright for himself. Then he thought about the detective, glanced down to the far end where O'Brien's dappled nag usually stood, the man doting on her like a child, hand feeding her oats, slipping her carrots from his coat pocket. Strange fella.

Saddling the two horses he felt better, had something now to offer to Mr. Coffin, knowing what was up. He was just passing Carr when he asked, "I see that horse the detective bought off Werner is gone—thing up and die? Can't say it'd surprise me if it had."

"Not even close. Don't know what he puts in those oats he feeds her, but it's working. He lit out of here on that horse not a half hour ago, mare moving like she was in the prime of her life."

"Maybe that detective was after ol' Bodine."

"Don't know what he was up to, but he'd been worked over pretty damn good by someone."

"Took a beating?" Shitty asked, now wondering if that was Coffin's doing when he left the bar.

"Looked like it, and fresh. When he said he was heading to Kerr Lake I told him he was in no shape to be hitting the trail out that ways. Warned him I did, that all the other fellas were leaving Kerr Lake, some nasty dealings out there, but off he went anyways. Folks just don't listen when they should."

Wasn't that the truth.

CHAPTER
FORTY-ONE

The cabin had a stillness about it. That was maybe a good sign. Modesto was leaning against Molly, sheltered in a small stand of thick white pines. They had been watching the cabin for several minutes, Modesto wanting to be sure he wouldn't be walking into an ambush. He knew Coffin must be behind him, but he had no idea about Bodine.

He was lucky Coffin was easily bored. After several minutes of kicking and spitting and cursing, Coffin said, "Fuck it, finish him off boys," and left, heading back to the Bucket of Blood. The two men left behind took a few more half-hearted swings at him then drifted off themselves. He was able to pull himself up and half-walk, half-stagger to clean himself up a bit then make his way to the livery, no one even noticing him. But now he was glad he had Molly to lean on.

The horse nudged Modesto's arm.

Modesto smiled, "You're right. No point stalling. Wait here and keep an eye out. Hopefully I'll be out shortly with Lucy."

Modesto was quiet on his approach, had no choice but to move slowly, every part of his body aching, his ribs feeling like they were pushing through his flesh with each step. He listened hard for any warning from Molly, or from within the cabin, but the stillness of the woods persisted, not even the sound of rustling leaves.

He gently pushed the door open. The place was dark, just embers in the stove.

"Lucy?" Even with his eyes adjusting to the dark it was hard to see. "Lucy? Are you here?"

Then a stirring, "That you O'Brien?"

He followed her voice, her curled up in the far corner, shivering, touched her brow, feverish. She said, "I know you'd come this time too. I'm so cold."

"Just a bit of the fever, Lucy, just needing some rest, but I have to get you out of here for now."

"Why?"

"Coffin. He's on his way."

"Can't leave, what about Lily, if she comes and we're not here."

"I doubt she'll head here, but we can watch the road for her. We will set up somewhere so you can rest, wait for Lily, and as soon as we can we'll get you both out of town."

He helped her up as best her could, wrapped a blanket around her shoulders and said, "Don't think I can carry you this time, Lucy, you able to walk?"

"Course I can walk."

Once out in the daylight, Lucy said, "What happened to you?"

"Coffin."

"Why didn't he kill you?"

"I think that was the idea but the two gentlemen he rustled up to finish the job finally got bored."

"Lucky you."

"Lucky me indeed."

They got to Molly, Modesto saying, "Wait here, I'm just going to get us a few supplies."

He left the door open so he could see clearly enough to find Lucy's rucksack, an extra bedroll, and their water canteen. As he was closing the door, he saw a pack of cards sitting neatly at the very centre of the small wooden table. Waiting. But not for him.

"Let's make haste," he said to Lucy and Molly, tucking the bedroll in behind the saddle. He hung the canteen over the saddle horn, helped Lucy up best he could and passed her the rucksack. "We're going to circle around, then follow our tracks back a short way down the trail. We'll find a good spot to wait for Lily."

"What if we run into someone?"

"I passed several prospectors on my way here, but they were only interested in getting as far away from Kerr Lake as possible, more monster rumours I think. The only person interested in talking was an old woman needing help with her calf."

"Could you help her?"

"She couldn't find the calf, strange, it was right there, a lovely little thing, just up the trail a ways. I said I would take her to the calf and then in the morning take it to Cooley's cow for nursing. I offered her a ride on Molly, she thanked me but said no, said she would hold the horse's tail and follow us to the calf, and she took hold of the tail and walked with us a bit. I said it was a chilled evening and she told me the winds were going to come up, told me to trust the east wind. When I turned to ask her name, she had gone, and then the calf too."

"Disappeared? Did she wander off?"

"I don't know if she was there in the first place. But if so, I hope her calf is fine, a lovely little thing."

"Was it Biddy?"

"No, not Biddy. But maybe one of her stories."

"A story?"

"Perhaps."

"Not sure how a person can be a story. What kind of a story?"

"About how to behave when alone in the woods. Maybe that story."

"Your Gran had lots of stories I guess. I'd like to hear some of them."

"I'll tell you them all, but for now, let's get going."

He found an animal trail off the main road that had now been trampled hard by men coming and going, and a little further on there was a nice clearing with a few big cedars for shelter. It seemed like a good place to hide and wait for Lily. He helped Lucy get settled, draped the blanket over her and then set to gathering birch branches, a slight wind picking up and carrying Biddy through the treetops, her saying,

They're on the move, they're all on the move, there'll be no stopping them now

Modesto asked, who's on the move

The men and the east wind, and it's a dreadful brew that's blowing in.

"Is she here?" asked Lucy.

"Yes."

"Ask her, for me, ask her if Lily is ok."

"She doesn't always answer back, it isn't really like that."

"Ask her."

So he did, and he listened hard, the wind started up, stirring and rustling through the trees, then beginning to rattle through the high up birch branches and Modesto looked up and he heard,

You'll never hear or see the likes of Lily Nail again after tonight

Modesto wasn't sure what that meant.

Lucy asked, "Did you hear?"

"No, there was nothing, Lucy."

"You don't have to protect me, I heard, but it probably doesn't mean what you think."

Modesto was surprised. "You could hear her?"

High up and pulled by the wind, the birch bark started to flap against its tree trunks, and Lucy said, "I think everyone could hear this time," and then she said, "I'm scared and cold, come sit with me."

"I'm scared too," he said.

And he sat beside her, covering her in his green coat, and Molly stood close to them, and they all waited under the fitful winds and the moaning trees.

CHAPTER FORTY-TWO

The bear had spooked their horses something fierce. Shitty and Coffin were just at the start of the road out to Kerr Lake when a black bear charged up out of the woods, running across the trail right in front of them. Coffin's horse bolted, sent him tumbling into the mud. Shitty jumped from his own horse, hoping to grab hold of Coffin's chestnut, but then both horses bolted off down the trail. Hard to believe their bad luck but there they were, both men walking, horses nowhere to be seen. And the bear had just scrambled across the trail and disappeared back into the bush, leaving them be.

"Fucking bear, fucking going to find it and skin it alive," Coffin yelled, "must've been four hundred pounds, if not bigger."

"Well, I don't think so, in fact I think it might have been Bilskey's bear if I'm not mistaken, and that one, well it was a fairly small bear, weren't but a year old," Shitty saying, but Coffin said, "Shut your mouth Shitty, you ignorant bastard. I'm telling you, I'm going to fucking skin that bear alive. No one will believe how big it is, not till I kill it and drag its hide right into the Bucket of Blood to show them."

Shitty, figuring it was just easier, said, "You bet Mr. Coffin."

Shitty stopped listening to Coffin's cussing, of the bear, the road, the horses. He was too busy counting the number of men they were passing, men heading back towards town. Must be least a dozen or so, some were riding, others hauling wagons, some even walking, but all loaded down with supplies, keeping to a crisp pace, not slowing to make time for any gossip. Shitty, wanting to know where everyone was going, yelled over to a prospector he recognized, "Hey Mac, packing 'er in?"

Mac slowed, but didn't stop. "Veins pinched out, we're headed north up to the Porcupine, heard there's gold, lots of it."

"But that slab of silver!" Shitty said, 'You were working ground close to it!"

Mac shook his head, "Another body out by Kerr Lake. Just ain't worth it."

"Another body?" Shitty asked, "A drowning?"

"No, this fella wasn't drowned, he was torn apart."

"You seen it for yourself?" asked Coffin, combative.

"No, Fred Levers and John Shannon heard it from the young Clem fella that'd been working ground out by Moberly. Said two fellas came across the body on the other side of the lake."

"Rumours, nothing but fucking clothesline gossip," spat Coffin.

"Not sure what you know of this country, Coffin," Mac said, stopping and turning around to face him, "and if you want to think they're rumours, go right ahead. But I know there's something bad out there, like the land itself has been woken up and is angry. And I've heard that thing, whatever it is, heard it screaming, and I've heard it thrashing through the woods at night. It's enough to make a man rethink everything. Hell, I might even head back down south, give up this prospecting business altogether, go back to teaching."

Shitty kept wondering about that, about the screaming and the thrashing, as he and Coffin walked on in silence. Every now and again Shitty thought he saw their horses, but it turned out to be just a deer, or a shadow, or wishful thinking. So, when he saw an old woman standing by the side of the trail, he kept staring at her, thinking she too would turn into a shadow. But she didn't, and when they got even closer and she was still there, and then another twenty yards or so further along the trail he saw a small light-coloured calf, Shitty said, "Well, that's a strange sight."

Coffin, then seeing her too, said, "Where the fuck did she come from?"

She was small, and the closer they got, the smaller she seemed, hunched over a bit, her coat too big for her, the bottom of her skirt caked in mud. They could see now that the calf was the colour of cream, with dark eyes and a placid demeanor.

When they had almost reached the old woman, Coffin said, "You smell rank old woman."

"It's the smell of death upon me," she answered.

"Can't help you with that, I'm not Jesus you know," Coffin said.

"No sir, you're not, but could you find a little kindness in your heart and help an old woman find her beloved calf? She's missing."

Coffin and Shitty exchanged a glance, both laughed, and Coffin asked, "Are you blind or daft, old woman?"

"I am blind sir, and I cannot find her."

But the old woman was looking straight at Tommy, eyes watery but dark, focused, and he said, "You don't look blind to me."

"Sure, I'm blind, and I've tired myself from walking and searching for my wee calf, and I could use some rest. Could you fetch her for me?"

Shitty muttered something, turned to head up the road, but Coffin grabbed his arm, said, "We don't have time for this, let's get going."

"Well, we gotta pass right by the calf, take no time to run it back..."

"No, something isn't right with this one, leave her," he said, and then to the old woman he said, "go home, your calf will follow."

"I have no home."

Coffin glanced around, as if expecting to see her cabin amidst the stumps of blasted cedar, said, "Of course you do, you're not right in the head."

"I had a little cottage, but some men came and blasted it to smithereens. Said there was silver beneath the ground."

"Was there?" Shitty asked.

"No. Nothing there but the rubble of my home."

Coffin laughed, said, "Bad luck all around then," gave Shitty a shove, said, "Let's get moving."

"Bad luck all around indeed," the old woman called after them, "and you yourselves won't be spared."

Coffin turned, midway between the old woman and the calf, "What does that mean?"

"You're going to lose your way."

"We know where we're going."

"That's not what I saw in your eyes."

Coffin swore under his breath, resumed walking, so she called after him, "A warning then for you, even though you showed me ill will. Go back to where you came from. There's something terrible waiting for you. A part of your past broken loose from its moorings."

"You're talking nonsense."

"I'm telling you what I see."

"Mad old bitch, said she was blind and here she is seeing things," Coffin said to Shitty just as they were passing the calf. Shitty glanced over at it, feeling a bit bad, but his feet were hurting something awful and Coffin was right, they had to find their horses.

Then they heard her voice, clear as anything, as if the calf itself was saying it, right beside them, and all around them, "They're going to fight you tooth and nail. Tooth and nail. Tear you limb from limb."

CHAPTER
FORTY-THREE

The voices sounded far away, but the slap to his face brought Bodine right into the present. Found himself flat on his ass in the middle of a trail, Coffin crouching down in front of him. Bodine was wondering if he was losing his eyesight, everything was out of focus. And his cheek was burning something awful and Coffin, the words now decipherable, was asking, "What the fuck are you doing out here in the middle of nowhere?"

That was a good question.

Coffin said, "Get the fuck up Bill."

Bodine wasn't sure he could. He was sore all over, but the sore you get from lying on hard cold ground, cramped and old feeling. He put his hands down to brace himself, finally said, "Can't really get my bearings here, Tommy," and he heard Coffin curse and say, "Shitty, get Bill up on his feet," and Bodine felt Shitty behind him, grabbing him under his armpits and hauling him up. Bodine was a little surprised at how strong Shitty was, said, "Hey, slow down, that hurts."

"Sorry Bill."

Shitty said to Coffin, now talking as if Bodine wasn't even there, "Should I haul him onto the wagon? It must be nearby somewhere."

"Yeah, go find the wagon."

"Going to set him back down, he seems wobbly. And right confused," Shitty said, then asked, "Where's the wagon, Bill?"

Bodine wasn't sure where the wagon was, wasn't too sure about anything - didn't recognize where he was, hard to think when he was so sore. Bodine said, "The wagon, now I'm not too sure about that…"

Shitty said, "Think he must've got himself a bump on the head."

"Fuck off and get the wagon," Coffin said.

Bodine could hear Shitty stumbling off, said, "I don't feel so good."

"You tell me right now why you're out here like this?"

"I don't know Tommy. Honest to God. I don't know, don't even know where I am."

"I'll tell you where you are Billyboy, you're close to Butch's cabin, out by Kerr Lake."

Kerr Lake. Right. Butch's cabin. The pieces coming back to Bodine.

"That right?" Bodine said, "Well, I don't know how I got here."

"Do you remember the wagon?"

Yeah, Bodine did remember the wagon.

"Maybe," Bodine looking around him, trying to get his bearings. What had happened?

Coffin leaned in very close to Bodine, asked, "The woman with you. Do you remember her?"

How could he forget? Remembered the sweet smell of flowers, remembered the tilt of her head, the red hat against the bright green trees now just beginning to unfurl their buds. Remembered thinking he could see why Tommy had followed this woman from state to state and now into this wilderness. He remembered the irresistible draw and how close she was to him.

"Can't seem to find the dang wagon, Mr. Coffin," Shitty called.

"Where is it, Bill," Coffin asked, "where's the wagon?"

"Don't know. Can't rightly remember much about anything."

"First, we lose our horses," Shitty said, walking up to the two men, "well, your horse Bill, and now this, the wagon gone! Ain't this just the damnedest."

"Quit your jabbering," Coffin said, "And get back out there and look for the damned thing. It's a fucking wagon you're looking for, open your eyes man!"

"Didn't want to get myself turned around. Might have been what happened to old Bill here, maybe stopped and went looking for something, got himself lost."

"Didn't get myself lost," Bodine said, "why don't you mind your own business Shitty, shooting off your mouth about stuff you don't know anything about."

"Now hold up a minute there, not like you have much to say about how you landed out here in the middle of nowhere..." Shitty started, but Coffin interrupted, said, "Both of you shut your mouths. Sky's turning on us, got a storm is coming in, best get set up somewhere. Maybe we can make it to the cabin. How far we got Bill?"

"Can't rightly say, Tommy, not too sure where we are right now, hard to guess."

Coffin stared at him. "You're turning out to be a great disappointment to me, Bill. By the time we find that cabin you better start remembering Billyboy, because I'm finding out one way or another what the fuck is going on around here."

• • •

When they finally found the wagon, it was tipped over on a steep angle in a ditch, the harness loosened and the horse nowhere to be seen. Bodine and Shitty staring at the wagon, but Coffin staring at Bodine. "When you ran the wagon off the road Bill, how did you manage to get yourself back up and down the road where we found you?"

"Can't rightly say."

"Can't remember?"

"No, guess not."

"Can you say anything that is fucking useful then Bill?"

Frowning, Bodine said, "Yeah, maybe my guns are in there. Check there Shitty, 'neath that blanket, my guns, they there?"

And Shitty slid down by the wagon, said, "Yup, gun belts here."

"Give it to me, Shitty," Coffin said, taking the belt, then asking Bodine, "Did you see anyone?"

"No, course not, would have said so if I had. Now pass over my guns."

"Would you?"

"What's that mean Tommy? Got nothing to hide from you. And I think it's only right you give those guns over here, they're mine."

Coffin didn't say anything.

Bodine said, "You got something on your mind Tommy, maybe best you say so. If I say I can't remember, I can't. There's the truth of it."

"Waiting for you to make some sense Bill. You leave town in a wagon. Why take a wagon? Shitty said there might've been a woman with you? Then we find you out cold in the middle of the trail to Kerr Lake. But no wagon. So you must have been with someone or run into someone else. As much of a fucking idjit that you are, I can't see you throwing yourself off the wagon, then the horses unhitching themselves and running off. And you remember guns but not the horses? And no woman? And you want me to believe you?"

Bodine said, "We go back a long way Tommy, you got no reason to doubt me."

Shitty said, "That ain't what that woman said, looking at his cards…"

"Shut up, Shitty," Coffin said.

"Well, I was just saying what I heard …"

"I said shut your mouth."

"What woman?" Bodine asked.

"One of them Nail sisters," Shitty said.

"Which one?"

"Don't rightly know, but she was quite a jezebel," said Shitty.

Jezebel? Yeah, he knew the jezebel. "What cards? What did she say?"

Coffin ignored Bodine's question, said, "Shut up about the cards. We're talking about what the fuck is going on here! Something is going on here, and I'm going to find out."

"You're letting all of this superstition get to you Tommy, com'on, you know me!"

"I thought I did Bill, but you got some explaining to do. Now we got to get moving, maybe on the way to the cabin we'll find the horses, the woman, or your goddamned memory. How about that Bodine?"

"Tommy! It's me, ol' Bill, your partner."

"You listen to me, partner, everything was set, everything! Butch said he had taken care of everything, that we were going to be rich and could go home. You said you killed Moberly, how do I know you didn't kill Butch as well, try and take everything? I don't want to believe it, but I'm having a hard time seeing things any other way."

"I had her with me," Bodine saying it quietly, like a confession.

"What?"

"Lily Nail. I had her with me. In the wagon."

"When? When did you have her?"

"I left town with her, after she was in the Bucket. Pretended I was one of Carr's drivers. She wanted to go out and see her claim, out by Kerr, I figured it might have been the one Butch was after. I was going to bring her out to the cabin, secure her there and come back and get you. Try to take care of things."

"That woman got the drop on you?" Shitty asked.

Bodine shook his head, "Don't know what happened. Maybe that detective and the other one ambushed me, must've hit my head because I can't remember anything, last thing I remember was taking her claim papers and then it was like I was being sucked up out of the wagon, maybe they was up in the trees waiting, grabbed me somehow, or maybe a mini hurricane or something like that, are there things like that?"

"Maybe a real strong whirlwind, but it'd have to be dang strong," Shitty said, "and I gotta say, ya don't hear much about those happening up here ..."

Coffin interrupted. "Shut up Shitty. And you Bill, you ran into a fucking hurricane did you? You're trying my patience. And I can tell you it wasn't O'Brien that drygulched you, I took care of him myself. And you told us that other sister was up at the railway camp. But now she's here? You just can't get your story straight. Show me those claim papers, where are they?"

Bodine patted his breast pocket, "Right here."

Coffin held out his hand, "Let's see."

Sighing, Bodine reached for his pocket, his face falling, then checking his other pockets. "It was right here, put it away just before ..."

"Do you think I'm stupid Bill?"

"No, Tommy, really, I took them from her, for you! To get the claim for you!"

"Jesus to Christ man, you're giving me some tall tale about a wagon missing its horses, Lily Nail, a hurricane, and a lost mining claim. I don't even know who you are anymore. The Bill Bodine I knew was someone I could count on. Fuck."

"Tommy..."

"Shut up, let me think," Coffin said, staring at the ground, then said, "This is what we're going to do. We're going to find the cabin, and we're going to hurry before this storm hits. And then I'm going to put you in a chair, going to sit you down, and you are going to tell me the truth."

"I am telling you the truth!"

"I can't take this bullshit and confusion any longer. Now let's go. If you don't tell me what I want to hear, I'm going to kill you."

CHAPTER
FORTY-FOUR

The morning wasn't like any other morning Shitty had ever seen. Woke up and thought it was still nighttime, iron clouds bunched up to the east. By the time they had reached the cabin the night before, they had been raw with bug bites and the night had turned cold. It had been late, very late, the three of them stumbling around in the dark trying to find the damn cabin. So there was no sitting Bill down in the chair then, just them crawling into their bedrolls and falling asleep. No one talking much.

And the night itself had been fitful, winds blowing every which way. Shitty didn't get much shuteye, and now he just wanted to be back in bed, and back in town. Instead they were out looking for the horses, walking in silence, Shitty feeling scared, didn't like the way things were sounding. Coffin had been up early, kicking at the bedrolls, saying, "We're finding the horses first. So right now Bill, your memory better start working."

And so they'd all stumbled out of the cabin, bleary-eyed and wary. Overhead the dawn was just breaking, the sky a dull red, the clouds layered and moving, Shitty thinking it didn't look too good up there, like waves of blood. Shitty didn't normally find himself thinking such things and it bothered him. He wondered about telling Coffin he was heading back to Cobalt, would the man just let him go, now that he was so cross and belligerent? He was wondering about this when Bodine said, "You got good eyesight, Shitty, what's that?"

"Where?"

"There, on the far side of the clearing, that light."

Shitty squinted, saw a sort of glowing patch, a small body of water in front of it. Hard to tell the water from the light, sort of reddish but maybe purple cast to it too? Reflection maybe. "Don't rightly know, Bill," said Shitty, "strange looking though."

Bodine said, "Maybe we should have a look. Could be a sheen on the rocks. Maybe it's one of them silver veins."

"Hard to say from here, but I don't think it could be silver," Shitty said.

"Why's that, Shitty," Coffin asked, as if only just then hearing their conversation, "you an expert now? One of them mining men?"

"Well, it just doesn't make sense, I mean that colour, looks like one of them sunsets. And it looks like it's moving, and rocks don't move, do they?"

"You smart mouthing me?" Coffin turned to Shitty, the muscles in his neck tight, "You be careful, keep spouting off, and you're going wind up at the bottom of one of those trenches."

"Didn't mean anything by it, Mr. Coffin, I was just saying…"

"I know what you were fucking saying, but what I'm telling you is to keep your mouth shut."

The three men fell silent and they stared at the glowing vapours stirring along the edge of the bush in the distance.

"Maybe," said Bodine, "it's a small fire, a campfire."

"I don't think that's a fire either Bill, now if you look …"

"Shut up Shitty, no one asked your opinion."

They kept staring, no doubt about it, there was something over there. Coffin turned to Shitty, said, "Go have a look."

"What?"

"You're the expert. Go on."

"You want me to go on all the way over there? Have to go around that water to get there!"

"Best start walking."

Shitty Mitty glanced over at Bodine, hoping for some support, but Bodine just looked away.

"I just don't see what's to be gained by me tramping through all this bush, it's probably just some reflection off the water," Shitty said.

"I want to know what that is, that's what's to be gained," Coffin said, "last thing we need is someone to be sneaking around out here."

Shitty looked away from Coffin and back towards the redness. It was shimmering. Must be some trick of the eye.

"What if it's the fellas that ambushed Bill here? What am I supposed to do?"

Coffin was wearing Bodine's holster. He took out one of the guns, held it out to Shitty. "Use it."

"Shoot them?"

"Shoot anything that moves, now get going."

Shitty didn't want to be alone. Not like he believed in the monster, he told himself, but something blood thirsty was going on out here and he didn't want no part of it. Didn't want to get ambushed either, hard to say what had happened to Bodine, finding the man flat on his ass in the middle of the bush. That didn't make no sense. And now Coffin was spooking him, seemed to be turning on him, getting mean and crazy. Maybe he could just get to the other side of the lake then slip away, head back to town, let the man cool off a bit.

"Alright, I'll head over there. What are you two going to do?"

"Don't worry about us, we'll keep ourselves busy. Just get going."

"Well, if I'm gonna head over there, I'd like you two fellas to wait here till I get back."

"We'll wait, Shitty," Coffin said, "we got nowhere to be right now."

• • •

Shitty lost sight of the light as he'd rounded the far edge of the small lake. Trying now to picture it from the other side, trying to remember exactly where the mysterious light had been, but he was mixed up, not sure now if he was even headed in the right direction. He glanced back towards where he'd come from. No sign of Coffin or Bodine. Damn. Maybe he just couldn't see them from where he was. Coffin said they'd wait, and at the time Shitty hoped he had meant it. Maybe they up and left though.

"Goddammit, Milton," he said out loud, "sometimes you're just too damn stupid."

A snapping of a twig just a few yards to his left caused Shitty to stand still, hold his breath and stop talking to himself. He waited a few seconds but there was no more sound. He started breathing again.

He scanned the woods lining the lake, then saw it, the red again, suddenly brighter, then fading and then going out entirely, like it was extinguished. What foolishness, tramping around the woods trying to find some red light. Shitty's stomach grumbled, hungry now without breakfast, or even much of a supper. Maybe he could get himself a rabbit. Wasn't sure about the gun though, never carried one like this before.

Sound again to his left, sure now it was a hare, maybe a squirrel, either way might be some eating to be had. He steadied himself, started to move slower, saw a flash of something pale in the underbrush and he fired. The form seemed to falter, then scramble away.

"Damnit!" Shitty said, plunging now towards the form, but as he got closer it seemed to grow longer, slipping along the ground, not the shape of a hare at all. Changing colour too? No, he must have winged it, he was just seeing some blood staining. Caught a glimpse of it in the underbrush, seemed bigger, a marten maybe, but then he came up short as the woods gave way to a rock outcropping. And standing up on the outcropping was Lily Nail, appearing as if she came right up out of the rock.

Vivid in the scarlet jacket, she was just standing there, staring at him, and Shitty was thinking there was definitely something wrong with his eyes, because he was having trouble focusing, her edges seemed blurry, but it was clearly her and there was blood dripping from her hand and her face was scratched, and he said to her, "What are you doing out here?"

"Minding my own business until you shot at me," she said, her voice thick somehow, like maybe she was talking underwater, and Shitty thought for a moment he might be having a stroke, was that what they called it, a stroke? Because something was happening to him, to his sight, her arms now looking too long, and she was too pale, her red jacket now seemed white, but ghostly, like mist.

He said, "I didn't shoot at you."

"You surely did."

And he watched as she seemed to dissolve and reform, and he felt his gun drop from his hand and he was rubbing his eyes as she changed, becoming very tall, and she came down from the rock with her edges shimmering like water, and her hair was long, like tentacles, and it was pale too, and grasping, and it slithered down along the rock and up all around him and he tried to move but he was held fast, the hair tight like a rope around him, and the tentacles found his throat, stroked it, and she said, "You're right, that scar isn't at all like a smile."

CHAPTER FORTY-FIVE

"We burn them out," Coffin said.

Bodine and Coffin had waited for Shitty, Bodine saying the man couldn't be trusted, probably slunk back to town. Coffin said Bodine wasn't really in a position to judge another man, and that they had both heard the gunshot—poor Shitty probably ran into the Nail sisters and was now lying dead in the bush.

And he'd been right. After some looking, they found the man. Except Shitty wasn't exactly shot or lying dead on the ground, he was up some six feet, snagged on a sharp tree branch. The two men stared at him for a few seconds, Coffin then marching over to him, pulling on one of the legs dangling down but the body was wedged between a tight set of branches.

Coffin barked at Bodine, "Get over here and help!" and they each took hold of a leg, struggled to lift the body up and then pull on it until they were able to free it from the branch, the body then flopping face down onto the ground.

Coffin turned Shitty over, stood back, said, "What the fuck happened here?"

After a bit more time simply staring at the body, and then checking around the clearing to try and figure out what happened, Bodine found his gun and said, "Let's head back to the cabin. Standing around all day looking at Shitty ain't going to bring him back."

And that's when Coffin had said they should burn down the forest.

Coffin nodded towards the expanse of woods in front of them, said, "Between here and Kerr Lake, they're somewhere in there. We can flush them out."

"What?" Bodine said, sort of laughing, "We can't do that, that's crazy. We don't know where they are. We don't even know if it is them out here."

"It was."

"Could have been anyone. Might have been a hunter that mistook Shitty for a bear or a deer. And Shitty never did pay attention. Or it could have been Shitty himself."

"What the fuck are you talking about, he's halfway up a tree, how do you think he got there?"

"Maybe he climbed up, hiding, got shot there."

"Do you see a gunshot wound?"

"Well, no…"

"He wasn't shot. But he shot at something. And he's been torn up, like he was dragged. And his neck's bleeding something awful. That wound of his opened up."

"Had that since he was a kid," Bodine said, leaning down for a closer look, "Seems torn right open. Maybe a cougar."

"That was no cougar, no, this was them."

"The sisters?"

"That's right."

"Come on Tommy, that just doesn't make any sense. How could those two do this to Shitty. In that amount of time? He wasn't smart, but he was strong enough. And a good hunter. No, that's just crazy. And don't see how starting a fire is going to help. Let's just head to the cabin, figure things out there."

"Used to be able to count on you Bodine, through thick and thin."

"What? Now hold on there, you know you can count on me. I just don't know what we're doing out here. Fellas are getting killed out here, all those prospectors, now Shitty. I say we get ourselves back to town, get on that train and get the hell outta here."

But Coffin didn't say anything, scanning the edge of the forest, not listening so Bodine said, "If we ain't going to bury Shitty, we gotta get out of here. This place is giving me the creeps."

"You feel it too," said Coffin.

"Feel what?"

Coffin, starting to pace, said, "Them. It's like they're out here, watching us, prowling around out here."

"No, that's not it. I just don't like standing around with a dead body. Let's head to the cabin, okay Tommy?"

"We'll go, but we're flushing them out first."

"What do you mean, flushing them out?"

"They'll have to come out once the fire gets going, will probably head for the cabin, it's cleared all around there and there's water. That's where they'll come. Right to us."

Bodine couldn't believe it. "You really want to start a fire?"

"Why not?"

"You can't just start a fire, there could be fellas working out here."

"No one's working out here, that monster talk has everyone packing it in."

"Maybe they know what they're doing then? Maybe whatever that monster is got Shitty. Let's forget the cabin, we can just walk back to town. Trains leaving all the time, we can get on one and never look back."

"Not a monster out here Bill, it's those two witches. I'm telling you, there's something wrong with them. They're unnatural."

"You can't torch the whole place."

Coffin started to gather brush, said, "Sure I can. Come on, start piling it up."

"There's a wind coming up."

"All the better to burn with Billyboy. That wind will chase them right to our cabin."

"Then what will you do?"

"What I should have done five years ago."

Didn't take Tommy long to get a nice big stack of branches together. Then he started to drag branches to form a path leading towards the underbrush and spruce trees, said, "Don't stand around, you lazy bastard, help me out. We want this here fire to take off fast."

Bodine said, "Not lazy Tommy, just don't think you should burn down the forest."

"Why not? It'll just make it easier for the dynamite boys. Doing them a favour."

"You said yourself fellas are clearing out, don't need to dynamite out here. Let's clear out too," Bodine said, the wind picking up, now rattling the treetops around them, Bodine worried that as soon as the fire caught, the wind would be bringing the fire with it wherever it went. "If the wind changes, we could get trapped out here."

Coffin had finished his berm of twigs and debris, was now hauling a few heavier branches onto the pile that now ran right across the clearing, meeting the forest edge where some stumps had already been hacked down and tossed into a pile. "That should do it," Coffin said, wheezing a bit, throwing one last thick tree branch onto the pyre.

"Tommy, look here, this isn't a good idea, the winds, they're getting stronger, this here fire could turn…"

But Coffin was snapping his matches till one caught and the crackling started, and Bodine said, "Jesus Tommy, no," scared at the force with which the fire took hold, chewing through the pile then snaking out along the berm, spitting sparks now with the wind picking up and Bodine started to stomp on the small flames, panicked, saying, "Good Christ Tommy, this is already out of control."

"It's my fire Bill. Mine. I started it, look at it," the fire crackling and starting to roar as it found the tree Shitty had been in, tearing over his body to get to the winter-dry lower branches now barely in bud, "it's fucking beautiful."

"You're not thinking straight Tommy."

"I'm thinking just fine. And you're wasting our time talking Bill, can't stop the beast once it's let loose. Let's head back to the cabin, wait for the witches," Coffin said, smiling as he watched the fire, eyes shining with pleasure and pride, then added, "maybe play a few rounds of cards."

CHAPTER FORTY-SIX

Molly was restless, her energy causing both Modesto and Lucy to stir, then Lucy murmuring, "Oh no, smoke," and both were up.

They must have dozed off right away, and while they had slept the wind had come up, blowing in hard from the west, disorienting, the big white spruce and cedars madly waving their branches, bending way up at their crowns. Molly was fussing, tossing her head, Modesto saying, "Yes, we'll get going. Just need to get my bearings."

"There," Lucy said pointing, "the smoke plume."

And yes, a greyish-green haze seemed to be hauling itself up and over the treetops.

"Alright, listen carefully, Lucy. On the way to the cabin, just south of it, the stream widens, follow it and it should take you to the lake. If you get there you might be alright."

"We need to find Lily."

"Listen to me please. Follow along the ridge behind us and it should bring you to the stream. Follow it and keep to the high ground. I'll take Molly and go find Lily, you just need to help me up."

"How are you going to find her? She could be anywhere. What if we can't get to her?"

"No, I sense she's nearby, she wouldn't leave you for too long, you know that. I'll find her. Or she'll find us."

Eyes on the churning rolls of charcoal smoke swelling up over the trees, Lucy said, "You be careful O'Brien. You make sure you come back to me."

"Molly and I will be fine. Just get to the water. I'll come back."

Lucy watched as he disappeared up onto the road, then turned and headed towards the ridge. Scrambling up, the rocks were sharp, hurting her still sore hands. Once on top of the ridge everything was black-green treetops, smoke now starting to drift and tumble into every gap in the forest below. At least she couldn't see flames yet, but it wouldn't be long. That was good, but what was bad is that she felt disoriented, wasn't sure which way to go. Couldn't hear any water over the winds now, the mood on the land disturbed, resentful, and she went up a little higher but still could not see which way was best to go.

A crashing sound behind her made her think stampede, and she looked for the closest tree to get between her and the noise, found a big aspen, wide in girth and old. She hugged herself to it and waited for whatever was coming.

"Well I'll be damned," she said to the aspen as the black bear burst through the underbrush, 'doesn't he raise a racket for such a small fella."

The bear scampered across her path, seemed to look at her with his small porcine eyes squinting through the smoke, then barrelled up the trail and along the crest of the ridge. Creature seemed pretty certain of which way it was headed, and she had no idea herself.

Lucy decided that in its melancholy look was an invitation to follow. So she did.

CHAPTER FORTY-SEVEN

"Sit down and deal."

The two of them were on their second card game. Bill Bodine was halfway out of his chair, thinking of just up and leaving, seeing the smoke drifting over the forest in the near distance, not sure now if Coffin was able to even think straight, the man not being himself at the moment, moods swinging wildly.

"Tommy, the winds, they're really whipping things up out there."

"Can't you see which way the wind's blowin' Billyboy?" Coffin said, "Pull yourself together. We'll be going in soon to mop up."

"We might get hemmed in by the fire."

"I said deal Bill."

Bodine sat back down and gathered up the cards, said, "We're taking a chance Tommy, a big chance, and for what?"

"For Butch! What is wrong with you? Have you forgotten they killed Butch?"

"This has nothing to do with Butch."

"What does that mean?"

"I just think, well, I think this has more to do with you and that woman."

"That right Bill?"

"Think about it Tommy. We've trailed after the Nail sisters from city to city to even all the fuck the way up here, and for what? Every time we get close they vanish. It's like, like they're ghosts or something."

"I told you, they aren't natural."

"You're obsessed with them though! It's all we've done for the past few years, tracked them all over the goddamn place! I don't want to keep doing this."

"That's why," Coffin said, "we're finishing it here. Tonight. This is it."

"It's over for me Tommy. Jesus, look at what happened to Shitty, I don't want to end up like that, or burnt up because this damn thing gets out of control. I don't know if those two are witches, or whatever they are …"

"How'd you lose your horse and wagon?"

"Not this again Tommy, I told you, I don't know."

"Think about it Bill. You were with her. And then, according to you, the next thing you know Shitty and I are finding you passed out on the trail. Unless you're lying to me, the only other explanation is she put some sort of spell or hex on you. Took off with your horse and wagon."

Bodine thinking about it, trying to remember, seeing her turn to him, saying, "You know, you look very much like a man I used to see around Butte," and he said, "Ain't that a coincidence" and she said, "Oh, I don't think so." And then next thing he knew his body was being lifted, and it was hurting everywhere and then there was blackness. He said to Coffin, "I just want to get as far away from them, and here, as we can. A clean start, no more chasing after those hellcats."

"I'm not disagreeing with you Bill, but we have to finish it with them. Right here. Are you going to stand with me or not?"

Bodine sighed, "I've been your friend all along Tommy."

"Then prove it. Stay and see it through. Now deal the cards."

Bodine sighed but started to snap down the cards, quiet, trying to keep his eye on the smoke outside that seemed to be getting thicker and blacker each time he looked. He took a look at his cards, Coffin looking at his own but then Bodine could feel the man staring at him, his cards turned face up and spread out on the table in front of him.

"What the fuck games are you playing here Bill?"

"What?" Bodine confused, looking from Coffin to the cards, "What's the problem?"

"You dealt this hand?"

"Well of course Tommy, you just saw me. Just the two of us in here."

"What does that mean?" Coffin asked, now standing up fast, knocking his chair over as he went.

"What's going on?"

"Look at them!" Coffin yelling.

"Well I give you it ain't the best hand but …"

"Call 'em out! Now!"

"What?"

"Call out the cards! What are they?"

"Alright, okay, well, you got a four of diamonds, eight, four and seven of clubs, and the ace of spades," he looked up uncertainly, "that's what I dealt. Fair and square."

"I knew you were up to something, your fucking lies," Coffin's eyes boring into Bodine, "She got her claws into you somehow, maybe it is a hex, are you under her fucking spell, Bodine? What happened to you when you were in the wagon with her?"

Bodine, still sitting, staring at the cards, said, "I don't know what's going on Tommy."

With that Tommy grabbed hold of the table, sent it flying sideways, catching Bodine in the legs, Bodine protesting, scrambling up and Coffin coming at him across the table, grabbing hold of him and shoving him hard towards the door, bellowing, "Get out! Get out before I kill you!"

"Christ, Tommy," Bodine sputtering as Coffin hauled opened the door and shoved him outside, Bodine staggering forward a few feet and Coffin looming in the doorway, "Stay the fuck away from me, don't ever want to lay eyes on you again." And with that the door slammed shut.

Bodine looked up, could see the turgid black smoke billowing up along the treetops, could hear the crackling and spitting of the fire.

"Fuck, Tommy, open up, we got to get out of here!" Bodine yelling as he looked around frantically for something, anything, then seeing Butch's shotgun propped up against the wall of the small lean-to that was used to store firewood, thinking once the shed caught the whole place was going to go up in flames, there'd be no saving anything. He turned and banged on the door, called Tommy's name, pleaded with the man he had called friend since they were boys together. The door stayed closed.

He grabbed the shotgun and started to run.

CHAPTER FORTY-EIGHT

Her hand was bloodied. She was sitting on a large flat rock near the water's edge. There were three ravens with her, one perched right beside her on the rock, its back to Modesto as he dismounted and approached, the other two on a jumble of rocks behind her. They were watching him closely. The raven next to her was large, his feathers shaggy around his legs. He was pecking at her hand.

Modesto stood and watched, trying to be sure he was seeing what was actually there: Lily and three ravens, her hand reddish, inflamed, and one of the ravens was feeding from, or at, it. The shore of the lake stirred with the winds, the rocks behind her grey and angular.

"Come and help me," she said.

"Your hand. It's wounded?"

"The bird is stitching it shut. I was shot."

He approached cautiously, asked, "Shot by who?"

"That dreadful man that goes by the name of Shitty Mitty."

"Why?"

"He thought I was a hare."

Modesto bent to look at her hand, reached out but the raven took a quick jab at him, so Modesto pulled back his hand, asked, "Were you?"

"A hare? Oh, I don't know," she said, sounding impatient, "But you could wrap my hand."

"Your doctor hasn't finished."

Lily murmured something, closed her eyes and Modesto could see the fine violet veins criss-crossing them, and then realized he could also see the veins running down along her arm like a river, the tributaries branching off and pulsing only to be interrupted by the thick red line bound with black lines. The raven's handiwork.

With her murmuring, the raven hopped away, then raised itself up with a few strong flaps of its wings to settle on the rocks with the other two of its kind.

Modesto crouched beside Lily, trying not to be distracted as her body was now fading to a pale grey, seeming to be absorbed into the rock. He took his handkerchief and wrapped her hand carefully with it. She said, "You're very gentle."

"I'm afraid the raven might enact harsh punishment should I undermine his care."

"Where is my sister?"

"Safe I think. She was headed to water."

"Was it wise to leave her? The fire is spreading."

"She'll be fine, but she wants you to come with me."

"I can't."

"Does she know?"

"She suspects."

"She won't be happy that I left you here wounded, come, you can ride Molly and we can find a way out of here together."

"No, I need you to go. I'm not finished."

"Finished what?"

"My task."

"Which is?"

She smiled but did not answer, instead said, "See what I am seated on?"

"A rock?"

"Silver."

"Ah, yes, I see that now. That's quite the slab. What will you do with it?"

"Try and find the people of the original owner to start. Lucy says he is still around."

"The murdered man?"

"Yes. She says she sees him," Lily shrugged, "so we can try and right that wrong somehow, I don't know, then keep a bit of this silver, get a cow for Lucy, a few chickens. Use a bit when we need it."

"Is it yours?"

"Legally yes. On paper."

He looked at the mark of her hand on the rock, the browned blood stain on the grey. She followed his glance, smiled, said, "Blood for silver."

"Worth it?"

Shrugging, she said, "You can't take without giving. In the future I will try and find what the rock wants or needs."

"What are you?" he asked.

"I'm Lily Nail."

"Yes, you are. But you are also something other than Lily."

"I'm simply angry, Mr. O'Brien. Pure rage."

"That rage could transform your physical self?"

"Yes, I suppose it has. And every other part of me as well."

"How long have you been like this?"

"Oh, I've always been angry, no reason not to be, but not like this. Something happened to me in the forest. Something opened up, slipped in and changed me."

Even as she said it, Modesto could feel energy radiating from her, the flowing of her now violet blood stronger, faster, forming eddies and waves, and he was unable to tell if it was inside his head or separate, part of Lily and not himself, and she said loudly, her voice almost pushing into his mind, "Now please, go back to my sister and make sure she is safe."

"Yes, of course," he said, "how will we find you?"

"The ravens see everything," she said, "so not to worry, we'll find you."

He stood, started towards Molly, but paused, saw the streams and rivers and violets and silvers running through her and he could not be sure he even really saw what was Lily, and he asked, "How did you get here?"

She sighed, said in a voice of water and rock, "Don't you know? I came in the pocket of Biddy Savage."

"How though, how could that be?"

"From the four corners of the Dublin Gulch, the soil itself carried on the east wind, it found me, settled inside, lying in wait. Now it's been stirred."

CHAPTER
FORTY-NINE

There had been no sign of her. Modesto had retraced his steps then followed the creek heading away towards the cabin. The fire was closer, traveling up high in the trees. It was loud, both the roaring of the fire itself and the cracking and splitting of trees that were in its path.

He had caught sight of Bodine staggering through the bush, his neckerchief covering his mouth, weak protection from the smoke. The man looked dazed, wasn't more than a hundred feet from the cabin, but was headed away from it. That meant Coffin was alone. And if right now he was unable to find Lucy he might as well try to deal with Coffin. Eliminate the threat. Or at least one of the threats.

So now he found himself watching the cabin again, just like before except this time he knew Coffin was inside, seeing the man's face appear at the window every few minutes, his expression both frightened and expectant.

"What to do Molly, what to do?" The horse was patient even though Modesto could sense her tension, the fear of the fire. He was afraid too. His entire left side still ached, his shooting hand now all but useless. A few more minutes passed, the time dragging on, the sky getting darker with the smoke and the wind.

He could call Coffin out, but the man could choose just to stay put. Then what? Maybe instead he should send Molly out. Make him wonder about Modesto, not left for dead after all? Might make him curious enough to come out. If he recognized the horse. Either way, the man would be needing a horse to get out of there and wasn't any sign of horses by the cabin, and Bodine had been on foot. Maybe the horse would lure him out.

So send Molly out, draw Coffin out of the cabin. To shoot him from the cover of the cedars or give the man a chance? Lucy would say just shoot him.

He tried clenching his hand. It hurt, but he thought he could manage a shot.

"What do you think Molly? Should we try?"

The horse emerged from the cedars slowly, ears forward, careful. Halfway between the cedars and the cabin, Coffin's face appeared in the window. The horse stopped, uncertain, and Modesto was about to call her back when the door flew open and Coffin was there moving towards her, but the horse shied away, reins dangling and swaying as the creature trotted to the far edge of the clearing, Coffin cursing, but Modesto realized that Molly wasn't spooked by Coffin, but by something up on the cliff.

It was Bodine, lying flat out, shotgun trained on the cabin. Behind him the woods were erupting in flame, the winter-dry conifers turning to torches, fire rushing up the trunks, all appetite, consuming needles, bark and branches. And it was like Bodine simply did not know the fire was almost on him.

"Tommy!"

Bodine's voice sent Molly skittering back towards the cedars, Coffin turning, trying to find the source of the voice. Between the deafening sounds of the fire and the thick smoke settling in around the cabin it was hard to tell where the voice was coming from, Coffin searching for the source, looking this way and that.

Modesto tore his eyes away from Coffin to Bodine. It was odd, the man calling again to Coffin. Was he warning him or calling him out, ready to shoot his life-long friend? No, Modesto could see that Bodine's gun wasn't trained on Coffin but on the far side of the cabin, and then he saw the blue shirt lean around the edge of the cabin and draw back again.

Lucy. Come home to her cabin. His other beautiful pearl-handled pistol in her hand.

Maybe Coffin thought he was hearing things, or that it was the fire calling him out, because he decided to go for the horse, moving slowly away from the cabin, prompting Lucy to slip around the corner. Now she was behind him. But plain as day.

Bodine's scream of warning to Coffin came quicker than his shot fired at Lucy, but slower than the cracking of the huge spruce behind him. It loomed over him, like some giant's torch, and the cracking of its great trunk was deafening and terrible. It swallowed whole his words of warning and caused him to spin around as he fired, the bullet sent off into a nothingness of flames and smoke.

Coffin and Lucy both heard the shot, turning and then watching as the tree wavered over the half-crouching figure of Bill Bodine and then he threw himself off the cliff, tumbling a few times then disappearing into a thicket of spruce and dogwood that was then showered with sparks and debris as the mammoth conifer crashed to the ground.

Biddy was crowing

No turning back, no turning back, he is getting his just desserts
Just desserts

Modesto was glad she was there, but knew it wasn't enough, he was waiting for the ravens, could see them far off in the distance, smoke-coloured phantoms, soaring overhead, three of them, then a few more and then a dozen.

In the few seconds that Lucy turned to watch the tree, Coffin had reached her, digging his hand into her hair and yanking her off her feet, her gun flying from her grasp, now dragging her towards the cabin and Modesto saw her there, her feet flailing, trying to haul herself back from Coffin's fierce momentum and Modesto felt the black ribbons furling and unfurling in his mind, the pain along the side of his head intense as he started to move, like it was splitting, a slithering, a letting loose of the black ribbons, or were they snakes.

And Biddy just said, *we need to go now*, and Modesto stepped out of the trees into the clearing, called, "Tommy Coffin!"

Over the howling winds he called again, "Coffin!" He wasn't sure Coffin would even hear him, the raging wind churning up everything in its path, dragging the fire along with it by the scruff of its neck, twisting and swallowing sound.

But Coffin turned, surprised, "You!" but unable to fully look at him, troubled by Lucy squirming and flopping at the end of his arm like a fish tossed on shore, so he yelled, "like a bad penny O'Brien, thought I'd left you for dead."

Left for dead, no, left for Biddy, she said, and for this, to witness this, the end, the end

Get ready little Moddie, get ready for the east wind

Modesto couldn't feel his arm, and now the hand with the gun was feeling numb too, wasn't sure he could even keep hold of the gun. What use could he be?

But as Coffin stopped to yell at Modesto, Lucy managed to get her feet under herself, scrambled to turn and then threw herself against Coffin, digging her nails into his eyes, him yelling "Jesus Christ you fucking bitch," and trying to throw her off but she kept clawing at him, the fury of her making it hard for him to get a firm hold of her, but when he did he shoved her to the ground, pounced on her, grabbing her by the neck and cussing, but by then Modesto was there, sending his boot into Coffin's side, knocking the man off balance and giving Lucy a chance to get free. Modesto yelling, "Lucy, inside the cabin, the ravens, they're coming. Now!"

If Lucy knew or didn't know what he meant about the ravens, she still made for the cabin door. She hesitated in the doorway as Coffin pulled himself to his feet, not seeming to be worried, his gun some six feet away, Modesto yelling, "The door! Lucy, shut the door!"

He relaxed when he saw it shut, Biddy saying, *she's gone now, gone to hallowed ground, beyond the reach, beyond the reach* and with that several ravens settled on the edge of the cabin's roof, Coffin seeing them, stepping back and away from the building, the black birds hunched and silent, and Coffin had to shout, "Are you going to shoot me O'Brien?" and throwing open his arms, "Go ahead, shoot!"

Concentrating on raising his arm, feeling the metal slipping from his hand and then the sting, ripping into his shoulder as Bodine staggered into the clearing, and Modesto thought how odd that he was shot with his own gun, the gun Lucy had dropped, and he knew then that it wasn't strange at all, but meant to be, the gun's purpose, why he kept them all these years. He felt himself fading as he saw the east wind knotting itself together behind Bodine, the wind almost taking form, turning from black to purple as it caught branches and debris in its maw, now rushing up and Bodine was there and then he wasn't, tossed and thrown upwards, now banged against one tree and then another as if he was suddenly a rag doll in the hand of an enraged, giant child, and it seemed as if he was still screaming when it was over and he was dropped to the ground in bits and pieces.

Modesto heard Coffin say, "Jesus Christ almighty, he's been torn limb from limb."

And Biddy was up with the ravens, her too hunched over but cawing, *your reckoning Tom Coffin, now's your reckoning*, and Tommy Coffin turned as if to run, but then stopped, Lily there, as large as life, at once herself and something utterly different.

Of all the things Modesto had ever seen, of all the things he sensed and hadn't seen, nothing compared to what he saw once Lily stepped out of the gloom and took hold of Tommy Coffin.

She became tall, so very tall, and almost translucent, with lesions of ash against her violet, icy skin, the entire surface of her smouldering of smoke. Utterly radiant. That long thin appendage that had stalked his mind since he first saw her at the train station took hold of Tommy Coffin by the shoulder. And just the touching of him seemed to unleash something both dreadful and beautiful and made Lily into an unheard-of thing. She was like a madness, and then an ice hide stretched over her twisting limbs, long and transparent, muscles now visible, and Modesto felt himself grow faint just at the sight of the coursing veins of deep dark purple, and her free hand went to her face and dragged the hide down and away and then the lungs like night moths, fluttering above the heart, and the heart large, too large, and then an unearthly terrible sound and the hair from her head stood out like branches studded with thorns and a terrible, wild wrath now whipped around them until a viscous fog of witchery engulfed both her and Coffin.

The last thing the man saw before he was no more was Lucy's face in the cabin's window.

CHAPTER FIFTY

S he could see him ebbing away, leaves collecting in his collar. Lucy asked, "What will I do without you?"

"You'll never be without me."

During the height of the storm, after Tommy Coffin had been obliterated, Modesto had been dragged back into the woods by the wind itself, the smoke and flames all around him until the east winds finally turned the fire back on itself, leaving it smouldering but exhausted. Lucy had taken Molly, searching and calling for Modesto, until finally seeing him, sitting propped up against a charred, but still standing, aspen. He was soaked in blood, his fine coat now all red and green.

"There it is, the red and the green that I saw," she said.

Modesto looked down, said, "I only see the green. I love this coat. It is keeping me warm, but it is cold all around me."

Lucy was now crying. "Where will I go without you and Lily?"

"Stay here, have your garden, and your cabin. She's somewhere close by. She's coming."

"Are you sure?"

"Yes. She would never leave you. And she will be fine. She will need some tending though, her hand, she's wounded."

"What if all the men come back."

"They won't. Not now, not with the monster."

"Oh Moddie …"

"Go now Lucy. Take Molly and go. You both need water, and rest. Take care of her for me. Leave, please, and don't look back as I go."

"But you're so alone."

"No, Biddy is here. Right beside me. Don't worry. Go."

Lucy started to walk, did not look back as the wind stirred the ash, and the blackened leaves drifted over Modesto as he smiled and drifted and felt the winds taking him, winds the colours of violets and ravens. He slowly eased himself down, stretched his limbs, feeling the heat of the land beneath him, heard then the whispering of the worms through the hot soil, singing sweet songs, how did they know the old songs, the songs of Biddy Savage? What a chorus to welcome him.

CHAPTER
FIFTY-ONE

Lucy and Lily stood at the edge of the forest, Molly beside them, the three keeping vigil, waiting as he faded and left. Three ravens sat nearby along a thick, charred aspen branch, preening one another. And when the sun had settled and left the sky a darkening turquoise, and when the first of the stars began to show themselves, Lucy told Molly about the starcows overhead, and then the three of them walked together back towards his resting place. There was nothing of him there and there was everything of him. Lily waited as Lucy and Molly went to the charred tree, Lucy leaning on Molly, stroking the grey mane, clearing out bits of ash, combing it smooth with her fingers.

She knew that soon enough the aspen saplings would push their way up through the charred forest floor. She would watch for him there amongst those saplings, for her pale-limbed lover. And she thought to herself, yes, really, what difference between a man and a tree, if both were able to live upright lives.

HISTORY & HAUNTING

This is a story set in a time of rupture, in the very early 1900s, when a monumental change happened to both the land and people in the Timiskaming District of Northern Ontario—both those already here and those drawn to the place. It was a place of outrageous occurrences and tragic outcomes. A few people got very rich.

Here are some events that actually happened in the strangeness and chaos that was Cobalt during the early days of the silver rush: a miner died from being kicked by a horse, a man was pushed onto the railway tracks by a coal shed, and a bear got drunk in Jamieson's Meat store.

There was also scandal and violence associated with a railway company up near Driftwood City that drew the attention of the authorities from both the French and Austrian embassies.

Carbolic acid was a common choice in many suicides during the early 20th century; death by train decapitation did not, as far as I know, occur in Cobalt, but a case did occur (and a man's head found a fair distance away from his body) in Butte, Montana.

The First Nations in the Timiskaming area have their own stories of strange creatures and beings that inhabited the landscape—I feel that is appropriate to briefly refer to them, but it is not my place to describe or explain them. There have, however, been sightings in the Cobalt area of a being that was called Old Yellow Top or the Pre-Cambrian Shield Man, a creature understood to be adjacent to a Sasquatch. There were sightings in 1906 near the Violet Mine, in 1923 by two prospectors working out by the Wettlaufer Mine, in 1947 by a mother and son along the railway tracks in Cobalt and finally in 1970, by the driver of a bus taking miners out to the graveyard shift at the Cobalt Lode Mine. Old Yellow Top, however, is not the creature in my story. Nice to know, though, that he has been kicking around for a while.

And the character Kit Murphy came from a real life troubling. This is what I remember: I was in grade school—circa 1966—and a group of Grade 12 boys dragged a classmate out into the schoolyard, held him down and cut his hair—it was considered too long hippie hair. Much of the school, along with some teachers, watched. Apparently, at that time, this sort of behaviour was not unheard of, and in some schools, teachers themselves would shave boys' hair –long hair being thought unmanly. I don't know what eventually happened to the young man whose hair was cut, but it made a lasting impression on me.

For more source information, please feel free to check out my Facebook page and/or website. There are many excellent histories available about the silver rush, Indigenous silver mining, claim jumping and the all too rapid and chaotic growth of Cobalt.

ABOUT THE AUTHOR

Brit Griffin is the author of the climate-fiction Wintermen trilogy (Latitude 46) and has written essays, musings, and articles for various publications. Griffin spent many years as a researcher for the Timiskaming First Nation, an Algonquin community in northern Quebec. She lives in Cobalt, northern Ontario, where she is the mother of three grown daughters. These days, she divides her time between writing and caring for her unruly yard.